I0818107

THE BROKEN

J.J. HERNANDEZ

The Broken

Published May 2021 by Moon Reign Publications

www.authorjjhernandez.com

Edited by Ginny Glass

Book Cover Design by ebooklaunch.com

ISBN 978-1-7371013-2-1

ISBN 978-1-7371013-0-7 (paperback)

ISBN 978-1-7371013-1-4 (ebook)

To the loves of my life Hazel, Nikki, and Kat. Thank you for having more faith in me than I had in myself.

For Diana,
my friend, my hero, my mother

CHAPTER ONE

SUMMER 2010

THE CAR WAS a 2004 Honda Accord, gun-metal gray, nondescript, and inconspicuous. It'd had three previous owners and was stolen off a used car lot in Union City, New Jersey, two nights ago.

Now, two rivers to the east, the car traveled west on Ditmas Avenue beneath an unusually bright crescent-shaped moon. The night sky brought little reprieve from the late summer heatwave, going on its second straight week of no rain and 100-degree days.

From the passenger seat, Julian Serrano surveyed the scene. Despite it still being early in the evening, the streets were empty. The suffocating heat had pushed everyone to seek air-conditioned refuge indoors.

"I'm going to take Ninety-Second," Angel Guerra said. His right hand gripped the steering wheel firmly. He held the e-cigarette close to his mouth, nervously inhaling every few seconds.

"Why?" Julian said. "Just stay on Ditmas till Remsen."

"If we take Ninety-Second, we can cut up Bedell and park on the backside. Whoever's with Hector won't expect it."

"There's no point." Julian kept his gaze on the scene outside his window, and although he was annoyed, he kept his voice low and even. "They're expecting us, remember? We don't know how many have shown up, and people might be watching the back. If we park on the backside, they will figure something is up."

"Damn, you're right." Angel closed his grip on his e-cigarette, holding it tight in a closed fist and close to his temple as if preparing to make a phone call. "I didn't really think it through."

In the backseat, James "Jimmy" O'Donnell sat quietly. The soft tapping of his typing on his cell phone was the only sound in the car. Julian figured Jimmy was exchanging text messages with one of the many ladies he kept on the hook. Typing some bullshit about how much he cared about her when the truth was, he didn't give a damn about any of them. Jimmy just enjoyed the attention, and ladies threw a lot of their attention his way.

The Honda passed through an intersection while traveling west on Ditmas Avenue. Julian looked down at the floorboard. He noticed the car's momentum had caused his shotgun to slip slightly off the duffel bag it'd been lying on.

Julian gazed pensively at the shotgun. He didn't much like using them. They were too loud, too messy, and too hard to conceal.

He preferred his .38 snub-nosed revolver. Expended rounds didn't automatically eject from revolvers, so he didn't have to worry about police finding his fingerprints or DNA on empty shells. It only held five rounds, not a lot, but more than enough if you were an accurate and discerning shot. But the shotgun was an attention grabber, and they needed everyone's attention for what they planned.

Angel turned the Honda onto Remsen Avenue.

"There," Julian said. "The tire shop."

"I don't see nobody," Angel said.

"Just pull over here."

Angel stopped the car a block away from the tire shop, and they waited. Julian scanned the terrain for several minutes, looking for anything unusual. It had been a while since he was last inside A+ Tire Shop.

It was a small, single-story, twenty-five-year-old building with a small one-room office serving as the business' reception area. The rest of the building consisted of a two-car garage for installing and repairing tires. An eight-foot high, barbed wire-topped chain-link fence surrounded the property. A mosaic of used tires was pressed against the fence as if displayed in an art exhibit. Seven cars in various stages of disrepair were parked on the sidewalk outside the fence.

"Alright, go ahead and park on the corner," Julian said.

Angel parked the Honda on the northwest corner of Remsen Avenue and Foster Avenue and turned off the engine. From there, they had a clear view inside the fence. Angel took a drag from his e-cigarette as he leaned forward and eyed the space inside the tire shop's fence.

"There's Hector's Cutty," Angel said, noticing the black 1978 Oldsmobile Cutlass parked alongside the building.

Julian nodded. "He's already inside."

Jimmy shifted in his seat. "Let's get it."

"Give it a few minutes," Julian said, grabbing the shotgun off the floorboard. He brought it close to his face and double-checked the small nylon bag covering its ejection port. Julian had taped it there to catch any empty shells that ejected from the shotgun. Confident the bag was secure—he pumped a shell into the breech and placed the shotgun back on the floorboard.

Julian grabbed the duffel bag and lifted it onto his lap. He unzipped the bag and looked inside. Six separate bundles of newspaper cut into shapes of U.S. currency neatly held together with a rubber band lay neatly in the bag. Each stack was topped with a one-hundred-dollar bill. On top lay a snub-nosed Smith & Wesson 640 revolver.

Julian glanced back at Jimmy and passed him the revolver. Jimmy grabbed the gun and eyed it contemptuously. When it came time to put in work, Jimmy was big on speed, efficiency, and looking good. And for him, the revolver didn't carry enough rounds, it took too long to reload, and worst of all, it looked like shit.

Julian put the shotgun inside the duffel bag and zipped it shut. He quietly took several deep breaths as he checked the scene outside their car one last time.

"Alright, let's go."

It got hot inside the Dodge Magnum a lot faster than Sgt. Frank Hawkins had anticipated. He had turned off the engine and the air conditioning in the Magnum as soon as the sun had set an hour ago. The tire shop was located on a street with many commercial businesses. Cars parked along the roadway with engines running after business hours attracted attention, and attention was the last thing he wanted whenever he conducted surveillance.

Now, whoever was in the beat-up Honda was just sitting there, and Frank was growing frustrated. He felt the sweat underneath his shirt and was tempted to turn the car back on. He eyed the keys dangling from the ignition and decided he didn't want to ruin a good case over a sweaty shirt.

"Looks like they're finally getting out," Katalina "Kat" Esposito said from the front passenger seat.

He could smell the stale coffee on Kat's breath and imagined she could taste it on her tongue. She had transferred into his narcotics unit three months ago, and she seemed to be getting comfortable around him. But he didn't think she was so relaxed that she wasn't self-conscious about the smells emitting from her body.

They had been working nonstop over the past twenty-four hours to put the operation together since he'd gotten word of the deal from one of his confidential informants. As they approached the fourth hour of surveillance, he was getting tired and figured she was exhausted.

Frank sat up. "The one getting out of the passenger seat is carrying a duffel bag."

Hector Franco hated to wait.

His dyslexia made reading difficult, so he didn't like to read. Having ADHD made watching television for more than a few minutes at a time unbearable, so outside of using it for background noise, Hector didn't watch television. He was limited in what he could do to keep himself occupied, so he was relieved when Isaac's guy showed up. At least now he had someone to speak with to pass the time.

Hector eyed the man curiously. He'd introduced himself as Ben and wore a dark blue short-sleeve Polo shirt tucked into faded blue jeans. The guy was slightly built, and his blond hair was cut short. Besides the faded scar on his forehead and the small *Hanzi* tattoo on the inside of his right wrist, he was plain and unassuming, which Hector figured was precisely the point.

"Do you ever get nervous?" Hector said.

He was leaning on the office's reception counter directly across from the desk where Ben was sitting. Ben held a twelve-ounce bottle of Corona in one hand, and his other lay on top of a purple and yellow Los Angeles Lakers gym bag. Earlier, Hector had watched him remove the bag, which apparently contained three kilos of uncut cocaine, from the left rear wheel well of a white Nissan Altima.

"Nah," Ben said.

Hector sucked his teeth. "Man, I don't believe that shit. You're driving across the country with your ride full of uncut white and you saying you don't get nervous?"

"I've been doing this for a while now, and the one thing I've learned is cops are too arrogant for their own good. They think they have it down, but the problem with that is I know what they know. All the cops go to the same schools to learn the same shit from a bunch of ex-cops. The people who put on those schools are so desperate to make some cash that they don't screen anyone, so I go to as many as possible."

Hector smiled. "So, you're just sitting there with them? Chit chatting and shit."

"Yup. The cops spend their breaks eating bad food and telling stories, trying to impress each other," Ben said. He took a long drink from the Corona. "I just hold up a wall and listen. They talk about what gets their attention when they're out patrolling. Technically, it's illegal to profile people. But they do it anyway, except they try to sell it as profiling vehicles and driving patterns, not the drivers themselves."

Ben moved the bag from the desk to the floor, by his feet and out of Hector's view. "I don't get nervous because I know what they're looking for, and they're not looking for someone who looks like me."

Hector imagined himself in a classroom surrounded by cops and almost laughed out loud. The thought of sitting in a room with a bunch of fat cops, all of them too stupid to realize they were within arm's reach of someone they were learning to catch, was pure comedy.

Hector was just about to ask some follow-up questions when Julian texted him to let him know they were outside.

KAT WATCHED as the three men entered the tire shop. Frank grabbed the vehicle's radio mic off its hook and keyed up to speak.

"Subjects just entered the tire shop. We'll start our approach after I get word from the CI that the deal's done. We'll take them as soon as they come outside. Don't let them get in the car. The last thing we need is a pursuit."

Frank repeated information he'd gone over during the mission briefing earlier. It bothered Kat to hear it again, and she imagined it pissed off the rest of the team as well. Most of them had been cops a while and probably didn't feel they needed to be reminded of the obvious.

Kat was sure Frank knew it, too, but he just didn't care. He was an old-school, hard-nosed cop who believed in thoroughness. He had been on the job for over fifteen years and had been on hundreds of high-risk operations. There was nothing anyone could say or do to make him change how he did things.

"I bet they're loving you right now," Kat said.

"I really don't give a shit."

She glanced at him. Since the Honda showed up, he'd incessantly tapped his foot on the vehicle floor. After three months, she was still getting used to Frank's idiosyncrasies. She knew the man was already hyperaggressive, but he got really worked up during operations.

When they got close to any sort of action, Frank's nervous energy would manifest itself through one of his two very annoying body ticks. He'd tap his foot or crack the knuckles on his hands, which drove her particularly mad.

"Here, chew this," Kat said, passing him a stick of gum.

Frank took the gum and smiled. "I guess we've moved past the honeymoon period." He cupped his hand over his mouth and smelled his own breath. "Do I offend? You know, all that coffee you've been drinking isn't doing me any favors either, don't ya?"

"I figured maybe we'd try chewing gum and give the foot-tapping a rest for a while."

Frank glanced down at his leg. "That bad, huh?"

"After three months? Yeah, it's pretty bad."

JIMMY WALKED IN FIRST, pushing past Hector as he held the door open for them with neither a look nor a word of acknowledgment. Julian figured Jimmy, who at a shade over six feet stood about six inches taller than Hector, either didn't see Hector or didn't feel he deserved any acknowledgment. Julian was willing to bet it was the latter.

Angel and Julian followed behind Jimmy, each greeting Hector with an elaborate handshake-hug combination. Julian scanned the room. It had been a while since he had been in the tire shop. Nothing had changed except for the additions of a worn-out dark-brown leather couch and a white mini-refrigerator.

The small office's walls were still the same shade of light green, only dirtier and slightly faded. The concrete floor was stained and cracked and probably hadn't seen a mop in a few months. The familiar smells of new rubber and old engine oil filled his nostrils, and the combination still nauseated him.

Julian spotted Isaac's delivery guy sitting at the desk. "What's up, bro?" he said, walking to the desk as Angel took up a spot behind the office's reception counter.

"How are you guys doing?" The delivery guy stood up, greeted Julian with the obligatory shake-hug combination, and introduced himself as Ben. They sat on either side of the desk, and Julian placed the duffel bag on the floor by his feet.

"You guys want something to drink?" Hector rubbed his hands together nervously. "I got Stellas and Coronas in the fridge."

"Nah, we're good," Julian said. "We gotta be somewhere in an hour. Just need the white and we're out."

"Works for me." Ben looked around the room and smiled. His smile left his face when he spotted Jimmy standing against the wall, staring a hole through him with big, black, empty eyes. "I'd like to get back on the road as soon as possible. I have a long trip ahead of me."

"Did you bring what we ordered?" Julian said.

"Course he brought it, Julian," Hector said. He had moved away from the door and was sitting on the couch. "Why the fuck else would he be here?"

"Chill, Hector." Julian gazed at Hector and motioned for him to calm down. "I don't see a bag or nothing, so I'm just asking."

"Isaac sent what you asked for, son." Hector leaned forward on the couch. "I seen him pull the shit out the car myself."

"Then where is it?" Jimmy said. He was standing by the couch where Hector was sitting. His voice was low and intense.

Julian felt the air in the room grow dense with tension. "Alright, listen. Everybody, just chill." He glanced at everyone in the room but held Jimmy's eyes a few seconds longer. His voice was even and calm. "It's a simple transaction. I have the cash right here in this bag. Show me what you brought—you count the loot, and we can all be on our way."

"Listen, man, that works for me." Ben was sitting straight up in his chair. "I just deliver what they give me to deliver and pick up what I'm told to pick up. It's right here under the table. I'm going to grab it so everyone just stay calm, alright?"

Ben kept his eyes on Julian, waiting for some sort of signal it was safe for him to grab the bag. Julian nodded at him, so he reached down and pulled a purple and yellow Los Angeles Lakers gym bag from underneath the desk. He placed the gym bag on the desk and leaned back in his chair.

"There." Ben pointed at the bag. "That's what I brought."

Julian pulled the bag close to him, unzipped it, and eyed its contents. The three square-shaped packages were completely covered with gray duct tape. He was confident each duct-taped covered package concealed 2.2 pounds of tightly packed, Saran-wrapped cocaine. Isaac's product was as pure as it came, so pure it could be stepped on three times and still be a sought-after party favor.

Julian poked a hole in one of the packages with a small pocketknife. When he removed the knife's blade from the hole, white powdery trickles, like sand, fell onto the package. He touched the powder with his right index finger and rubbed it between his thumb and index finger.

"It looks good." Julian lifted the duffel bag that lay at his feet onto the desk. He stood up, unzipped the bag, and removed the shotgun.

He pointed the shotgun at Ben. "There's been a slight alteration to the deal."

FRANK'S CELL phone vibrated loudly in the quiet car, alerting him of an incoming text message. He removed it from the front breast pocket of his shirt and read the message.

"Fuck."

"What?" Kat said.

Frank ignored her question. He picked up the radio and keyed the mic. "It's turned into an armed robbery. We're going to have to make entry. Go! Go! Go!"

"JULIAN, MAN, WHAT THE FUCK?" Hector said.

Julian focused on Ben, but Hector's movements were evident in his peripheral vision. Hector started to raise himself off the couch when Jimmy hit him in the nose with the butt of his gun. There was a sound of crunching cartilage, and blood exploded from Hector's nose. He brought his hands to his face and collapsed onto the couch.

Julian remained focused on Ben, who seemed strangely calm despite a shotgun pointed at his face. Holding his gun loosely by his side, Angel moved from behind the reception counter and stood behind Ben.

"What happens now?" Ben said.

"Now," Julian said. He lowered the shotgun as he removed the three packages from the Lakers' bag and placed them in his duffel bag. "We're going to take what you brought and what we brought, and we're going to leave."

"What about me?"

Julian zipped up the duffel bag. “After we leave, I don’t care what you do.”

“How do you think this is going to play with Isaac?” Ben said.

"To tell you the truth, I'm not worried about Isaac.” Julian lifted the bag off the table. “He’s just coming up, but so are we. Now, it’s just a question of who gets—”

Two loud bangs on the front door shook the room. The door nearly came off its hinges as it flew open. A glove-covered hand crossed the door’s threshold and tossed something inside the office.

“Fuck,” Julian said.

The bright white light from the small explosion left him momentarily blinded. Although his ears were ringing from the loud noise, Julian could hear someone yelling commands for them to get down and drop their weapons. His vision cleared up just as the cops entered the office, clearly identifiable from the badges around their necks and “NYPD” printed on their body armor.

There were cops everywhere. All carrying guns and yelling. He tightened his grip on the shotgun. He had to decide.

Death.

Prison.

Laila and Tito.

Julian put his shotgun and duffel bag down and lay face down on the floor. He thought about Jimmy and Angel and wondered what they would decide.

He closed his eyes and waited for the sound of gunshots.

They never came.

CHAPTER TWO

Spring 2015

At eighty-five miles per hour, the video recording system mounted in Diana's patrol car turned on automatically. The red light indicating that the system was operating had started flashing. She had passed eighty-five three seconds ago and was fast approaching one hundred.

The information communicated over the radio was being updated so fast that she could barely process everything. The most recent information indicated an unknown number of suspects were firing weapons inside a large office building. Civilians were inside the structure when the shooting started.

Holy shit, this is it...

Diana patted her chest several times, double-checking that she was wearing her ballistic vest. Her hand trembled slightly.

"Get it together. Breathe. Everyone is watching. Don't be scared." She remembered the in-car audio recording system that turned on with the camera and was embarrassed she was speaking out loud.

Dumb ass. Now, the peanut gallery will have something to pick apart.

She was the first arriving officer. The tall office building, its size eclipsing the morning sun, was on her left as she approached the incident location. She didn't want to park too close and risk alerting the suspects, so she parked her vehicle away from the building. She exited the vehicle, drew her 9mm Glock from its holster and moved tactically, using the building and other structures for cover as she made her way to the front entrance.

Keep it tucked. Don't want to get shot because I left my big Puerto Rican butt exposed.

As she approached the building, a group of civilians stood just in front of her. They seemed frantic and waved for her to enter. They were yelling, but their words were unintelligible.

Stay focused. Keep moving. Go toward the threat. You're a bad bitch, and before this day is done, everyone here will know it.

Diana reached the front door and took a few seconds to gather herself. She listened for movement or sounds, anything that would give her an indication of where the danger may be. There were gunshots and screaming from deeper inside the building.

She opened the door and quickly entered. The building had no windows, so ambient light was minimal at best. She moved steadily from room to room, and despite the darkness, she used her flashlight as little as possible. She didn't want to give away her location, and her eyesight was adjusting to the darkness, so she didn't want to screw that up.

Don't leave a room without checking the blind spots. Don't leave yourself exposed.

There were more gunshots followed by screams for help. The sound of her own breathing was loud in her ears, and the palm of her hand was sweaty on the grip of her gun.

Get there, but don't rush. When you rush, you make mistakes. Can't afford to make mistakes—too much on the line.

There was a shape in front of her. The flash from her gun's muzzle slightly distracted her, and the force from the fired round threw her off balance. The acrid smell of the propellant filled her nostrils. She tried to refocus on the figure in front of her.

Did I miss? I can't tell. It's so goddamn dark in here.

The audible alarm was deafening. Diana yelled commands that could hardly be heard over the loud noise.

Damn, I missed. Get your shit together. You're a sitting duck. Get off the X.

Diana squatted and moved to her left, away from the threat. She took cover behind a wall, waited two seconds, and leaned slightly to her right—the target was in view. He was holding a shotgun.

She fired two rounds.

Got that prick center mass. You got this, girl. Keep moving.

There was screaming to her right. She slowly made her way down a long hallway, her weapon at the low ready. The screaming grew louder—she was getting closer to the source. She reached the end of the hallway and could go either left or right.

Decide. I can't stand here forever. Someone needs help.

There were more screams to her right. She pivoted in that direction, cleared the opening, and entered another room. She moved to clear a blind spot when she heard the sound behind her. She turned around and saw them. The woman was standing directly in front of the man. His right arm was wrapped around the woman's neck. He held a gun in his left hand and was using her as a human shield.

Diana aimed for the center of his forehead and squeezed the trigger.

As SHE RETURNED to the building's main entrance, Diana went through the last few minutes in her head. She knew she had made some egregious mistakes during the training scenario, including missing several shots she'd fired at targets.

There were two weeks left in training at the Basic Peace Officer Course offered by the Orange County Police Academy, and she had yet to successfully complete an active shooter scenario set up inside the Shoot House. It was the Academy's giant enclosed maze of loud sounds and blinding images. All designed to disorient and unnerve trainees while they make their way through shoot-or-don't-shoot scenarios.

After being inside the darkness of the Shoot House, Diana was momentarily blinded when she walked back into the daylight. When she regained focus, she spotted Marvin Douglas, the Academy's head law enforcement instructor, standing to her left. With his shiny, bronze-colored skin, broad shoulders, and ramrod-straight posture, he was impossible to miss.

She was angry, disappointed, and a little depressed. Instructor Douglas was a man of dignity and discipline and the last person she wanted to speak with now.

Nope. Not now, not today.

Diana hurried her pace and kept her eyes focused directly ahead of her, trying to avoid eye contact with Instructor Douglas. She figured she could get back to the main training building, change, and get gone before anyone noticed. The workday was almost over so it shouldn't be a big deal.

“Rivera,” Instructor Douglas said.

She stopped walking and turned to face him.

Damn.

“Yes, sir.”

“Get changed and come see me in my office in thirty minutes.”

DIANA KNOCKED SOFTLY on the open door and waited until Instructor Douglas permitted her to enter his office. He was turned away from her, working on his desktop computer, which sat on a Maplewood desk which was positioned directly beneath a six-foot Maplewood bookcase.

“Rivera,” Instructor Douglas said. She was surprised when he said her name without turning to see who was knocking. Her surprise lessened when she spotted her reflection in the small mirror mounted to the top of his computer monitor. “Come in. Have a seat.”

The top three shelves of his bookcase were filled with books. Always curious about what others read, Diana scanned the book titles as she entered the office. Most of the books she believed she could have predicted would be in a former law enforcement lieutenant’s collection, books on leadership, management, and motivating others. She was pleasantly surprised to see two books in his collection: *The Beautiful*

Struggle by Ta-Nehisi Coates and *The Critique of Pure Reason* by Immanuel Kant.

She thought his office was surprisingly low-key for a person with his reputation. Before his very successful tenure as the Academy's head of law enforcement training, she'd heard that the man had spent 25 years knocking heads and winning awards with the NYPD.

Despite his position and achievements, his office was much smaller than she would have expected. His desk looked old and used, and the only items on it were a large desk calendar covered with handwritten notes and a Marine Corps coffee mug he used as a penholder. Except for a framed photo of Joe Rosenthal's *Raising the Flag on Iwo Jima,* the office walls were completely bare.

Instructor Douglas finished typing and turned his chair around to face her. "We need to talk about today and where you stand overall."

"Yes, sir."

Instructor Douglas was a large man, even sitting in a chair. He towered over every person at the Academy, and his considerable height was proportionate with his weight, which she guessed was about 240 pounds. Instructor Douglas was soft-spoken despite his imposing size and measured with his remarks. She could tell he chose his words carefully.

"You did not perform well today," Instructor Douglas said. "Actually, you were just short of terrible."

Carefully chosen words, as always.

"Yes, sir, I know."

"You completely bypassed a suspect in one of the rooms, and you missed shots on two targets. One of which involved a hostage." He leaned back in his chair and interlocked his fingers over his stomach. "Want to tell me what happened?"

"I don't have any excuses, sir." Diana held his intense gaze. "I heard gunshots and screaming, so I moved toward the threat as quickly and as carefully as I could. I guess I was moving too fast."

"It's not that you were moving too fast. Moving fast can save lives. However, people should only move at a pace that allows them to perform their duties safely and efficiently. The problem is you were moving too fast for your skill level.

"Yes, there was a perceivable threat, and we expect you to move toward any threat as quickly as possible. But we don't want you moving so fast that you overlook suspects. And we definitely don't want you moving so fast that you miss shots, especially when accurate shots on target may save an innocent life," Instructor Douglas said.

"I understand, sir."

"I know I'm not saying anything you haven't heard from the other instructors. Your performance today isn't really what I wanted to speak with you about."

"It isn't?"

"No, it isn't. The course is almost over, and despite your performance today, you're on pace to graduate with the rest of your class." Instructor Douglas leaned forward in his chair. "But I have to ask—do you really want this? Do you want a career in law enforcement?"

"Yes, sir, I do. I've worked hard to get to this point."

"I know you've worked hard. But therein lies the problem. Despite all your hard work, you're still having difficulty with this part of the job —the tactical part—the shooting. Yes, it's only one part, but I'm sure you would agree it's an important part."

Was that sarcasm?

"Yes, sir, I would agree with you. That's why I'm working to get better, and I believe I can get to where I need to be."

"I have no doubt you can get there—eventually. However, our decisions can have significant repercussions if we react too slowly or make bad choices. We're literally in the life-saving business and don't have time to wait for eventually."

Ouch.

"Academically, you're at the head of your class. You're one of the most intelligent people I've ever met. There are a lot of other career fields where your talents can make you very successful."

Please, don't do that. Don't treat me like I'm too weak to get through this. I'm tired of people worrying that I'm not strong enough to get through hard times.

"I want to finish what I started here, sir." She felt the emotions bubbling up but forced them down. She sat up straighter than she had been and maintained eye contact with him. He returned her gaze but did not speak for several seconds.

What's that look? It looks like empathy. Like he's telling me, he understands where I'm coming from. He's telling me he's sat where I'm sitting, and like me, he chose to fight.

He leaned back in his chair, steepled his fingers under his chin, and looked up at the ceiling.

Or that's a look of pure contempt, and he's saying you're a loser, Rivera. Get the hell out of my office.

"Okay, this is what's going to happen. You're going to take the weekend. Go home and be with your family. Discuss everything with whomever you trust most and think about what you want to do. If you come back Monday and tell me you want to continue, we'll get back to work."

"Yes, sir." She got up to leave.

"Have a good weekend, Rivera. See you Monday."

Oorah, sir.

HER ENTIRE BODY ACHED. At thirty-five years of age, the bruises on her body and her pride took a lot longer to heal than she remembered. Diana sat in the warm bath, listened as Maxwell serenaded her from her phone, and thought about where she was and how she'd gotten to this point. She thought about the options she had and the decisions she was going to have to make.

I can quit. I can go back to Wall Street and find another financial analyst job. If not, there are a lot of things I can do in the private sector. Jobs where I'd make a whole lot more money.

Maxwell stopped singing, and her cell phone rang. A picture of her sister Rosa flashed on the phone's screen.

"Not tonight, *mana*." Diana let the phone finish its ring sequence and waited for Maxwell to resume his serenade.

I'm thirty-five years old. Why am I putting myself through this? Yeah, the academics are easy, but I feel so out of my element with everything else. It's almost over, and I can still barely get through physical fitness training without throwing up. I can't shoot for shit, and I feel like an asshole whenever I have to move around like I'm some sort of Navy SEAL.

She took a sip of wine and noticed the Maxwell song had ended and Prince's "Under the Cherry Moon" was playing.

This is just training. At some point, I'll have to do this stuff for real.

Prince was singing about dying in someone's arms when the phone rang, and Rosa's picture flashed on the screen again. Diana decided to answer or risk her sister showing up to check on her.

"Hi, Rosa." Diana hoped her sister would hear the impatience in her voice and take the hint, and this would be a short conversation.

"¿*Que milagro*? You finally decided to answer the phone," Rosa said from the other end of the line. "I've been calling you. You okay?"

"You've called once. And, yes, I'm fine. I was unpacking when you called, and I left my phone in the other room. I didn't hear it ring."

"And you couldn't call me back?"

"I was busy. I'm still busy. Are you okay? Did you need something?"

"No, I don't *need* anything. I'm checking in to see how you're doing. How was your day?"

"It was fine." Diana's impatience had grown into frustration.

"You don't sound like it was fine," Rosa said. Diana had no response, so several silent seconds passed before Rosa moved on to what Diana knew was the real question she wanted to ask. "Have you heard from Derek?"

"Why would I hear from him?"

"It's been a few months. Now that you two have had some time—"

"Exactly, Rosa, it's been three months. He's not coming back. He left me when I needed him most. I don't want him back."

Diana was angry. It had been a few months since Derek had left, and their marriage had ended, but Rosa continued to ask about him. She knew her sister was worried about her, and although she appreciated her concern, she was tired of the questions and wanted to end the conversation. "I have to go. I'm unpacking and still have to finish some work before bed."

"Okay. Call me tomorrow. Please."

"I'll try. Goodnight." Diana ended the call.

She understood why Rosa continued to ask about Derek. Her sister believed in marriage and was good at keeping hers strong. She kept telling Diana that her marriage was just stressed after the trauma of losing Isabel, and maybe she and Derek just needed a break.

As much as she wanted to, Diana didn't believe it was just a break and hated acknowledging the pain it was causing her. As angry as she was at him for leaving, she loved Derek. She'd loved being married, and she'd loved their family.

She thought about the day he'd left. She remembered lying face-up in their bedroom and being exhausted after two hours of crying and yelling. She had gone home early after Chloe, their neighbor from two houses down, had called to ask her about the moving truck parked in their driveway. Diana had made the mistake of confiding in her about their rocky marriage, so Chloe had turned the dial on the nosey neighbor routine up to ten and was always on the lookout.

Diana had arrived just in time to watch her husband load the last few boxes. Although she had been expecting something like this—things had been different between them after they'd lost Isabel—she'd asked questions anyway. She'd thought if she forced him to stand and speak, they could somehow work through the heartache together. Diana slowly realized there would be no conversation, at least not the one she envisioned.

She realized the man she'd loved was inherently a coward. He'd taken some exhaustive measures to avoid having to speak with her. He'd taken a sick day from work and used a credit card she hadn't known about to hire the movers. Like the antagonist in a crime film, he'd been planning this heist for months.

She'd followed him around their house and watched as he double-checked for things he didn't want to leave behind. She didn't yell at him, and even though she was dying inside, she did not cry. She did not want to give him the satisfaction.

He eventually spoke to her. Derek stopped, faced her, and laid it all out. He told her he wasn't happy anymore, that something had died inside him after Isabel died.

He reminded her, as if she had somehow forgotten, that it had been almost a year since they lost their baby, and she wasn't getting any better. He'd told her he'd only stayed after Isabel died because he thought

Diana was weak and incapable, but he couldn't waste his life taking care of her. And she must have been standing too straight because he added the final gut punch of telling her he just didn't love her anymore, at least not how a husband should love their wife.

Diana waited until he and the movers drove away. When she was certain she was alone, she cried. And in an empty home, to no one in particular, she yelled. She'd gone from room to room, a bottle of wine in her right hand and a full wineglass in her left.

Can't waste his life taking care of me. That's what he told me—those were his words.

She'd finally reached his room, his "man cave." With the walls stripped bare of the giant flat-screen television and the ego-enhancing awards bestowed upon him by the sycophants at his advertising firm, the ugly dark-gray paint he'd chosen was fully exposed. Her shoes echoed as she walked around the empty room, and when she'd thrown the empty wine bottle at the wall, it had shattered, and the sound had been deafening.

She remembered sitting on the floor and staring at the new hole in the wall. She remembered thinking about what it would take to fix it herself and realizing she had no clue where she would begin.

I eventually fixed that hole myself. I didn't have much choice because I was broke, but I fixed it—and everything else in that house, for that matter. I picked myself up, learned what I needed to do, and fixed everything myself.

I did it once. I can do it again.

CHAPTER THREE

FALL 2018

JULIAN OPENED HIS EYES.

The alarm on his cell phone woke him from a restless sleep filled with bad dreams into a dark room that left him momentarily disoriented. He stared straight up at the ceiling and cleared his head. It took him a minute to remember where he was. He wasn't on a thin plastic mattress inside a cold, concrete cell upstate but in a clean, full-sized bed in his one-bedroom apartment on Dekalb Avenue in Brooklyn, New York.

The gray and white wallpaper had turned yellow and was peeling away from the walls, and the old wood floor howled in pain with every step he took. The water pressure sucked, and he didn't have Internet. But after spending the first two months of his release living with his cousin Miguel in Crown Heights, he finally had his own place. It wasn't the best spot, but it was his, and his alone. Julian didn't have to contend with a flatulent cellmate, and he could come and go as he pleased.

He sat in bed and placed his bare feet on the cold floor. He checked the time on his cellphone and saw it read 10 p.m. He had enough time to work out and be at his job by midnight.

Julian went into the bathroom, where he urinated and washed his hands. He splashed cold water on his face and looked at his reflection in the mirror. He was disappointed by the image that stared back at him. It reminded him of the time he'd lost in prison. Now thirty-seven years old, the crow's feet wrinkles around his eyes were noticeable from five feet away, and his hairline started about an inch higher on his head.

He returned to his room and worked out with dumbbells in front of a three-by-five mirror he'd mounted on the wall. Five sets of full-body exercises that left him sweaty and out of breath. He followed that with an intense core workout of crunches, leg lifts, and planks.

He finished with push-ups, three sets of fifty repetitions. Doing them reminded him of the push-ups he had done every day for eight years in prison. It was an unpleasant memory, but he wanted to remind himself of the shithole he'd just left behind and motivate himself to never go back—no matter what.

The Emerald Cleaning Service supervisor, Josh, sent Julian's crew to a twelve-story commercial building near Gramercy Park in Manhattan. They cleaned the building overnight and had to be done by the time it opened for business at seven a.m., so their five-person crew was hustling from the moment they stepped in.

They worked in pairs, each tandem taking a different floor, with the fifth person responsible for waxing and buffing the building's hardwood floors. Julian and his partner, Eli Dominguez, spent the first four hours of their shift on floors seven through twelve, emptying trash bins, dusting, polishing, vacuuming, and cleaning bathrooms. Music from the rap artist Ghostface Killah was booming out the portable speaker Eli had set up at the end of the hall. They were just beginning work on the tenth floor when "Nutmeg" from Ghost's *Supreme Clientele* album started playing.

"This shit right here is the best he ever put out." Eli's voice boomed out from the office he was emptying trash cans in, momentarily drowning out the rap lyrics emitting from the speaker.

Julian was out in the hallway applying furniture polish to one of the eight wooden plant holders that lined the walls. He figured Eli's voice would be raised even if they were in the same room. For a short man, Eli had a surprisingly deep voice that was as coarse as sandpaper. Even when he was in a good mood, everything Eli said had an aggressive tone and the cold hostility of a prison yard argument.

"The song or the album?" Julian said. Despite Eli being in another room and the music playing over the speaker, he didn't raise his voice.

"The album. His best song is 'Apollo Kids.'"

"Yeah, those are both dope. Most of his shit is, but for me, it's all about *Ironman* and 'All That I Got is You.'"

"The Mary J joint? Yeah, that song is fire. But you're wrong. His album *Clientele* is his top shit."

Julian chuckled because it was like this every time he and Eli worked together. They'd spend the night debating music, usually hip-hop music and artists that had emerged in the nineties and early 2000s. But since Eli didn't believe music preference was subjective, every debate had to end with someone being right and someone being wrong. The truth was that Julian agreed with most of Eli's opinions. But seeing him agitated made Julian laugh, so sometimes he would disagree just to get Eli worked up.

"It's great, no doubt. I just prefer *Ironman*. Every time I listen to that shit, it keeps him locked into number eight on my all-time MC list."

"Number eight?" Eli stepped into the hallway. "*¿Esta loco?* Are you mentally ill? There's no way Ghost is lower than top five on any list."

Julian smiled. "I disagree, but that's just my opinion."

"Bullshit. Name your top five. Quick, you shouldn't have to think about it."

"Alright. One through five—Jay, Rakim, Biggie, Nas, and Tupac."

"Now I know you're crazy. How in the fuck you got Jay Z over Nas? And where the fuck is Pun? How can any self-respecting Puerto Rican not have Big Pun on their greatest MC list?"

"He's on it but he ain't in the top five. He's more like top ten, maybe top twelve."

"*Carajo, hombre*. You should be ashamed of yourself."

"Alright, what you got?" Julian couldn't stop smiling at the sound of disgust in Eli's voice.

"Nas, Ghost, Biggie, Jay, and Pun. And that shit right there is the gospel. Lock it in."

"Are we talking the best or your favorite?"

"I don't understand the question. It's the same shit," Eli said with a hint of indignation.

Julian laughed out loud. "Come on. It's time to eat."

JULIAN AND ELI ate their lunch in the tenth-floor hallway. They sat on the floor, their backs pressed against the hallway wall. Eli sat with his knees bent, resting his elbows on his large, protruding belly. His long, dark hair, which he usually wore in a ponytail, like Steven Seagal in *Above the Law*, hung loosely on his shoulders.

Julian sat with his legs extended straight out, his feet crossed, and was halfway through his peanut butter and jelly sandwich. Eli had devoured his tuna sandwich within a minute of unwrapping it and was now about to empty a pudding cup with just his second spoonful.

"They don't put enough pudding in these things." Eli held the pudding cup over his face, bottom side up, looking directly into the empty container. He tried to gather whatever pudding was left in the cup by scraping its sides and bottom with a plastic spoon.

"Those things are filled pretty good," Julian said.

"Not good enough." Eli licked the back of the spoon.

"Want the rest of my sandwich?" Julian held the sandwich out, offering it to Eli.

"Nah, I don't like peanut butter. Ate that shit every day for seven years. I can't even stand the smell of it anymore."

He placed what was left of his sandwich back in its plastic bag and nodded. Julian had learned most of Eli's story in the four months they'd been working together. He knew how nine years ago Eli had spent a week binge smoking methamphetamine during the day and using a sawed-off Remington shotgun to rob fast-food restaurants at night.

When it was all said and done, Eli had robbed twelve different businesses and smoked over five ounces of meth. Even after all that, the cops were only able to connect him to one robbery. And they only made that connection because Eli passed out in his getaway car in a White Castle parking lot after being awake for five days straight.

"How much longer are you going to do this shit, Julian?"

"Work here?" Julian leaned his head against the wall behind him and closed his eyes. "Man, I don't know. Don't have much choice right now."

"Yeah, I remember those days. Fucking parole sucks, man."

He looked at Eli through a squinted eye and chuckled. "What are you talking about, bro? You only have this job because you were *on* parole." Julian closed his eyes. "What else would you be doing if your P.O. didn't get you this job?"

"You're probably right. I never thought I'd still be up at four in the morning cleaning fucking toilets and shit."

"From what you told me, you were up at four in the morning all the time, doing all kinds of shit. So, what's the difference?"

"The difference is, I was high as fuck." Eli extended his legs and placed his hands palm down on the floor on each side of his body. "Sobriety is hard as fuck. I can't even smoke weed."

"Man, you don't need that shit. You've been out for almost two years, right? And you did the first year of supervision. So, if you were able to get through that first year without getting violated, I'm guessing you've been clean this whole time."

"I never said I *needed* it."

Julian opened his eyes and peered at Eli. "Then what are you saying?"

"That it's fucking hard to be awake and sober at four in the morning."

Julian shook his head and chuckled as he raised himself off the floor. "Come on, let's get back to work. I gotta be somewhere in a few hours."

It was still early afternoon, and Diana had already had a productive Tuesday. She'd met with a parolee in her office in Park Slope and visited two more in Clinton Hill, one near Gates Avenue and the other on Lafayette. All three had just been released on drug-related charges, the cases Diana dealt with most often.

Next, she'd driven to Ascension House in Crown Heights to check on a parolee she'd worked with for a while. Ascension House was a transitional shelter program that provided temporary housing for women just released from incarceration. She parked her silver Hyundai Sonata on Union Street in front of the three-story building and went to the apartment of a middle-aged woman named Shelby Clair.

She had to knock three times before Shelby answered the door. She was forty-two, slim, and, despite her years of drug abuse, pretty. She wore a too-big Boston Celtics shirt over sweatpants. A thin silver necklace with a small crucifix pendant hung from her neck.

The sounds of a cartoon show emitted from the back of the apartment. Diana figured Patrick, Shelby's six-year-old son, was watching the cartoon. Diana made it a point to try to learn the name of every member of a parolee's immediate family.

"Hey there, Ms. Rivera," Shelby said.

Although large dark circles bruised the skin underneath them, her eyes were clear, albeit unwelcoming. Shelby had been working the overnight shift loading trucks for UPS, and since she couldn't afford childcare, she stayed awake during the day with Patrick. She only slept when he went down for a nap.

"Hi, Shelby," Diana said.

"I wasn't expecting you."

That's the point.

"Yeah. I had some stops in the neighborhood, and since I haven't seen you in a few weeks, I figured I'd drop by." Diana looked past Shelby into the apartment.

Shelby seemed to notice Diana's gaze. "I'm sorry, come in." She moved to the side and held the door open.

Diana entered the apartment, looking around as she walked a few feet from the front door to the living room.

"How's Patrick?"

"He's good. He's in the back, watching T.V. Do you want something to drink?"

"No thanks, I'm fine. How's the job?"

Shelby shrugged. Diana noticed her hands were shaking, and the track marks on her arms looked new. They were covered with scabs, and the skin around them was red and bruised.

"It's a job. They work you hard over there, but I'm not complaining. At least I got money coming in."

"Have you been going to meetings?"

"I try. But I just don't have much time between working all night and staying up all day with Patrick."

"I thought the people who worked at Ascension House helped with childcare?"

"They do as much as they can, but there are a lot of people with kids running around here."

"I get it, but you know staying clean is a condition—"

"I'm clean, Ms. Rivera. I promise."

"Okay, but sobriety is a process. You need support to go through that process. You need to get to as many meetings as possible."

"I'll try. I promise."

Diana held Shelby's gaze for several seconds. "There's a meeting over on Prospect Place in an hour. Get Patrick together. I'll drive you over and wait in the car with him until the meeting ends."

"Really, Ms. Rivera?" Shelby started moving toward the back of the apartment. "So, you believe me, right, Ms. Rivera? You believe I'm clean, right?"

I want to believe you.

"I'll believe the results of your urine sample."

"When do you want me to come pee, Ms. Rivera?"

"After the meeting, when I drive you to my office." Diana watched Shelby disappear into the back of the apartment.

God, I hope you're telling me the truth.

THE WALK over to El Borinquen was a lot different than Julian remembered. When he was a kid, he'd walk the streets wholly immersed in the sights, sounds, and smells of home. Kids playing handball on almost every block, the combined smell of garbage and fried foods filling the air, and music from Latin record stores colliding in midair with the hip-hop blaring from car radios.

Before Julian went to prison, he'd heard all the stories and complaints about the changing neighborhoods. He'd barely noticed the changes himself. And he certainly hadn't cared if a *bodega* or two went out of business.

But after being gone from the neighborhood for so long, the changes he once couldn't see were now obvious to him. The kids were inside on their media devices, the garbage had been cleaned up, and the Latin record store and fried food restaurants were long gone, replaced with designer coffee shops and doggy daycare centers.

El Borinquen had stayed the same, though. A hole-in-the-wall diner serving some of the best Puerto Rican food in New York City. It felt smaller than he remembered, but that was the only difference he noticed. The maroon-colored walls were still lined with pictures of Puerto Rican icons like Mark Anthony, Roberto Clemente, and Rita Moreno. And the booths, running along the wall, were still a weird shade of blue. He spotted Nikki sitting in one of them and made his way over to her.

Nikki Delgado, formerly Benavides, was Laila's older sister. They all grew up in the Bushwick Housing Projects and attended the same schools until high school. That was usually when the neighborhood's more intelligent and harder-working kids, like Nikki and her husband, Alex Delgado, started using the transit system to attend better schools throughout the city.

Julian and Laila started dating when they were seventeen, but Nikki, the protective older sister, disapproved. After Julian started making moves on the street and earning some cash, he and Laila moved out of Bushwick and into a two-bedroom walk-up apartment above Lopez Insurance on Forest Avenue. When Laila had moved away from her family, Nikki's disapproval of him turned to dislike.

"How are you doing, Nik?" He slid into the seat opposite Nikki. "You're looking good."

"Julian," Nikki said. She looked him over, and contempt was in her eyes. "You look the same. A little light on top, maybe, but the same."

"Yeah." He patted the front of his head at the hairline. "You know what they say, 'Father Time is undefeated,' and all that."

They exchanged awkward smiles, but the tension between them was palpable. Julian had tried a version of this meeting before. He'd asked Nikki to bring his and Laila's son Tito to see him when he had been locked up, but she'd refused. She'd said it was too long a drive, and she didn't have time.

He'd tried again when he'd first been released. He had called Nikki on the phone and asked about seeing Tito. She'd told him no straight up and hadn't even bothered with an excuse. After she'd shut him down for the second time, he'd reached out to her husband, Alex, for help. They went back a long way, and Alex did what he could, but Julian was tired of hiding from Nikki and wanted to be more involved in Tito's life.

Julian wasn't lying when he told her she looked good. He'd always thought Nikki was a good-looking woman. She and Laila had the same dark, wavy hair and delicate features. But, while Laila had deep brown eyes and tawny brown skin, Nikki was light-skinned, and her eyes were hazel-green. She looked more European than Latin. She had put on some weight but otherwise hadn't changed much.

He fumbled with the one-page menu. "And Alex? How's he doing?"

"He's doing well."

A few seconds of silence passed, and she stared at him with cold eyes as if trying to bluff him into folding his cards during a game of Poker.

"This place hasn't changed," Julian said.

"Places like this never do. That's what makes them places like this."

"I passed by the old neighborhood yesterday. The market that was across the street from P.S. 257 is gone, but otherwise, nothing—"

"I don't want to do this with you, Julian."

Julian was surprised by her abruptness and felt himself getting angry. He'd figured it would be a difficult conversation with Nikki. Laila got sick soon after he went to prison, so she and Tito moved in with

Nikki, and she took care of Laila until she died. After that, Nikki's dislike of him turned to hate.

He thought she would at least allow him to make his case, but he recognized her mouth twitch and dead-eye stare for what it was—a big, blinking "DO NOT DISTURB" sign.

"Like I told you over the phone, I won't let you see Tito."

"He's my son."

Nikki shifted in her seat. "I know he's your son. But he doesn't know you, and I think it's better if it stays that way."

"What do you mean by that?" Julian leaned forward angrily. "He's my son, Nik. He's only fourteen. He should know me. I need to know him. It's what Laila would have wanted."

"Don't talk to me about what my sister would have wanted. You have no idea what she wanted. It's your fault she's dead, and you're trying to talk to me about what she would *want*."

He turned his gaze outside the window, took a deep breath, and turned back to Nikki. He was angry but ashamed as well. "Nik, Laila had cancer. How can you say it's my fault she died?"

"Cancer is what's on the death certificate." She leaned forward, glaring at him through unforgiving, hate-filled eyes. "But heartache is what got her. She lost days of her life every day worrying about your sorry ass out on the streets doing dirt. That life was hard enough on her. After you got locked up, she was on borrowed time. Don't get it twisted. She died because she loved you."

Julian didn't know how to respond, and even if he did, he wasn't sure he could speak.

Nikki grabbed her bag and stood up to leave. She stepped toward Julian and leaned over to his ear, speaking quietly. "Stay away from Tito. It took a while, but he's healthy and happy. If you think I'm going to allow you to stroll back in and fuck all that up, you better think again." She stood straight up and walked out of the restaurant.

He didn't turn to watch her leave.

CHAPTER FOUR

ANGEL GUERRA'S *BODEGA* WAS ON JEFFERSON AVENUE, between Throop Avenue and Marcus Garvey Boulevard, in Bedford-Stuyvesant. It was on the bottom floor of a four-story building, the top three floors consisting of six walk-up apartments.

From the outside, the bottom half of the store's windows were covered with pictures of deli sandwiches and various grocery items they had for sale inside the store. Maria's Deli Grocery, named after his mother and the store's official owner, was printed in light-blue lettering on the dark red awning that covered the top of the store's windows.

Since Angel unofficially owned the entire building, he used it as a front and a laundry, cleaning his money by paying himself rent for the six unoccupied apartments. He even kept them furnished and the names on the leases were legit in case someone asked. Even if someone official came knocking, which they never did, he wasn't worried. He kept no product or cash inside the building, and his crew knew better than to act stupid around the shop.

Angel liked where his store was located. A few years back, Brooklyn started to change. The Nets moved into town, the Barclays Center opened, and everywhere west of Clinton Hill saw an influx of million-dollar real estate properties, billion-dollar companies, and hipsters.

Rich people liked to see that their investments were being looked after, so the NYPD always made a point of having plenty of cops proactively patrolling areas that, in the past, wouldn't have seen a cop unless they were called. Angel's *bodega* was smack dab in the middle—between the flourishing and the forgotten. Just close enough to where his shop got a taste of the new money but not so close that he had to worry about more cops in the neighborhood.

His spot was across the street from a Popeyes and T-Mobile Store. Where those stores now stood, before a greedy owner converted a not-so-large lot into two much smaller spaces, there used to be an Associated Supermarket. It was a halfway decent place where people from the neighborhood could buy their groceries from someplace other than a tiny, roach and rat-infested corner store. But like most halfway decent things in this neighborhood, the market went out of business.

He remembered when Carlos Paz and Artie Weisman tried to rob the supermarket. It didn't go as planned, and Artie and Carlos were gunned down for their trouble. It was just one of Angel's many memories of the old neighborhood, and he liked to tell it, especially when he had younger members of his crew around, as he did now.

"Artie and Carlos was always doing armed robberies. They would go in strong through the front door. It'd be middle of the day with people everywhere. They didn't give a fuck," Angel said.

"And they got away with that shit?" Devon Carter said.

Devon and Angel were outside Maria's, sharing a blunt. Angel stood with his back against the store's window, covering a picture of a Cuban sandwich, while Devon sat on a blue milk crate. They had just finished unloading a delivery truck of groceries into the store's basement through a sidewalk entrance. Angel used the basement to stockpile inventory and as an office for himself.

"They did for a while. They was both crazy, even before they got cracked out. They was always doing stupid shit, ever since they was kids. Strong armed robberies in Washington Square Park and shit. Then they started smoking rock, first Artie, then Carlos. After they started doing that shit, they *really* didn't give a fuck."

"Don't sound like nothing nobody around here ain't never done before. Including the smoking crack part."

"Yeah, you right about that. But those two was killers on a whole other level." Angel took a hit off the blunt but did not pass it back. "Stupid, reckless motherfuckers. Shotgunning people in broad daylight even when they was doing what they was told."

"For real?" Devon seemed a bit more interested after hearing the last bit of information. Angel knew Devon had witnessed dozens of violent acts and had been an active participant in just as many, so it took extreme examples of violence to keep the youngster interested in a story.

"Uh-huh. It got to where the streets would empty real quick when people saw those two coming down the block." Angel took a second hit off the blunt and passed it back to Devon. "Except they fucked up and tried to pull that shit in the Associated when Kyle Sinclair was in there shopping. You know Kyle?"

"Nope."

"He grew up on Van Buren. Went to P.S. 305 with him back in the day, but all he did was hoop and never really hung out. He was a good ballplayer—played D1 ball for St. Johns. He became a cop and moved back into the crib he grew up in. He did his shopping in that Associated and was there when Artie and Carlos tried to take it down.

"They walked into that Associated, shot the first motherfucker they saw, and *then* started hollering orders and shit. Kyle was on the backside, wearing regular street clothes but still strapped. He was buying milk or some shit, sees them doing dirt, creeps up from behind, and blasts both those fools."

"Damn, that's foul." Devon sounded unimpressed. He took one last hit off the blunt, dropped it on the ground, and used the sole of his sneaker to crush out what was left of its heat. He stood up, raised his arms above his head to stretch his back, and yawned.

Devon had been on this earth for twenty years and probably had heard a thousand of these stories. Tales of neighborhood outlaws who had the balls to take what they wanted but were too reckless, too strung out, or just too stupid to live long enough to enjoy what they took.

"Yeah, old Kyle became semi-famous off that shit too. There is a ten-second clip on channel seven news of him getting a medal from the mayor. And all Artie and Carlos got was smoked," Angel said.

"They was crack heads. Who gives a fuck?"

"You're missing the point."

"What point?"

"Yeah, Artie and Carlos was cracked out and doing dumb shit. But they was able to do that for a while. They would've had stacks of loot if they didn't spend it on rock. Five-O wasn't even close to catching them. Even with them smoking that shit, it was just their bad luck that Kyle was in the Associated that day.

"They was bold as hell. They would've lasted a lot longer if they'd kept their heads clear and not been so reckless. You gotta be bold in this game—no two ways about that, but you gotta be smart too. Or else you end up dead, and some soft-ass motherfucker gets famous."

"Alright, man, good story," Devon said dismissively.

Angel took a deep breath to calm himself. He looked past Devon at the silver Chrysler 300 pulling up to the curb and its driver, Jimmy O'Donnell. Even though it was after four in the afternoon, Jimmy was just getting his day started. The man was a few months short of thirty-nine, but he was trying hard to avoid the realities of his age. With no wife or kids, he spent his nights doing two things—carrying out Angel's directions and laying down with one of his ladies.

Jimmy leaned his head and shoulder out the car window. "What's up, Angel?"

"*¿Como estas, mi pana*?" Angel nodded at him and smiled.

Jimmy made no move to exit the car, but Angel didn't take any offense. He knew Jimmy was in pain and probably hungover. Angel figured if he got close enough, he could smell the Johnny Walker Black on his best friend's breath.

Jimmy used booze to chase the painkillers he took every morning to manage the ache in his left knee. The pain and a slight limp had been the result of getting kneecapped while he was serving time in Clinton Correctional. He had slowed a bit and was soft in the middle like most guys approaching middle age, but Jimmy was still a stone-cold killer, and Angel trusted him.

Angel glanced at Devon. "You all set for tomorrow?"

"Yeah. Angel, man, I really appreciate you letting me do this one," Devon said.

"Ain't nothing, son. You earned a shot. Do this right, and you'll have more opportunities down the road."

"You ain't gotta worry about nothing, I got this."

He was being honest when he'd said Devon deserved a shot. Devon had been putting in work for him since he was sixteen years old. Started as a lookout and moved up to where he had his own corner. Angel had decided to bring him closer when he saw how good Devon was at putting bodies in the ground. At twenty years old, the kid already had at least ten bodies on him, and Angel figured that count might be low. Devon was a killer, no doubt, almost as cold as Jimmy.

"All you gotta do is take the shit over to Lugo up in Crown Heights. He should be handing you sixty back, and don't let that motherfucker short you neither."

"I got it, Angel. Don't worry. Ain't no motherfucker gonna short me."

"Alright, I'm just saying. Two keys ain't much, and sixty grand ain't shit, but doing good in this business is about your reputation. If motherfuckers think they can just take shit from you, you won't last long."

"Ain't nobody taking shit from me, and I plan to live forever."

Angel smiled. He appreciated the arrogance of youth. "Forever? Really? You'd be the first, especially for people in this game. What makes you so special?"

"There ain't no place in heaven for me, and hell is full. Ain't nowhere left to go."

Angel laughed out loud.

THE TALL MAN looked strung out to Julian. He had big, empty eyes that didn't seem to blink, and an old, dirty New York Rangers hat covered his head. The guy stood in line at Tony B's Pizza on Third Street, near Fourth Avenue in Brooklyn. Julian and Ms. Rivera had already ordered and were waiting near the front door for their food when the man went all in on his Samuel L. Jackson impression.

The pizza shop was a small, family-owned restaurant with limited space for patrons to dine inside. The interior service counter had five stools for customers, and three small round tables lined the wall across from the service counter. Despite its limited space, Tony B's was a popular neighborhood establishment that had been featured on one of those "this is the best place ever" shows on *The Food Network*.

To accommodate customers who could not find a seat inside, the restaurant set up a small section of its counter to service customers standing in line outside. This is where most of its customers placed their food orders and where the man, seemingly unhappy with his own life, was throwing his tirade.

"How the fuck is you out of sausage?" the man said.

The employee, who looked like he may have done some time himself, peered down at the man, seemingly bored with the conversation. "Like I said, my man, we're out of sausage. It happens sometimes."

Julian was surprised. Despite the employee's hard look, he didn't raise his voice.

"I ain't never heard of no pizza shop running out of pizza toppings, especially meat toppings. Meat is like the number one topping for pizza. Everybody wants some kind of meat on their pizza." The man seemed more animated when he noticed he had everyone's attention.

"It is what it is, guy. You want the slice or not?" the employee said.

Most of the customers, Ms. Rivera and Julian included, were uncomfortable with the scene but did not intervene. For Julian, between growing up on these streets and spending time in prison, staying out of matters that didn't concern him was second nature. He figured his parole officer, Ms. Rivera, didn't want to get involved unless a law was broken. He remembered her telling him once that while technically she was law enforcement, she wasn't a cop.

"Goddamn right, I want the slice. Put some extra cheese and mushrooms on that motherfucker," the man said.

THEY SAT on a bench outside Washington Park, across the street from the pizza shop. It was cool outside, according to the weather update on Julian's cell phone the temperature was in the mid-fifties. But the sky was clear, and the bright sun offered warmth and comfort despite the mild temperature.

Ms. Rivera didn't seem to mind meeting Julian outside the workplace. They were a few blocks from her Park Slope office. She could have easily mandated that they meet there, but he was pretty sure she preferred being outside by how restless she acted whenever they met inside her office.

Ms. Rivera used a napkin to wipe her mouth. "Pizza's good at that place."

"Best in Brooklyn," Julian said.

They both finished the rest of their pizza slices without speaking further. He collected their trash into one bag and tossed it in the garbage can against the park fence, directly behind their bench.

"So, how's it been going?" Ms. Rivera said.

"Fine."

She nodded and looked directly into his eyes, silently challenging his response.

He smiled at her. "I'm serious, Ms. Rivera. Everything's fine."

"*Fine* is a vague response at best. *Fine* doesn't tell me much."

"Well, I'm kind of in a vague situation, so fine is probably the most appropriate response."

"What does that even mean, 'vague situation?'"

"Just that some things in my life are a bit uncertain now—a bit unclear."

He gazed at her, and as usual, her eyes disarmed him. Ms. Rivera had big, expressive brown eyes that she used to communicate her thoughts and feelings while making it clear she was strong and not someone to be messed with.

But there was something else in her eyes. Behind the focused strength was a sadness that made her more human to him. It made him feel as if she was a good person and that he could trust her.

She hadn't shown him that side at the beginning, which had been another lesson for him not to be too quick to judge people based on the first version of themselves they presented. After spending time together, Julian realized that how Ms. Rivera had initially acted toward him was how she treated everyone she worked with when first meeting them.

When he got out of prison five months back, he was instructed to report to Ms. Rivera, his parole officer, at her office in Park Slope within twenty-four hours. He had entered through the main entrance on Second Avenue and, after clearing security, had sat in the building's waiting room.

About ten other ex-cons were in the room, all Black and Latino. A few had their heads down, focused on whatever they were looking at on their cell phones. Most stared straight ahead at an empty space. Their looks were a mixture of boredom and sadness, as if the empty space they were staring into was a television show full of bad memories and worse news.

Then, Ms. Rivera entered the room. She shook his hand, her grip strong, and her eyes cold. They went into her small, windowless office. The walls were blank; the only furniture was an old, scarred desk, two chairs, and a cheap four-foot wooden bookcase that doubled as a shelf for an old, beat-up printer.

They'd sat down and discussed his conviction and parole. He'd done eight years on a twelve-year bit for Aggravated Criminal Possession of a Weapon, which meant he had four years of supervised release to look forward to. Of course, he didn't mention he was really in that garage to buy a few keys of cocaine, but someone had snitched him and his boys off to the cops.

She'd handed him the New York State Parole Handbook, and they had gone over the conditions of his parole—predictable rules like not leaving the state of New York without permission or being around people with criminal records.

Last on the list, he had to comply with any special conditions imposed by his parole officer. The last rule, he figured, was a catchall thrown in to give parole officers a stronger leash to tie around parolees. Although having a job wasn't one of the official rules, Ms. Rivera used that last one to mandate that he maintain lawful employment.

"You have to have a job," she'd said to him.

"Yeah, unless we're living in a dystopian society where I can trade a plant for groceries like Kevin Costner in *Waterworld*, a job is pretty high up on my list of priorities."

She'd sat back in her chair and folded her arms, surprised and, what he thought might be, slightly amused by his comment. "I'm serious. Having a job is not specifically outlined in the rules, but I mandate it for everyone I work with."

"Ms. Rivera, believe me, I get it. I will find a job as fast as I can. I already have a line on one through my cousin."

"Really? Where?"

"Emerald Cleaning Service. It's a janitorial company. They have contracts with a lot of the big companies in Manhattan."

"And what would you be doing there?"

"Their Chief Financial Officer spot just opened up. I'm under consideration."

She'd leaned forward in her chair. "Don't play with me, Serrano. I have a series of questions I must go over every day, ten times daily. You'll make this a lot easier for both of us if you just answer the questions straight. I appreciate a good joke—I do. But you're just being a condescending prick, and you're pissing me off. Now, I know this is your first time on parole, but let me enlighten you on something—pissing off your P.O. is definitely the last thing you want to do."

He had been slightly surprised by her reaction. He'd heard tales of parole officers being checked out, doing just enough to stay out of trouble and keep their jobs. He'd figured he'd see what kind of hand he had been dealt. If the stories were true, he could skate through the mandatory supervision. But her reaction had let him know she wasn't the one to be played with.

"Apologies, Ms. Rivera. It was a bad joke. I meant no disrespect. To be honest with you, I'm just nervous. I have a lot riding on this going right. I'm trying to rebuild my life."

She leaned back in her chair. "I asked what you would be doing because I dislike assuming anything. Especially when I look at your records and see you earned your bachelor's degree while you were incarcerated."

"I appreciate you not assuming anything, but your assumption probably would have been right. I'm going to be cleaning offices. I can't waste time waiting for some imaginary job that's never going to come."

"I agree that you need a job sooner rather than later. But why make it sound like something better than working for a cleaning service is a pipe dream?"

"Because I can't imagine it's anything more than that. I don't know if a lot of companies are chomping at the bit to hire an ex-con with a Liberal Arts degree."

"If you really believed that, why did you bother getting it?"

He'd thought about her question. "Boredom? I don't know. I spent my first six months at Eastern pissed off, eating ramen and getting fat. After a while, I started attending group meetings with this pastor, Danny Watson. He was a good man. A former addict who turned his life around. He talked a lot about self-improvement, intellectually and spiritually.

"After a while, I became less angry and started reading everything I could get my hands on. When Pastor Danny brought up the idea of taking college classes, I decided to take a course and see if I could do it. Pretty soon, my routine consisted of early morning workouts and afternoon classes."

"Sounds like you found a way to be productive the eight years you were inside. And I'm sure it helped with the parole board," Ms. Rivera had said.

"I suppose it did. I know it helped make the time go by faster."

She'd looked at him and smiled warmly. "Fair enough. If you're clear on everything you must do, and you don't have any questions, we're pretty much done."

"I got it, Ms. Rivera." He got up to leave when she stopped him with another question.

"Why *Waterworld*?"

Her question had surprised him. "What do you mean?"

"I mean, why reference that movie when you made your point earlier? There are a lot of other, way better post-apocalyptic movies you could have used for your analogy. Why that one?"

"I don't know. Most people think it's bad, but I liked it as a kid. And I think people just shit on it because that's what everyone else is doing. Very few people look past the movie's flaws and appreciate the things it did well. I think it's underrated myself."

"Interesting."

"What do you think about it?"

"*Waterworld*? I think it's hot garbage."

After that first meeting, she started treating him differently. She was never overly familiar or unprofessional. She'd conduct her home and work visits, and they'd meet in her office as scheduled. But after a while, their meetings would sometimes happen over lunch outside her office, almost as if they were friends.

"How's everything else?" he heard Ms. Rivera ask, pulling him back to the present. "How's your son?"

Julian turned his gaze toward the park, where some kids played basketball. "He's fine. I don't get to see him much, but he's doing good."

"What was his name again?"

"Tito. After my uncle. I wanted to name him Piri, but his mother wasn't having it."

Ms. Rivera raised an eyebrow and smiled as if she was both surprised and pleased by this information. "As in Thomas?"

"Yeah."

"Piri Thomas, really?"

"Why does that surprise you?" He was more amused than offended by her reaction.

"I came up in the New York City public school system, too. I *know* they're not teaching about Puerto Rican authors and poets."

He chuckled. "No, they are not. At least they weren't when I was in school. *Down These Mean Streets* was the first book I ever read. My mother gave it to me when I was twelve. I really liked it, so I read more of his writings as I got older. I liked the name, but, like I said, Laila wasn't having it."

"Are you two still together?"

"She died. About a year after I went inside."

"Oh, I'm sorry," Ms. Rivera said. She was silent for a few seconds. "So, who's giving you a hard time about seeing Tito?"

"Laila's sister, Nikki. He lives with her and her husband, Alex. After Laila died, Nikki petitioned for custodial rights. I was locked up and broke. Not in any position to really fight it. Probably would have lost regardless. It was for the best, anyway. She and Alex are doing well. They have a nice house out in Bay Ridge."

"You're probably right about it being for the best. But now that you're out and working, have you talked to the sister about being in Tito's life?"

"Oh yeah, I've tried, but she's not having it. Nikki doesn't want me anywhere near him. Alex and I go way back, so he's been helping with that as much as he can. But Nikki, she's uh...she's strong-willed. To tell you the truth, she's probably right to feel that way. Tito was six when I went in. He doesn't know who I am. It doesn't help that Nikki only knows the fucked-up version of me. She blames me for a lot. To tell you the truth, she's not wrong."

"What do you mean?"

"That's a much longer story." He read a text message on his cell phone. "And I have to be somewhere."

"Alright. Before I forget, get me the address where your son is living. I'll need it for your file. You're doing well, Julian. Keep at it."

"That's the plan. Take it easy, Ms. Rivera."

"You too."

DIANA WATCHED Julian as he walked away and smiled to herself. She believed he was trying, but she knew he wasn't as reformed as he made himself out to be in her presence. Julian was charming and very intelligent, but Diana was not naïve. She knew his criminal actions went beyond what was in his file. She figured he committed criminal acts he had never been held accountable for, and she suspected some of those acts were violent.

But when Diana looked into his eyes, she sensed a paradox. The good man trying to do right by the people he loved intermingled with violent, focused aggression. What, or whom, that aggression was focused on was unknown to her, but she wanted to trust the good man would win out in the end.

Underrated indeed.

KAREN'S HAIR gave off a weird mix of cigarette smoke and flower-scented shampoo that filled Devon's nostrils. She slept with her back to him, so he spooned her. He wanted to put it inside her again—get one last nut before he headed back to Angel's spot with the money, but he couldn't stand the smell of her hair.

He was worked up after making the deal with Lugo. He'd had so much adrenaline running through his body he'd had a full erection as he'd driven to Karen's apartment in Bensonhurst. He'd been on top of her as soon as she'd opened the door, and the smell of her hair hadn't bothered him at all. He'd become a lot more aware of it after he'd climaxed for the second time.

He rolled over, looked at the small black bookbag on the floor, and smiled. For him, the bookbag represented his success and future. Now, Angel would know he could trust him and would bring him closer. He wished Angel had seen him inside Lugo's spot over on Bedford. Even though Lugo had three of his boys there, Devon had walked in with no fear in his heart. He'd played it real cool and had even sat down and smoked a blunt while he'd counted the cash.

He was going to make sure Angel heard about what'd happened. Go see him at the *bodega* after they open and tell him the story while they shared a blunt. Soon enough, Devon would replace Jimmy as Angel's number one, and then he would start seeing some real cash.

Jimmy was cool. He'd let Devon borrow his car after they'd finished the deal earlier. But the man was old and broken and couldn't hardly walk. Devon knew Angel and Jimmy were close, but Angel was a businessman in the end. After Angel saw how Devon had handled business tonight, Angel would have to realize that having him close was good for business.

Devon knew he should get up and leave. He wasn't supposed to stop in the first place, but he wanted to get it in with Karen, and now that he had, he was tired and felt his eyes getting heavy. He started falling asleep to images of himself living in a beautiful apartment on the Lower East Side when he heard the crash at the front door.

He sat up and looked toward the front door just as it flew open. Two men, both dressed in dark clothing and carrying shotguns, entered the apartment. Devon went for his Ruger LC9 handgun, which lay on the floor beside him.

"Don't bother," one of the men said. His voice was slightly muffled by the ski masks he and his partner were wearing.

Devon left the gun where it lay and turned back toward the intruders.

"What the fuck ya want?" Devon yelled.

Karen sat up and held the bedsheet to her chin. He was surprised she wasn't screaming.

"The cash," one of the men said.

"What cash?"

One of them walked to the bed and smashed the butt of his shotgun into the side of Karen's face. Devon felt warm droplets on his arm as she fell sideways onto the bed and screamed in pain.

"The cash." The man repeated the words as he pointed his shotgun at Devon.

Despite having a shotgun pointed at his chest, Devon stared straight up at the man defiantly. He thought about Angel's words earlier about being bold *and* smart. Devon wanted to be bold and fight—he didn't want to give up Angel's money. But he knew he had to be smart and survive this day. If for nothing else, so he could find these two and kill them.

"It's in the book bag." Devon sat up straighter. "You two motherfuckers ain't gonna make it. I'll find you."

The blast from the shotgun echoed loudly inside the small room. When Devon saw the white flash, he thought he heard the man laugh, and everything went black. The last thing he thought of was how the two men came in strong through the front door.

Just like Artie and Carlos.

CHAPTER FIVE

Julian recognized the man playing defense against him from around the way. He had seen the guy playing ball in the park before but hadn't known his name until one of the other players called him Darrell.

He gave Darrell a quick jab step followed by a pump fake. Darrell didn't go for the fake and flashed a "you gotta do better than that" smirk.

Julian went for the jump shot anyway.

Darrell took a hard swipe at the ball but got Julian's wrist instead. The blow forced the ball into the air and out of bounds.

He'd been playing Julian close since the game started, but he'd dirtied up his game a little after Julian took him to the hole on three different possessions. Julian's team kept winning, so he was on his third straight game and was starting to get tired legs.

Julian played ball at Prospect Park twice a week. It was one of the things he was consistent about doing since getting out of prison five months ago. He'd eased back into the sport—playing three-on-three with whomever he could find, just trying to get his game back. He had played some at Eastern, but those games were different. The games at Eastern were unorganized and chaotic, the equipment was terrible, and most of the competition was mediocre at best. He spent most of his time doing other things besides playing ball, so his game got rusty.

After a few weeks of three-on-three with decent competition, he'd started getting into full-court games on the center court, where all the real competition played. Initially, it was slow; he was an unfamiliar face, so he wasn't chosen for a team. He had to "call next" and wait till he was the one choosing a team. After a few weeks, his face and skills became familiar to the better players, and he didn't have to wait long to get into a game.

The first team to eleven won, and Julian's team was down eight to ten. He set up at the top of the key and took the check from Darrell. Julian passed the ball to Alex at the right elbow, made his way to the post, and called for the ball.

Darrell was about six-one, so Julian, who stood just under five-eleven, didn't have to look up at him. But the three inches in height didn't account for Darrell's unnaturally long arms. Despite his height, Darrell was maybe 170 pounds and not very strong.

He took a pass from Alex and dribbled with his back toward Darrell, trying to bully his way closer to the basket. Darrell leaned into Julian, using his weight to try and keep Julian away from the basket. He thrust himself backward with each dribble, crashing into Darrell's chest and face over and over. He shoulder-faked right, then spun back to his left and shot a fadeaway jumper. Darrell jumped, extended his unnaturally long left arm, and swatted the ball into the tree line.

"Get that shit outta here!" Darrell yelled.

He glared at Julian and exchanged congratulatory fist bumps with his teammates as he sauntered back to the top of the key. Julian followed behind and took the check from him. He passed the ball to a teammate, whose name he didn't know.

Tito sprinted along the baseline, to a spot just above the three-point line. The guy guarding Tito seemed tired from chasing him, so he gave Tito a lot of space. The unnamed teammate threw a bounce pass to Tito. Alex set a back pick for the unnamed teammate, and he slipped to the basket. Tito threw the guy a bullet pass, and he lay the ball in the basket without breaking stride.

"Ten to nine us. Ball up," someone from the other team said.

The only woman on the court was on the other team. She took the inbounds pass from one of her teammates and brought the ball up court. Alex picked her up at half-court, but that was a losing battle. She was a great ball-handler and had been killing Alex off the dribble the entire game.

"Alex, back off her," Julian said.

Alex didn't listen and stayed close to her until they reached just above the free-throw line. She stopped, faced Alex up, and surveyed the court. She backed up to give herself some space and dribbled the ball back and forth between both hands. She dribbled the ball slow and low to the ground back toward Alex, who stood in a defensive position at the free-throw line.

When she was about to reach him at the free-throw line, she held the ball high in her left hand for a split second. A hesitation long enough that tricked Alex into leaning too far to his right, a quick crossover dribble, and she had a direct line to the basket for an uncontested layup.

"Game!" someone from the other team yelled.

THEY DECIDED to have lunch at the Chipotle on Seventh Avenue. It was Thursday afternoon, and the restaurant was full of customers, but they found an empty table inside. Julian ordered a bowl with double chicken, brown rice, black beans, medium sauce, and guacamole. Tito had three small steak tacos with lettuce, tomato, grilled vegetables, sour cream, and hot sauce.

"I still say Uncle Alex was playing her too close. Especially since she was blowing by him the whole game," Tito said.

"Maybe," Julian said. He was careful not to speak critically of Alex or his game. "It's tough, man. He just wanted to play good defense and help us win the game. No one knew she'd have a crossover like Iverson."

"More like Tim Hardaway."

Julian smiled as he watched Tito take a bite of his taco. "What do you know about Tim Hardaway? He was way before your time."

"A lot. I love the NBA. Especially stuff from the nineties. Uncle Alex got me into it. I watch a lot of the old stuff on YouTube and NBA

Classic. Hardaway with the UTEP Two-Step, killer crossover. Run TMC with him, Chris Mullin, and Mitch Richmond."

"Damn, I'm impressed," Julian beamed.

This had become their routine over the past five months. As soon as he was released from prison, he tried to connect with Tito through Nikki, but she wasn't having it, so he went through her husband, Alex.

He and Alex went back a long way to Mrs. Dash's first-grade class at P.S. 257. They were close through junior high school, but then Alex started traveling over the Williamsburg Bridge to Lower East Side Prep in Manhattan.

Alex did well in school, earned an academic scholarship to Rutgers, and became one of the top people at a construction company. Julian ended up at Eastern District High School, where they handed you a diploma if you stayed in class long enough every day to be counted toward their federal funding and could manage a passing score on state exams.

Alex started bringing Tito to the park every Saturday. They would play ball for a few hours and finish their day with a long lunch somewhere. It had been slow going initially, trying to get to know each other, so it'd been the three of them the entire time. After a while, Tito became comfortable with Julian. It helped that he seemed eager to know his father, so Alex would play ball and then slip away for a few hours, giving them time alone.

"What's your favorite team from that era?" Julian said.

"The Knicks. Who else?" Tito finished his second taco and started on his third.

"Yeah, I guess that was a stupid question."

"I love that team. I've seen every game that's available on the Internet. John Starks, Anthony Mason, and, of course, Ewing. They would have won the championship in 1993 if Charles Smith could have made a layup."

Julian lay his head face down on his folded arms. "Man, that was heartbreaking. Freaking Charles Smith."

He raised his head, and they shared a chuckle. He stared at Tito, amazed at how much he looked like his mother. Considering how short Laila had been, his son was taller than Julian would have expected. He had his mother's delicate features and tawny brown skin, and his light brown hair was cut short.

But the dead giveaway, the one feature that cemented the boy's gene pool in his mind, was the boy's eyes. Tito had Laila's big, round, brown eyes. The kind that peered into your soul and held your heart captive. Although they had been spending more and more time together, they didn't speak much about Laila. Julian wasn't sure if it was him or Tito avoiding the subject.

They finished their meals silently, but Julian wasn't ready for their time to end. "So, what's up with that school of yours? You like it there?"

"It's okay. Nothing special."

"What about the girls? I bet you're killing it with the ladies."

Tito gazed down at the table.

"I'm sorry, man. I wasn't trying to embarrass you."

"I'm not embarrassed. I just..." Tito kept his eyes fixed on the table.

"What?"

"I don't know how to talk to them. I want to. I really do. I just...I get so nervous. I don't know what to say."

Julian smiled. "Shit, man, is that it? I'll let you in on a little secret. None of us know how to talk to women, and we all get nervous around them."

Tito lifted his head, his eyes wide with curiosity. "Really?"

"Absolutely. Man, your mother and I were together for a while, and I still would get nervous when I saw her. Not bad nervous—the good kind. The kind that makes your heart beat a little faster with excitement. The kind that makes it hard to say even the simplest thing because you want everything you say to have some profound meaning.

"You just need to be brave for the few seconds it takes to walk up to her and speak. You'll be surprised. They're usually nervous, too, and are looking for an opportunity to talk with you. But even if she doesn't speak to you, at least you tried. Then you'll know you can do it, and you can try again with someone else."

"Does it get easier the more times you try?"

"No, not really. The butterflies are always there. But that's a good thing. The butterflies let you know you're alive."

They smiled together like old friends.

DIANA COULDN'T STOP GLANCING at her date Carter's fingernails. She wasn't staring, but her attention would return to them every few minutes. Even in the bar's dim lighting, she could tell he had his fingernails professionally manicured from the perfectly trimmed edges and high gloss of the finishing polish. It wasn't a deal-breaker or anything. She found him very attractive, but it was curious and somewhat distracting.

They had met for dinner at Paradiso, A small, family-owned Tuscan-inspired Italian restaurant on Greenwich Street in Tribeca. It was an intimately lit, long, narrow space with a grand mahogany bar at the far end. Twelve matching circular mahogany tables filled the restaurant, six on each side of the room.

She had spaghetti with black pepper and pecorino while he ate paccheri cooked in meat sauce. She ended her meal with a small cup of lemon gelato while he finished with two fingers of twelve-year-old scotch. After dinner, Carter invited her to continue their evening over drinks, so they walked two blocks south to The Lucky Tavern on Harrison Street.

"My hand to God, it's a true story," Carter said.

"Why in the hell would he do that?" Diana laughed and took a sip of her vodka tonic.

"I guess he just had a meltdown. The stress finally got to him."

"So, he walked into the professor's office and peed on the man's desk?"

"Yup. Didn't say one word. Just unzipped, did his business, and walked out." He took a drink of his Dewar's.

"Did that happen a lot at Howard University?"

Damn, he's good-looking.

"At Howard? No. At Johns Hopkins—a lot more often than you'd think."

"Really? It's kind of surprising to hear so many of our future physicians are headcases."

"Well, it's not really that many, but it does happen. At least it did when I was there. And if we're speaking in relative terms, we're all head-cases to some degree or another."

Um, okay. Where's he going with this?

"Interesting observation. Say more."

"We all have quirks. Little idiosyncrasies that the next person may find curious or strange, even disturbing. Those opinions are just that—opinions. And aren't based on any objective facts."

Now we may be veering off into bullshit territory.

"I was with you till the last part. It's true we have norms, and people who go against those norms may be perceived as strange or *as 'head-cases,'* as you so eloquently put it. But there's a big difference between someone who, say, tattoos their entire face and someone who whips out their dick and pisses on their professor's desk."

He brought his drink to his mouth, smiled, and held her eyes with his. "That's a good point. Now I'm convinced. He was insane." He chuckled and sipped from his glass.

She found him attractive and mildly interesting, but he was undoubtedly arrogant and not very funny. The arrogant part she could deal with—he was an oncologist at Mount Sinai St. Luke's Hospital, and most of the doctors she knew were varying degrees of arrogance—but the unfunny part weighed heavily on her.

She only agreed to meet him after a friend had been relentless about fixing them up. She had been divorced over three years and dated sparingly. Her friends knew this and tried arranging dates for her every chance they got.

"So, you're a parole officer. What's that like?"

Here we go.

"It's never boring, I can tell you that much," she said.

"I wouldn't imagine it would be. Is that something you always wanted to pursue?"

"No, not at all. After college, I worked on Wall Street for a while. I was a financial analyst for a small brokerage firm. But I quit after I got married and moved out to Edgewater."

"New Jersey?"

"Yup." She took a sip of her drink.

"So, what happened? To the marriage."

Nope, that will not be a topic of discussion this evening.

"It ended—like most marriages do." She didn't say anymore and took another sip of her drink. He must have picked up the hint from the long silence because he steered the conversation away from marriage.

"So, you didn't always want to be a parole officer, and you can clearly do whatever you want. So, why are you doing that?"

"I don't know. I thought about going back to the financial world for about two seconds and then realized I hated that idea. Some of the money people on Wall Street are the worst kind of criminals, getting away with some vile stuff. I didn't want to go back there.

"One day, when I was visiting my sister upstate, I was driving behind a police car in Newburgh, and recruitment information was printed on the back window, so I called the number. Ended up speaking with one of their sergeants and gathering some basic information.

"I was thirty-five at the time, I had never held a gun, and I wasn't very physically fit. I realized I was completely intimidated by the idea, but I was tired of being intimidated by anything, so I applied. The department hired me and sent me through a Basic Peace Officer Course," Diana said.

"So, you started in Newburgh?"

"Yeah. I was there for about a year. You know where that is?"

"Upstate? Yeah. I've heard that's a pretty rough little city."

"It can get busy, but I really liked it."

"Then why did you leave?"

"I wanted to move back to the city."

"So why not NYPD?" Carter finished his drink and motioned toward the waiter for another.

"I loved helping people, and I enjoyed being on the job, but I got tired of most of the bullshit we had to do. We spent most of our time arresting addicts and mental health consumers, people who needed counseling and resources, not thirty days in a cell. But seeing addicts off the street, even temporarily, appeased the taxpayers and community leaders, so we kept up the perverse game of Whack-a-Mole."

"It sounds unorganized and like an obscene waste of resources."

"I don't know if I would say that. Everyone I worked with was a good person who was doing a tough job. It's just that the purse strings are held by people who have never done the job." Diana finished her drink. "Anyway, I figured most of the people in the system are locked up for minor drug offenses. Maybe I could do more if I had the opportunity to work with them one-on-one."

"You're an idealist."

"No, what I described is definitely the reality of the situation, so I'm a realist."

He laughed and glanced up when he noticed the waiter was standing there with a fresh drink. The waiter put the drink down in front of him and took away the empty glass.

Carter lifted his glass. "To being a realist."

A corny toast? Why did you have to go and ruin it? Cue violent eye roll.

She lifted her empty glass, touched his glass with it, and quickly placed it back on the table.

This could be a deal-breaker.

"So, what now?" Carter said.

She surveyed the bar. The crowd had thinned, and the staff was cleaning up. Three other couples were sitting at some of the tables, and a few people sat on stools by the bar.

"Now? Now I order an Uber and go home," Diana said.

And you're drunk and not very funny.

"The night is still young—let's go somewhere else. Anywhere you want, just name it."

"Yeah, the night may be young, but I'm old and want to go home."

"You're not old, and you're very beautiful."

And you're fine as hell, I'm buzzed, and comedy is overrated.

"You can come home with me if you want."

He smiled and signaled for the check.

CHAPTER SIX

THE CLERK WENT HEAVY ON THE MAYO.

When Frank had ordered the turkey club on white, he'd given the guy specific instructions he wanted light mayo and heavy spicy mustard. He must've been on the guy's "pay no mind" list because he watched the moron screw up the order through the glass case displaying cigarettes and Lotto scratch-off tickets.

Frank decided to let him finish making the sandwich. He wouldn't pay for it anyway, so what the hell. The clerk wrapped the sandwich in white deli paper and placed it on the counter.

"Seven-eighty-five," the clerk said.

"That's not what I ordered," Frank said.

The clerk's chubby face looked confused, but his expression quickly changed to annoyance. "What do you mean, man? You ask for Turkey Club. That's Turkey Club."

The counter was elevated about three feet, so Frank had to look up at him. The clerk's short arms and stubby fingers indicated he was shorter than the average man. Frank figured he enjoyed the height advantage the counter provided. The clerk had a heavy beard that seemed to be overcompensation for the lack of hair on his head. His English was broken and heavily accented.

"Yeah, I asked for a turkey club. What I didn't ask for is for you to drown it in mayo. It looks like the creampied vagina of a 40-year-old porn star fresh off filming a gangbang scene."

The confused look returned to the clerk's face. "What?"

"Look, Pablo, or whatever the fuck your name is, make me another sandwich." Frank pushed the sandwich across the counter. "That one's not going to work."

The clerk began to respond but seemed to think better of it and didn't say anything. He went back to the table and made a fresh sandwich. Frank watched him through the glass till he was done.

The clerk placed the fresh sandwich on the counter. "Seven-eighty-five."

He sounded angry but kept his head down and didn't make eye contact. Frank picked up the second sandwich and placed a five-dollar bill on the counter. He grabbed the first sandwich off the counter as he exited the store.

He walked one block south on Bedford Avenue and got into the passenger seat of a black Ford F-150 extended cab parked on the street. He closed the passenger door and tossed the sandwich with the heavy mayo on his partner's lap. Heriberto "Eddie" Sotelo, who was focused on the residence at 92 Bedford Avenue, was startled when the sandwich landed on his crotch.

Eddie picked up the sandwich. "What's this?"

"Turkey club. They had a two-for-one special going on." Frank unwrapped his sandwich. "Anything new?"

Eddie placed the sandwich on the dashboard and turned his attention back to the residence, a low-rise, three-story row house with a red brick façade. The outer glass door and front door were separated by a small vestibule. Frank knew from experience that the interior was divided into three separate apartments in row houses like this one. They only cared about who and what was in apartment 1A.

"Nothing. No one in or out. Far as we can tell he's still in there," Eddie said.

"Tony and Kat check in?"

Frank had left his side radio in the truck when he'd gone for food, so he hadn't heard if the other members of his team had radioed in.

Antonio “Tony” Bruno and Kat Esposito sat in a dark blue Chevy Impala on Bedford, two blocks south of where Frank and Eddie were parked.

“Yeah, about ten minutes ago. Nothing to report on their end.”

“Anything from Joe?”

“Nah, not yet.”

Frank took a bite of his sandwich and wiped his mouth with his forearm. "We're gonna lose this collar if those cocksuckers don't hurry up with that warrant.”

Frank had submitted his search warrant request as soon as he’d received word from his confidential informant that there were at least two kilos of cocaine inside apartment 1A. He had the fourth member of his team, Joseph "Joe" Sullivan, hand-walking the warrant through the Brooklyn District Attorney's Office, and it was still taking too long. It’d already been six hours since he’d submitted the request, and last he’d heard, it was still on the desk of an assistant district attorney.

All they needed was a judge to sign off, and they'd be good to go. Frank knew they were on a clock, and he was anxious. They had a few more hours before the information he’d used as probable cause to justify the request went stale, and they wouldn't be able to move on the location.

Frank took another bite of his sandwich and chewed aggressively as his tapping foot thudded loudly on the vehicle floor.

Eddie glanced at Frank. “Frank, you gotta relax, man. It’s only been a few hours. We’ll be fine.”

“Those fucks move too slow. They have no consideration for what we’re doing out here. That cocksucker is sitting on at least two keys, and who knows how much cash."

“The process is the process. Joe is in their face, but nothing or no one is going to make anyone in that office move any faster than they want. You know this, so why get worked up?” Eddie shifted in his seat. He was either cramping up for sitting down so long or bored with the topic of their conversation. His abrupt change of topics was evidence it was more than likely the latter. “So, what do we know about Mr. 1A?”

Frank put what was left of his sandwich inside the wrapping paper and balled it up. He opened the window, tossed his trash on the ground outside the truck, and took a long drink from the bottle of water he'd left in the vehicle cup holder.

"He took delivery of two keys on Wednesday, so it's already been two days. I'm sure he's stepped on it by now, so we should get double that—at least. Outside of that, nothing much. My C.I. says he's small-time, but he's trying to come up.

"Apparently, he was fronted a key two months back, and he was able to move it quick. He paid what he owed plus an extra twenty-five percent within a week. Been ordering up pretty steady ever since," Frank said.

"Always on consignment?"

"Nope. He's been paying upfront. I guess he didn't want to pay the extra twenty-five percent."

"I don't blame him. Twenty-five is steep. So, are we going to book him or work him?"

"That's up to him. There isn't much for us to gain, busting a small timer moving one or two keys at a time. I'd rather work it up to the connection, but we'll see how it goes." Frank took another drink from the bottle of water. "We'll know within five minutes if he'll flip."

"You think?"

"This job is eighty percent reading people. If you ask the right questions, it shouldn't take you more than five minutes to figure out if he's going to be of any use to us."

"Five minutes, huh, Frank?" Eddie said sarcastically. He turned his attention back to the residence. "Okay. I'll bite. Tell me more."

"I didn't think I'd be giving a class on interview and interrogation, but we got some time to kill, so why not. Here's one for you—mispronounce their name."

"What?"

"First thing you do when you sit down to interview a perp, before you say anything else, you mispronounce their name."

Eddie scoffed.

"What do you do if someone mispronounces your name? You correct them, right?" Frank said.

"It's pretty hard to mispronounce Eddie, but I suppose I would if someone did."

"Yeah, of course you would. So would I, and so would anyone with any sort of pride. You mispronounce a perp's name. Their first name, last name—it doesn't matter. Just keep mispronouncing it. If they don't correct you, then you know they're a weak motherfucker, and they'll be signing the snitch agreement within the hour."

"Bullshit."

"Nah, brother, them's the facts see." Frank did his best James Cagney impression. "Believe me—after twenty-three years on the job, I've learned a trick or two."

Frank heard the text alert from his cell phone. He pulled the phone from his jacket pocket and read the message.

"Judge signed the warrant. Let's move."

THE TACTICAL GUYS from the Emergency Service Unit parked their Bearcat a few houses down from the perp's residence. Six members of its Apprehension Tactical Team, the A-Team, exited the vehicle and moved quickly to the front of the residence. Both the outer door to the vestibule and the front door to the building were unlocked, so they made it inside quickly.

There wasn't enough room inside the building for both teams, so everyone on Frank's team, except him, waited outside. He wanted to be part of everything during his investigations, so he followed the A-Team into the building.

They didn't have a "No Knock" search warrant, which meant the Apprehension Team had to knock on the door, announce themselves, and that they had a search warrant for the premises. Frank hated "Knock and Announce" search warrants because it gave perps time to destroy evidence.

When he first started on the job in 1995, Rudy Giuliani was mayor, and the "Broken Windows" approach to law enforcement was how they did business. This meant that everything from panhandling to dope dealing was dealt with the same way—aggressively. Judges were tripping over themselves to sign any and all search warrants.

Now, with police misconduct part of every news cycle and a district attorney up for reelection, Frank would have needed proof the entire Sinaloa Cartel was waiting inside the apartment to get a "No Knock" approved, and even then, it would still have been a maybe.

As they entered the building, the front door to apartment 1A was to their immediate left. There wasn't much room on the right side of the door, so the entire team lined up on the left side, behind the protection of the operator holding a ballistic shield. Frank waited impatiently at the end of the lineup for them to make entry into the apartment.

Inside the apartment, he was expecting to find two to four kilograms of cocaine, cash, and Andre Lugo. He used to move grams and ounces to college kids at NYU, but word from Frank's C.I. was that Lugo was trying to expand. He was buying more weight, stepping on it a few times, and supplying a small crew of four dealers.

Three loud knocks echoed in the small hallway.

"NYPD, we have a search warrant for this apartment!" one of the SWAT guys yelled.

They waited a few seconds, listening for movement inside the apartment.

"Breacher up," another operator said.

The second man in the lineup was carrying the battering ram—a twenty-three-pound piece of steel designed to force open locked doors. He moved to the front of the lineup, holding the ram by handles on both ends like a large gym bag. The officer twisted at the hip and spun his entire torso from right to left, keeping his feet planted on the floor. He struck the door directly above its lock. There was a loud crashing noise as the door flew open. He moved quickly out of the way, allowing the team to enter.

"So, he just kept on playing video games? Even after you guys smashed in his front door?" Tony said.

"Yup." Frank was standing in the kitchen washing his hands. "He didn't budge till one of the tac guys made him move."

"Freaking youngsters and their video games. Not even an M4 rifle pointed at their head can get them to put down the controller." Tony chuckled.

Lugo was handcuffed and sitting on the couch. Tony was standing over him and going through his wallet, looking for identification. Tony had been a member of Frank's current team the longest. They'd worked patrol out of the Sixty-First Precinct in Coney Island together for a few years before Frank became a detective and transferred to Narcotics.

Tony was a big man. A former defensive lineman when he'd played college football at Hamilton College in Clinton, New York. He put his size to good use for a while with the Violent Felony Apprehension Squad before finally hooking back up with Frank in Narcotics.

The A-Team had cleared out, and Frank's team was finishing their search of the two-bedroom apartment. They'd found four kilograms of cocaine and a forty-caliber Glock handgun hidden inside a hole in his bedroom closet. A small floor safe containing eighty thousand dollars was located beside Lugo's bed.

Frank strutted into the living room and sat on a chair directly in front of Lugo. "Andy, my man, today is not a good day for you. You know what we found in here, right?"

Lugo stared at the floor and gave no indication he'd heard Frank.

"Andy, giving me the silent treatment is not the best way to go. If you talk to me, maybe we can come to an agreement."

Lugo did not respond. Frank glanced to his left and noticed Eddie was standing in the kitchen.

"Andy, you keep playing deaf, you're gonna get fucked. Our shit is rock solid—there's only one way to make this go away."

Lugo raised his head and glared at Frank. "My name is Andre, motherfucker. My lawyer's card is on the refrigerator. Call him and get him down here for me."

Frank smiled and stood up. "You can call him yourself when you get to Central Booking."

He glanced at Eddie, who was smiling and shaking his head. Frank shrugged and turned back to Lugo.

"Detective Sotelo, please escort Mr. Lugo here outside and get him ready for transport."

"You got it."

Tony helped Lugo to a standing position. He passed him to Eddie, who chuckled as he walked Lugo out of the apartment.

"Oh well, what're you gonna do." Frank shrugged. "You just can't help some people."

Tony smiled, and they pounded fists. Truth was, Lugo's response was exactly what Frank was hoping for, and he was anything but disappointed. He already knew who Lugo's connect was, but he didn't need the rest of his team to know. Lugo getting offended and lawyering up before he'd said any names was ideal.

"Is Kat still in the back?"

"Yeah, I think so," Tony said.

"Alright. Go help her finish packing everything up. Voucher the coke into evidence."

"What about the cash?"

"What cash?" Frank winked and grinned widely.

"Roger that."

Frank watched Tony walk to the back of the apartment and smiled. And why wouldn't he? The bad guy went to jail, nobody on his team got hurt, and he was eighty grand richer.

Today was a good day.

CHAPTER SEVEN

JAN ZAJAC HAD BEEN WORKING AS AN ELECTRICIAN FOR THE past month at a construction site on Linden Street near Fairview Avenue in Ridgewood. Diana had told Zajac she would visit him at work sometime during the week. She waited until Friday but didn't give him a heads-up. She thought his not knowing when she would show up would keep Zajac on his toes and keep him from missing work.

When she first arrived at the construction site, Zajac was nowhere to be found, so she waited by the entrance. Workers watched her through furrowed brows and squinted eyes. They were trying hard to convey that they were tough guys and weren't happy with her presence. After a few minutes, she spotted Zajac toward the other end of the site and made her way to him.

"How's it going, Jan?"

Zajac glared down at her, seemingly unsurprised by her unannounced visit. "It's going."

She could smell the alcohol on his breath. Zajac was a large man, six-foot-six and close to 300 pounds, with pale skin and jet-black hair graying at the temples. His nose was red and enlarged, and his eyes were tinted yellow around the dark-brown irises. Both were clear signs that Zajac spent most of his days looking for the bottom of a bottle.

They stood by a trailer, away from the heavy construction. Several of the workers eyed them as they spoke. Some looked at her as if she were the last bottled water in the desert. Others seemed hostile and suspicious, so she figured they picked up that she was some type of law enforcement.

"You been working hard?"

Zajac stared at her blankly, offering no reaction. His face was dirty, and his green T-shirt was stained with sweat. He seemed bothered by the question, almost as if the answer was obvious and she was stupid to ask.

"Why are you here?" Zajac said.

"I'm here to check on you. See how you're doing."

"I'd be doing better if you weren't here. You know what type of people work these sites. You being here has them all nervous."

"First, I really don't care how they feel about me being here. And second, you know these visits are part of your parole. So, why the attitude?"

"There's five different ways you could handle these checks, but you choose the most public one. If you're so hungry for the attention of men, I could think of one or two things you could do to get some good attention." A thin smile crossed Zajac's face, and he stared down at her menacingly, keeping his eyes focused on her chest.

Diana's blood ran cold, and she could feel her knees begin to shake. She made her own schedule and didn't check in with her office, so it'd be a while before anyone came looking for her if anything went down. Zajac was a violent man who was capable of much more then thinly veiled threats.

A former member of the Greenpoint Crew in Greenpoint, Brooklyn, he had done time for multiple assault and drug offenses, been paroled, and gone back on a first-degree assault conviction after he'd used a metal pipe to break a guy's arm over a gambling debt.

When he got out, everyone he'd run with in his youth was gone, erased by death, prison, or substance abuse. He was like a museum exhibit to the new generation—mildly interesting for a few minutes but inevitably dismissed and forgotten. The realization of his place in the world made Zajac angry and resentful, and when he felt cornered—extremely dangerous.

Diana backed up a step to create some distance between herself and Zajac. She took a defensive stance and held her hand near her right hip, where her gray blazer covered her 9mm Glock handgun.

"You need to think about how this can go in the next few seconds." Diana spoke slowly and deliberately, not wanting her voice to reveal any of the fear she felt. "I'm here for a simple visit, but if you want, I can violate your ass right now. I'll make sure the only time you see sunlight over the next five years will be during yard time at Five Points."

There was fury in Zajac's eyes. She could see the carotid artery in his neck pulsating, and his hands were balled into fists. "Don't come around here no more. I'll come down to your office when I can, and we can handle these bullshit check-ins there. But you don't show up here no more."

Diana relaxed her arm and softened her stance. She took a second before answering to collect herself. She didn't want him to hear the fear she was feeling. "Let's be clear on one thing—I'll go where I want when I want. You are a parolee. You're not running anything, and you do as you're directed. Is that understood?"

Zajac scanned their surroundings. Their exchange had caught the attention of several workers who were now milling about and watching them. "Yeah."

Diana noticed him looking at the people standing behind her. She wasn't sure if they would come to her aid if he attacked her or helped him beat the crap out of her.

"Is your boss in the trailer?"

"Should be."

"I'm going to go speak with him about your performance. You need to get to my office tomorrow and give a urine sample."

He walked past her without responding, close enough that his arm grazed her shoulder. Diana turned and watched him walk away to be sure he didn't attack from behind. She wasn't sure if the presence of potential eyewitnesses saved her from an assault or if he'd just calmed down on his own. Either way, she'd felt uncontrollable fear and was ashamed that she had.

They were chickenshit reasons, but she had more than enough cause to violate him right then and there. But Diana knew he wouldn't comply and feared what would happen to her when he didn't. She decided to wait. If he bothered to show up at her office, she'd have more officers ready to take him into custody if needed.

If he didn't show up, she'd violate him and have a warrant issued for his arrest—have the NYPD pick him up. She knew it was the smart, safe play but still felt like a coward.

She turned and walked to the trailer.

ANGEL WATCHED the television with the sound muted. He sat back on his dark brown leather recliner with an ashtray on his stomach and a tightly wrapped blunt in his left hand. His right hand was curled behind his head as he watched Keanu Reeves hang on to the bottom of a speeding bus.

"So, what do you think?" Angel said.

"I don't know," Jimmy said.

He sat slouched on Angel's couch. His head was leaned back, and his eyes were closed. Angel could smell the alcohol on Jimmy's breath when he'd first entered the apartment. He knew Jimmy wasn't quite drunk yet, but he wasn't far off either.

"You telling me you ain't heard shit? It's been almost a week."

"Nothing."

Angel shook his head. "Devon gets smoked, someone takes our money, and nobody don't know shit? That's bullshit. Somebody knows something."

"I agree, but I don't know who yet."

"Why the fuck didn't Devon come back here with my shit that night?" Angel spoke louder and with more intensity.

"I don't know. Like I told you, I went with Devon to do the deal, and after we was done, I told him to bring it back here. I didn't know he was gonna go lay down with one of his bitches."

Angel had spoken with Jimmy about this before. He had woken up the morning Devon got smoked, still groggy and a bit hungover from the night before. He hadn't even realized Devon hadn't come back with his money till Jimmy called to tell him Devon was dead. The girl he'd been with, Karen, called the cops after two guys had broken into her apartment and shot Devon in the face with a shotgun. Word was, she'd told the cops, two men had stolen some money from Devon.

He'd sent Jimmy to have a conversation with Karen. After going to work on her for a few hours, Jimmy came back convinced she was telling the truth about the two guys and the stolen money. Jimmy was never one to leave witnesses, so she'd been found a day later under the Williamsburg Bridge with her throat slit and her face so bruised her own mother barely recognized her.

"Jimmy, man, you should have stayed with him. Made sure he came back here with the money."

"You wanted to give the youngster a shot, Angel. I ain't no fucking babysitter. Once the deal was done, I expect that motherfucker to handle business and bring the shit back here." Jimmy sat up. "It's only sixty Gs. Who gives a fuck?"

"The money ain't the problem, Jimmy, and you know it. Some bitch ass motherfuckers thinking they can take my shit and there not be any consequences is the problem." Angel took a hit off the blunt. "You think it was Hawkins?"

"It wouldn't make sense if it was. I mean, why fuck with our arrangement? I wouldn't put it past him either, though. Hawkins is a dirty motherfucker. What do you think?"

"I don't know yet, but we gotta tighten the circle. We got too much business coming up to have shit be this sloppy."

Jimmy leaned forward and stared absently at the television. "You heard Julian's back?"

Angel eyed Jimmy suspiciously. "Yeah, so what?"

"I'm thinking we put him on."

"What's the matter with you? Didn't you just hear me say we have to tighten the circle? And you want to bring on *another* motherfucker?"

"Julian ain't just another motherfucker. We can trust him."

"No, we *could* trust him. He's been out the game. Locked up for like eight years."

"Exactly. He did his time, day-for-day. We know he won't snitch, and we know he can put in work. That motherfucker wasn't afraid of shit."

"Jimmy, man, that was yesterday. Being locked up changes people. And with his girl dying and shit—man, I don't know. I heard he's been out for almost six months, and he ain't come through here once, not even to say, 'what's up.' Seems to me like he don't want no part of this shit no more."

"He's on parole, Angel. You know how that shit goes."

"Man, don't nobody give a fuck about parole. Do you think he knows what happened? That I put Hawkins on us that night?"

"How could he? Hawkins kept everything quiet. And besides, I did time off that shit too. He knows I got locked up, so if you and me are still cool then he shouldn't be worried about you. As far as anyone knows, Hector was the snitch, and he got dealt with."

Angel glanced at the television and shook his head absently. "I don't know."

"Listen, let me talk to him. See where his head is at. If I like what I hear from him, I'll bring him through, and we can see what's up. What do you think?"

Angel took a hit off the blunt and thought about Julian and the work the three of them used to put in together. Julian had been kind of the leader when they were first coming up. He had been bold as fuck, and smarter than everyone else. Two good things to be when you're trying to make a name for yourself in this game.

But Julian had been too careful. It was taking too long for their little crew to get anywhere, so Angel made a move. He knew it was a risk to bring Julian back in after what he'd gone through and after being out of the game for so long, but Angel had big things planned, and he needed soldiers.

"Alright, man. Let's give it a shot."

CHAPTER EIGHT

Dr. Latonya Griffin's office was on the ninth floor of a twelve-story building on Maiden Lane in the East Village. Diana was already running late, so she was relieved to make it across the Brooklyn Bridge before rush hour started. Traffic on the Bridge was always heavy. But it was Monday, and the three-hour blocs in the morning and early evening, when the bridge filled with people traveling to and from the city, made it all but impassable.

She found a parking spot a block from the building and entered the doctor's office reception area just five minutes late for her appointment. Diana headed toward the sitting area while typing reminders on her phone's Note App, notes she would use later to write detailed reports of her meetings with parolees.

She had been in Dr. Griffin's office dozens of times, so she was comfortable navigating her surroundings while her attention was concentrated on other things. She sat down in her familiar spot, a single chair away from the bathrooms and water cooler, and waited to be called into Dr. Griffin's office.

"Diana."

She looked up when she heard Dr. Griffin's familiar voice call her name. "Hello, Doctor. Sorry, I'm late."

"No worries at all. Come on in."

Like the reception area, Dr. Griffin's office was elegant but simple. The large office's walls were painted a light but warm cream color. A wood desk, chair, and bookcase were all the same shade of reddish-brown and took up an area on the far end of her office. A laptop computer sat open on her desk, and the bookcase was filled with books, none of which Diana could identify from where she stood.

Diana made her way to the area set aside for sessions. The furniture in this space, two oversized gray-blue fabric chairs positioned so the chairs' occupants faced each other, was arranged to promote intimate conversations. There was no coffee table or other obstruction between the two chairs.

They each took a seat on one of the chairs and smiled politely. It had been over a month since their last session, but Diana felt no awkwardness. It hadn't been like that for her in the beginning.

Before her first session, Diana hadn't understood therapy and hadn't believed she needed it. She knew she was depressed and maybe broken, but she thought she could find her way through it on her own. How she'd grown up, the thoughts and feelings she was experiencing weren't acknowledged, much less discussed openly. That's how she'd lived her life, even after her daughter died and her marriage disintegrated.

"So, how have you been? It's been a little while since we last spoke," Dr. Griffin said.

"Yeah, I'm sorry. Work has been crazy. I just haven't had a lot of time."

"There is no need to apologize. Our time together is for you and based on what you feel you need. If you don't feel the need to come as often or at all, that is perfectly fine."

Dr. Griffin's mouth morphed into a wide, warm smile. The deep dimples in her dark brown cheeks emphasized its sincerity and made Diana feel safe—the same way she'd felt every time she met with Dr. Griffin.

For Diana, speaking with Dr. Griffin, with her strange accent that combined the buttery southern flavor of her native South Carolina with the razor-sharp edge of her adopted New York, was a calming and cathartic experience.

"I've started dating again," Diana said.

"That's good to hear. Is it serious?"

Hell, no.

"No, not at all."

"Any reason why not?"

"Nothing in particular. He's a nice man, very attractive. I'm just not in that place."

I have my own issues. Dealing with someone else's neurosis is not for me.

"And it's okay to feel that way. Even though it's been a few years, you went through a lot—"

"I slept with him."

Dr. Griffin leaned back a little and smiled. "Okay, I ain't mad at you. Do your thing, girl." They both chuckled. "Seriously, if you felt comfortable and safe to be with this person, good for you."

"I did. I jumped in faster than I ever had before, but it had been a while and...I don't know. I just wanted to, so I did."

I'm a woman. I have needs.

"There's nothing wrong with that, nothing at all. You're an adult and can live your life how you choose. If it made you happy, so be it. You deserve to be happy."

"Yeah, 'happy' is probably too strong a word. He wasn't very good. I would say I was sated."

They shared a laugh and settled into a brief, comfortable silence.

"So, those are new." Dr. Griffin nodded at the mala beads bracelet on Diana's left wrist. "How long have you been practicing Buddhism?"

Diana glanced down at her wrist and rubbed the Sandalwood Tiger's Eye mala beads between her fingers. "I wouldn't say I've been practicing Buddhism, but I have become very curious about it." She returned her gaze to Dr. Griffin. "I've been interested in Eastern philosophy since college but never really invested in learning about it. Nothing else seemed to work for me, so I revisited it. I've been reading a lot about it the past few months and recently started meditating." Feeling self-conscious, Diana covered the beads with her other hand. "I know it must sound a bit desperate."

"No, quite the contrary. Spiritual growth is a very important part of mental and emotional health. It's a good thing that you're exploring something you find interesting. Is it helping you at all?"

"I don't know. I guess. I don't think I'll ever be a true Buddhist. I don't know if I could commit to the whole monastic existence, but there are parts of the philosophy I really connect with."

"There's nothing wrong with that. I even think the Dalai Lama said, 'Do not try to use what you learn from Buddhism to be a Buddhist; use it to be a better whatever you already are.' Or something like that."

"Impressive."

Diana was surprised even though she knew she shouldn't have been. Dr. Griffin was a brilliant woman with a curious mind. It made perfect sense she would be able to quote the Dalai Lama off the top of her head.

"Not really. I just have a lot of time to read. Go on with what you were saying," Dr. Griffin said.

"I was saying that I find certain parts of the philosophy interesting and helpful. There's this whole thing about the mindfulness approach to grief and loss. Buddhism teaches that mindfulness is helpful during the grieving process because it helps acknowledge the universality of loss and accept the inevitability of loss as a part of life."

"And you find this idea of being *mindful* helpful?"

Diana thought about the question. It had been almost four years since her three-year-old daughter Isabel died, and she still found it difficult to move on. She had tried many different things to get through the heartache, but nothing seemed to work. She felt like she was perpetually stuck in the depression stage of the seven stages of grief, and she was trying desperately to get to stage seven—acceptance and hope.

"I don't know. Maybe. All I know is that there are days when I feel lost and inadequate— like I have no value. And there isn't a day that goes by that I don't feel sad at some point. I'm just looking for anything that will help get me on the other side of this," Diana said.

"Since Eastern philosophy plays such a significant role in this conversation, I want to share a story I once read. There was a woman named

Kisa who gave birth to a son. One day, when her son was still a baby, he got sick and died.

“Kisa carried his body around her village, asking if anyone could bring him back to life, but there was nothing anyone could do to help her. She was so desperate the other villagers thought she had gone mad. Finally, Kisa visited the Buddha about bringing her son back to life. He told her he could bring her son back. But first, she had to bring the Buddha a mustard seed from a household where no one had ever lost someone.

“Kisa went to every home in her village, but she couldn't find a household where anyone had not experienced the loss of a loved one. Eventually, Kisa realized that everyone had lost a family member. She now understood that death was inevitable. That it’s a natural part of life. When she accepted this fact, she was able to work through her grief and bury her son.”

I’m not an idiot, Doc.

“I understand that death is inevitable. But accepting that fact hasn’t helped make the pain go away,” Diana said.

"Then that may be the problem. If you're waiting for the pain to go away, you're only going to cause yourself more suffering. Obviously, the story shouldn't be taken literally, but some lessons can be learned if we understand the message. Trying to ignore or stave away our emotions is a losing battle, so why try? Instead, we should make peace with the emotions, identify the cause, and figure out how to use those emotions to make us stronger.

"Another lesson, or message, is that you're not alone. What you're going through is universal. Everyone, at some point, experiences pain and grief. Sharing this experience with other people may alleviate some of the sadness.

“Isabel is gone. It may become dull over time, but the pain will never go away. Rather than use that as an excuse to disappear, use her memory to fuel you. To push forward every day and live life,” Dr. Griffin said.

They were both silent for a few seconds. Diana stared at Dr. Griffin through tear-filled eyes. “You’re pretty good at this, you know.”

“I wouldn’t be so sure about that. I’m almost positive I butchered that story, so I may have screwed up the message. But, hey, whatever works, right?"

Chuckles and tears carried them through the rest of the session.

THE WALLS in Julian's old building's community porch were graffiti-covered. But he was focused on a small section near the top right-hand corner of the wall that seemed strangely familiar. At first glance, the images appeared as if a child had drawn them. Two pink-faced policemen, with fangs for teeth and holding brown-colored batons, stood on either side of a black silhouette. The policemen were drawn to appear as if they were using their batons to strike the black silhouette.

"See anything you remember?" Jimmy said.

"Some stuff, yeah. This is new." Julian pointed at the images he'd been staring at.

"That? Looks like a little kid got his hands on some markers."

"Nah, it's pretty good, actually. There's a good artist somewhere in this building."

"You bugging. That shit is kiddie scribble."

"Nah, man, it's a Basquiat."

"A what?"

"Jean-Michel Basquiat."

Julian glanced over his shoulder. Jimmy was sitting on a milk crate and focused on rolling a blunt.

"Never heard of him," Jimmy said absently.

"Artist from the eighties. Born and raised in Brooklyn. He started out as a graffiti artist—used to throw up SAMO. Whoever drew this copied it from one of his paintings,"

"*SAMO*? What's that?"

"Same Old Shit."

"Ha. He got that right. Where you learn that stuff from anyway?"

"Must have read it somewhere, I guess."

"Yeah, you was always reading. Must have a lot of time to read when you was locked up."

"Hell, yeah, I did. Ain't shit else to do in there. What'd you do?"

"Jerk off, gamble, workout, fight, jerk off some more. In that order, too."

They both laughed, and Julian thought about how not much had changed. New trash covered old streets, and rancid smells still filled the air. Different people sat on the same benches, talking the same gossip. New dope boys stood on the same corners moving the same shit. Gentrification was in full effect throughout the city, but this place remained unchanged.

For all the things that hadn't changed, Jimmy was not one of them. Julian thought his friend looked a lot older than thirty-eight, and somehow, he seemed physically weaker and less confident. Julian had noticed the subtle limp when Jimmy walked, and what had once been over 200 pounds of defiant arrogance was now 170 pounds of memories of what once had been.

He couldn't help but feel sadness when he looked at Jimmy. He, Angel, and Julian had run together, but Julian and Jimmy were best friends. They'd taken care of each other when they had been in the game. It was clear that this was another life that got screwed up when everything went down the way it did, and they were forced to go separate ways. They were each other's compass—without one, the other was lost.

"So, why ain't you come see me before today? I heard you been out like five months or some shit," Jimmy said.

"Man, I'm on parole. You know how that shit goes. I been trying to reconnect with my son, but his aunt ain't trying to have it. Between her and my P.O., I gotta fly straight."

"Nikki? Yeah, she always was a tough bitch. How is her fine ass anyway?"

"She's doing good. She married Alex Delgado. They're doing really good, actually."

"Alex Delgado? From the thirteenth floor? That motherfucker was soft as baby tissue."

"Nah, man, he's good people. He helped take care of my son while I was locked up. He's been hooking me up, bringing Tito around to see me."

"That's good. How old is the little man now, anyway?"

"Fourteen."

"And he remembered you?"

"Yeah. He was six when I got locked up. Young, but not so young he forgot me. Laila didn't bring him to see me when I first went in. She wanted to wait till he was a little older, but she died before she got the chance. Nikki took him in, and you know how that goes with her."

"Yeah. I'm sorry about Laila, man. And I'm sorry I didn't do more for Tito when I got out. I spent my first year out just trying to get my shit together, and before I knew it—"

"Don't worry about it."

Jimmy sounded remorseful, and Julian was honest when he said not to worry about it. He didn't expect anyone to care for his kid when he went inside. That was just the way it was for people in the life. It was all smiles and empty promises about being there for each other when things were good. But as soon as the bad times came, it was every man for himself.

"So, how's that job of yours?" Jimmy said.

"It's work. Money sucks, hours suck. Ain't much more to say about it."

"Yeah, ain't shit out here for ex-cons. No matter what they say about rehabilitation or second chances, the system ain't meant for people like us. Motherfuckers make it hard as hell to stay straight."

"I guess. All I know is I gotta find something better. The fucking apartment alone is killing me. I'm barely scraping by, and I definitely won't be able to take care of Tito on what I'm making."

"I feel you, fam." Jimmy sounded uninterested. He lit the blunt, took a long hit, and looked at Julian. "So, speaking of money, what do you think about coming back on? Working with me and Angel again?"

"*With* you or *for* Angel?"

"With us. What the fuck you mean 'for Angel?'"

"I heard Angel's running things now."

"Who'd you hear that from? Me and Angel are doing this together. He just handles the money and shit. You know he's always been good at keeping stuff organized."

Jimmy was getting angry. Even when they were kids, Jimmy was always sensitive about how people perceived him and his role in their trio. To people in the neighborhood, Jimmy was the muscle—the big, strong, remorseless killer. While Angel and Julian, more so Julian, were seen as the decision-makers.

Even though they all put in work and had bodies on them as well, Jimmy was the enforcer. He didn't seem to feel guilt or pity, which, combined with his size and strength, made him ideal for that role.

"I just heard Angel's the man. He has that little *bodega*, got all them youngsters working for him—"

"*Us*. They working for us. Me and Angel is partners. Like I said, he's good at keeping shit organized. Uses the store and apartments to clean our money."

"Really? You guys got it like that now?"

"You know it. Man, Angel got us into cryptocurrency, shell companies, all kinds of shit. It's got to where we don't even keep cash around. Except when we going to make a buy. Them Honduran cats don't fuck with no cyber money. They want cash in hand—know what I'm saying?"

"Yeah, I got it." Julian walked over and sat down on a milk crate next to Jimmy. "It sounds good. I gotta think about it. I still have questions."

"Like what?"

"Like what happened that night? How the fuck were all those cops there waiting for us? There was a fucking snitch, man. Who was it?"

"What the fuck you mean 'who was it?' It was Hector."

"You sure?"

Jimmy's eyes intensified and he leaned back slightly. "What the fuck is you trying to say?"

Julian thought back on the night everything changed for him. He remembered being disoriented from whatever the cops threw in the room and then making the decision to lay it down and not try to shoot it out. He also remembered how Angel and Hector weren't there when they'd finished loading them all into the transport vehicle.

He'd heard the cops talking on their radios about searching for one of the suspects who ran off. The story he got later was that Angel made it out of the building through a back door in the garage. Hector hadn't been charged because the cops identified him as the victim.

The narcotics detectives had pushed Julian for information about the one that had got away when they'd interrogated him. They'd told Julian that giving the person up would help him with his case. He hadn't talked, just asked for his lawyer, and ended up with a twelve-year sentence.

“Where was Angel? How the fuck did he get away? There were cops everywhere,” Julian said.

"I don't know how got away but he did. He got lucky, and we didn't. It just be that way sometimes. Instead of being all paranoid and shit, you should be congratulating him. Angel just did what any of us would have done if we could. It was Hector, man. How in the fuck he don’t get charged? He arranged the whole motherfucking deal. Even that white boy Isaac sent did three years.”

“Do you know that for a fact, or is that what you heard?”

“Julian, man, I don’t like what you’re saying. Angel ain’t no fucking snitch. He got more bodies on him than you. I been with him the last five years. I seen what he done. There ain’t no fucking way on earth he’s a snitch with all the shit he done the past few years. Including with Hector’s snitch ass. Angel went to see that motherfucker and beat the truth out of him. Threw that little piece of shit off a roof and finished it.”

“But you weren’t there, right? You don’t know what Hector said.”

Jimmy stood up and moved away from Julian. “It don’t matter if I was there or not. Hector was the snitch. Angel said so. I trust him as much as I trust you. Angel got his ass—case closed. Now we’re here and things are going good. We're making money, and I'm asking you if you want in. Simple fucking question.”

Julian stood up and ambled back toward the fence. He thought about where he was and how he'd got there. He knew confronting Jimmy was risky, but it had to be done. He had needed to look in his eyes and see how he responded, but he still wasn't sure about Jimmy.

Angel, on the other hand, was a different story altogether. Something went wrong that night, and Julian had lost everything. He believed someone he trusted had done something that put into motion a chain of events that took him away from his family and killed the woman he loved. He was pretty sure that person was Angel.

“Alright, bro, hook it up.”

CHAPTER NINE

FRANK USED A NICKEL TO REMOVE THE SCRATCH-OFF INK drawing of cash that hid the number on the card. The number that'd been revealed was more of an inkblot, but he was pretty sure it was forty-eight. It didn't matter anyway; forty-eight wasn't one of the ten numbers he had to match to win any money.

Frank had gone into the convenience store on the corner of Wilson Avenue and Bleecker Street to buy a cup of coffee. He'd walked out with a twenty-dollar scratch-off card that could payout as much as five million dollars. The picture on the front of the card depicted five rows with four stacks of cash in each row. The top of each cash stack hid a number underneath; if the revealed number matched any of the first ten numbers, then Frank would scratch the bottom of the matching cash stack to reveal the cash prize. He had twenty chances to win something.

Frank leaned on the hood of a gray Honda Civic parked in front of the Eighty-Third Precinct on Wilson Avenue. His cell phone vibrated in the front right pocket of his pants, alerting him of an incoming text message. He ignored it and kept his concentration on the scratch-off card. He bit his lower lip and used more strength than was needed to scratch the remaining nineteen cash stacks. Frank reviewed the hidden numbers and saw he had no winners.

"What's up, Frank?"

He turned when he heard his name and saw Bobby Sinclair standing in workout clothing. His patrol uniform was wrapped in dry-cleaning plastic and draped over his shoulder.

"Oh, what's up, Bobby?" Frank looked back down at the card. "Damn."

"What's the matter? No winners?"

"Fucking A-Rabs, all they sell is garbage. They been there at least ten years, and I ain't never hear anyone say they won something outta that fucking place." Frank crumbled the card into a ball and threw it on the ground. "You going in?"

"Yeah, but I'm not on till four. I was gonna get a workout in first. How are Gloria and the kids?"

Frank took a drink from his coffee cup and didn't respond immediately. He wasn't about to tell this tool bag that his three adult daughters hated him, and his wife Gloria walked out on him almost a year ago. She called him a degenerate gambler and took everything but the ice trays.

"They're good," Frank said.

"That's good to hear." Bobby moved closer. "Listen, are you still using the same guy to bet on football?"

"Who, Dino? No, why?"

"Just a little misunderstanding with my guy. Nothing I can't straighten out. I need someone else for this weekend's games."

"Bobby, if you owe, you know your name is no good till you get even. No one is going to take your action."

"I know that, Frank. You think I don't know that? I was hoping you'd lay them down for me."

Frank eyed the sad sack. Even on a Tuesday afternoon, he had that desperate look in his eyes, like a junkie begging for his next fix. He knew Bobby liked to gamble, especially the ponies. The story was that he'd won ten grand betting horses at Aqueduct on his twenty-first birthday and had been hooked ever since. Frank also knew that Bobby was well into his forties, divorced, and living with his parents in Astoria, Queens. Franks was on his own cold streak and didn't need Bobby "The Mush" making it worse.

"Sorry, man, I can't do it. I got my own shit going on. Besides, I ain't laying bets with Dino anymore. I haven't for a while. Why don't you just go up to Atlantic City? Or upstate to one of the Indian spots?"

"'Cause I'm on the rest of the week. I need to get some cash flowing ASAP."

"Sorry, man, I can't help you."

"Alright, Frank. I get it, man. Take it easy."

He watched Bobby stroll into the precinct and didn't feel one way or the other about not helping him. The truth was that Frank had his own problems. He owed money to two loan sharks—Demetrius Chloros in Dyker Heights and Jaime Escalante out in Far Rockaway, and the juice was running on both debts.

His cut from the split of Andy "My Name is Andre Motherfucker" Lugo's eighty grand got him straight with the vig on both debts. But the clock started fresh every week until the debts were fully paid. Between staying afloat with what he owed and getting caught up on alimony, Frank was back to square one.

He remembered the waiting text message and pulled his cell phone out of his pocket. He hoped it was good news, something that might help him get back to even. Frank saw the message from one of his informants and felt his adrenaline start to flow. The message consisted of two words.

A name.

Julian Serrano.

THE PLAY ENDED a little later than Julian had anticipated. It had been scheduled to start at one, but the actors at the Nuyorican Poets Café had been delayed in taking the stage.

He had checked the Café's website and saw they would be hosting a performance of *Bees and Honey* by Guadalis Del Carmen. He had never been to a play before and didn't know what this one was about, but he wanted to do something different with Tito. He knew of the Nuyorican Poets Café and understood its history and significance to the Latin community, and he wanted to share the experience with his son.

"What did you think of the play?" Julian said.

"I liked it. It was a little weird at first, watching the people on stage and being so close while they pretended it was just the two of them. But I liked that the actors talked like you and Titi. They sounded like people I know and spoke about things I've seen before, in real life."

Julian understood what Tito meant. It was his first experience attending a play, too, and seeing the actors on stage at the Café, with its small, intimate setting, was a bit jarring at first. But he'd got caught up in the actors' skills and the playwright's beautiful words, and he'd been mesmerized by the experience. He felt strangely proud that a work of art depicting the love and struggles of a married Latino couple in Washington Heights, complete with Spanglish dialog and references to Latin food and music, existed.

Julian laughed. "Yeah, watching the actors perform live was kind of weird at first."

"Did you like it?"

"I loved it."

They stood by the Café's main entrance on East Third Street in the Lower East Side. Tito glanced over his shoulder at a large mural of Pedro Pietri on one of the Café's walls.

"Who's that?"

"That's Pedro Pietri. He was a Nuyorican poet and playwright. He co-founded this place in the seventies with a bunch of other Nuyorican poets and artists," Julian said.

"What's Nuyorican?"

"We're Nuyorican. It just means people of Puerto Rican descent born and raised in New York City."

"That's pretty cool." Tito stared at the mural with concentrated interest.

"Yeah, it is. This place represents a great history of Latinos and other minorities achieving something special. It's something to be proud of. It's proof that you can do whatever you want if you work hard and aren't afraid to go after your dreams."

"Did you come here when you were my age?"

"Nah. This is my first time here. Honestly, we never left Brooklyn much when I was a kid. Even when we did, we weren't coming to a place like this. The only theater we knew about was the Commodore."

"What's that?"

"It was a crappy little movie theater out in Williamsburg. We used to pay two dollars to watch double features. That place was grimy. Your sneakers would stick to the floor when you walked."

"That doesn't sound good at all."

"Yeah, it was pretty bad. If we wanted something a little nicer, we'd walk over to Ridgewood. It wasn't anything too fancy. We'd pay a little bit more, and it was only for one movie, but it was a little nicer than the Commodore." Julian moved away from the mural. "Come on, let's get some food."

They walked east on East Third Street to a restaurant on Avenue C that served Chinese food. They both ordered pork fried rice and shared a plate of Chinese spareribs. They ate their food in silence, and in between bites, Julian stole looks at his son.

He had been planning this day for a few weeks, even managing to get a few hours of overtime at work so he would have some extra money to spend. Julian thought about the experience of the play at the Café and the surprisingly good meal he was sharing with his son, and he was glad he'd put in the extra hours.

They left the restaurant and walked south on Essex Street toward the train station on Delancey Street, where he planned to catch the F train back to Brooklyn. Alex agreed to meet at Brooklyn Bridge Park at six so he could pick up Tito, and they were running late.

This was always the hard part. When he and his son walked together in silence, both aware their time together was ending.

Tito walked with his head down.

"You good, big man?"

"Yeah." Tito kept his eyes focused on the ground beneath his feet.

"You sure? You don't look like you're good. You're staring at your kicks like it's the first time seeing them."

"Titi Nikki and Alex have been fighting a lot lately."

"Okay. Well, married people fight sometimes. It's nothing to be worried about."

He looked up at Julian. "I think they're fighting about you."

"Me? What makes you think they're fighting about me?"

"Because I hear Titi say your name, and then she'll say a bunch of curse words. I think she's mad that Alex brings me to see you."

"I'll be honest with you, Tito. Your titi and I don't really get along. We never did. Not even when your mom was alive. But we're working on it. Your Uncle Alex is trying to help get us all together. Maybe if me and your titi can figure things out, you and I can be together as much as we want."

"I'd like that."

"Really?"

"Yeah. I remember when it was the three of us—you, Mom, and me. I love Titi Nikki, and Alex, too, but I miss it when it was the three of us. I miss Mom."

"Yeah, I miss her too."

They reached Delancey Street and walked away from the light of day, down the steps, and into the waiting darkness of the underground station.

CHAPTER TEN

VERNON COULDN'T DECIDE BETWEEN THE PLAYSTATION Four Pro and an Xbox One X. Both had strong central processing and graphic processing units, but the Xbox was a little stronger in both categories. Both offered one terabyte of storage and were capable of 4K output for videos, but the Xbox X offered twelve gigabytes of random-access memory, while the PlayStation only had eight.

Each was black and sleek, and he thought either one would look pretty dope next to his big-screen television. The Xbox cost a Benjamin more, but he wasn't sweating that. These days, money wasn't a problem for him.

Vernon liked shopping at Best Buy, especially this one on Atlantic Avenue. The salespeople usually left you alone unless you approached them for help, and he didn't need any. He loved computers and electronics and knew exactly what he was looking for. He would bet a G that he knew more about this stuff than anyone in the store.

He settled on the Xbox and asked one of the people in the blue shirts to get it for him. He knew they wouldn't hand the items to him till he paid, so he walked to the checkout line. Vernon stood in line waiting for the next register to open, hoping it would be the dime piece working on register ten. She was beautiful and had a banging body to match.

Vernon was disappointed when his turn came up, and he was directed to the weird-looking guy on register five. The guy behind the register had greasy hair, wore comb-over style, and big Coke bottle glasses that made his eyes appear as if they were bulging out of his head. He looked like Milton from that funny-ass movie *Office Space*.

Milton rang up the Xbox and asked Vernon to enter his zip code into the little keypad. The zip code thing was always strange to him, so as usual, he entered five random numbers. Vernon pulled out his thick billfold, making sure it was visible to anyone watching, paid in cash, and strutted out of the store with his new Xbox.

He walked east on Atlantic Avenue and entered the front passenger seat of a black Ford Explorer parked on South Portland Avenue. Damon "Little D" Horowitz sat in the driver's seat typing text messages on his cell phone and didn't bother to look up when Vernon got in the Explorer.

"Damn, motherfucker, took you long enough. What'd you get?" Little D kept his eyes fixed on whatever he was typing.

"The Xbox."

"How much you spend?" He stopped typing and stared at Vernon.

"Six hundred."

"Damn. You twenty years old. Why in the fuck you still play with that kiddie shit?"

"Bitch, you only a year older than me and it ain't kiddie shit. You can do all kinds of stuff with this besides playing games. You can get on the Internet, watch movies, and other shit, too," Vernon said.

"Yeah, but you got it for the games."

"Yeah, you right." They both laughed. "Come on, man. We gotta get back to Angel's for the meeting."

Little D pulled the Explorer into traffic and turned left onto Atlantic Avenue. Vernon spotted the NYPD police car in the Explorer's side-view mirror. He reached down and pushed the butt of his HK45 handgun entirely under the seat, careful not to lean down too far. He didn't want to give them fools a reason to pull him and Little D over by moving around too much. The cops stayed with them for two blocks, then turned off on Carlton Avenue.

"Did you see it?" Vernon said.

"See what?"

"The fucking police cruiser. They was right behind us."

Little D glanced in the rearview mirror. "Nah, man, guess I missed it. Looks like they're gone now."

He stared at Little D for a few seconds, then turned his attention to the view outside his window. Vernon was tired of rolling with this kid and wished Angel would cut Little D loose, but he figured that wouldn't happen anytime soon. For whatever reason, Angel kept Little D close and gave him more to do every day, especially after Devon had got smoked.

Devon used to be Angel's A-1, but then he'd got sloppy. Decided to lie down with his bitch instead of handling business like he was told. Ended up with his face blown off and Angel's cash taken.

He guessed that was why Little D seemed to be moving up faster than him. Little D was stupid. Not the special education kind, but stupid enough that he did exactly what Angel told him, no more, no less.

Vernon figured after the bullshit with Devon, Little D's stock had gone up. Angel probably felt more at ease knowing he didn't have to worry about Little D doing anything besides what he was told to do. But Angel made sure Vernon was always with Little D, keeping the big dummy on point.

Vernon couldn't deny that it bothered him a little, maybe even hurt him. He had been loyal to Angel since he was sixteen, moving weight for him and putting bodies in the ground. But he wasn't given much to do except for babysitting Little D.

First, he'd been pushed aside for Devon. Making it clear to anyone paying attention, Angel was prepping Devon for big things. But that hadn't worked out too well, so he started giving Little D more to do, as long as Vernon kept watch. It didn't make sense to put the person who needed watching over the person doing the watching, but that's how Angel was doing things.

And then there was the charity case, Jimmy. Angel's partner from back in the day. A used-to-be tough guy hooked on painkillers and liquor. He limped around on that bum leg of his, barking orders like he was Angel's partner, too out of it to know he wasn't. He knew Angel trusted Jimmy. It was probably the only reason Angel kept the gimp around because Vernon didn't see him doing much else.

Now they were on their way to do security for a meeting Angel and Jimmy were having with one of their old partners. He figured Angel would probably bring another old head on, someone else who would take a spot above Vernon. Julius or Julian or Julio, it didn't matter what his name was. To Vernon, he was just another sorry-ass ex-con like Jimmy. Too broke and too stupid to know the game had passed him by.

He examined the reflection in the side view mirror. Since no police cruisers were behind them, Vernon relaxed and leaned back in his seat.

KAT WAS FOCUSED on the black Ford Explorer as she steered the Impala through traffic. Her partner, Eddie, sat in the passenger seat and used his portable radio to call off the sector car. They had spotted the uniforms parked on Atlantic Avenue, just west of the Best Buy, while waiting for the kid they'd identified as Vernon Miller to exit the store.

Eddie had given her ten-to-one odds that the uniforms would jump on Vernon when he exited the store. Vernon was wearing a bright white hoodie and expensive-looking white sneakers, and his fitted jeans were pulled down to where the backside of his boxer briefs was almost fully exposed. Combined with his "I just stepped on a nail" strut, Kat figured the uniforms would be all over the kid. But she knew better than to turn down the kinds of odds Eddie was offering, so she put up a dollar.

She was sure she'd made an easy sawbuck when the kid started strolling on Atlantic, and the uniforms didn't follow. She pulled out the cash as soon as Vernon got inside the Explorer. The uniforms were on the move before the SUV turned onto Atlantic. Eddie called them off, and she passed him a dollar.

They had been following Miller and his partner, the big kid ironically called Little D, around for two days since her confidential informant put them on Angel Guerra and his *bodega* on Jefferson Avenue. She wanted to work the case up a little before they brought it to Frank.

Kat knew better than to bring Frank a half-cooked cake, so she and Eddie were doing a lot of homework. Guerra didn't have much of a criminal history—just some petty thefts and assaults when he was a kid, but the informant was adamant he was moving major weight.

They spent a day watching the *bodega* on Jefferson Avenue, but outside of meeting with Miller, Little D, and a middle-aged white guy they still hadn't identified, Guerra didn't leave the store. They turned their attention to Miller and his very large partner, but the only thing they'd seen either of them move in the past two days was whatever Miller had in the Best Buy bag.

"It looks like they're headed back to the *bodega*," Kat said.

"Yeah, it looks that way. So, what do you think? Are we wasting our time?"

"I don't know. I don't think so. I hope not. We've already spent almost a week on this tip."

"So, how far do you want to go with this? You know how Frank is."

"Let's give it a little longer, see where it goes. It's Wednesday. What the hell else do you have to do?"

"Believe me, I can find something to do. I always have a hot little mommy lined up."

She scoffed. "Oh, please. With that lisp? I'd be surprised if you could say five words before they sent you away."

"Listen here, pal o' mine. Of all the things they want me to do with my mouth, talking is not one of them."

"If you say so."

They laughed and continued following the Ford Explorer as it turned left onto Bedford Avenue.

"Yup. They're going back to the store," Kat said.

"All right, we'll sit on it for a while, but I don't want to be out here all night. Especially if nothing's going on."

"Roger that."

JULIAN WAS SITTING in the front passenger seat of Jimmy's Chrysler 300, holding on tight as Jimmy drove dangerously fast down the narrow streets to the meeting with Angel. It was the first time Julian had been inside Jimmy's car, and he was surprised by how clean it was. Everything was shiny, the carpet looked vacuumed, and despite the smell of alcohol emitting from Jimmy's pores, the interior of the car smelled fresh.

"Did you just clean the car today?"

"Nah, it's been about a week. Why?" Jimmy said.

"Shit is spotless. I'm impressed."

"Why does that impress you? You think I'm a slob or some shit?"

"Nah. It looks like you just had it detailed an hour ago. So, when you say it's been a week since you cleaned it...I don't know. I think that's impressive."

"Well, first, you impress easy. And two, I'm not good with dirt. I need everything around me right. I can't tell you how many cellmates I had to beat down `cause they was dirty motherfuckers."

"That's a big change from when we were kids. You weren't too worried about cleanliness back then."

"Yeah, well, being locked up changes a motherfucker. You know how that shit is. People fighting every day for shit that don't even belong to them. I fought to keep my little space in that hellhole clean. I don't know why—I just did. Now, it's just who I am."

Julian didn't respond. He didn't need to. Being in prison was something they shared. The only difference was how each had dealt with their experience. He had chosen to lay low—get educated and mentally stronger. It seemed like Jimmy had decided to lash out and fight for anything that made him feel like he had even an inch of control over his life.

Jimmy turned the Chrysler onto Jefferson Avenue, and Julian knew they were close to Angel's *bodega*. Since being released from prison, Julian had repeatedly played the coming moments out in his head. Even as kids, he and Angel had never been especially close. They were more like friends-in-law, joined by their shared friendship with Jimmy but separated by a healthy competitiveness.

The three of them grew up doing dirt together. But as they got older and the work they were doing got more serious, Julian emerged as the leader of the trio. Healthy competitiveness grew into a tense rivalry.

Despite what Jimmy had said to him, Julian was still suspicious about what happened eight years ago. Those feelings, combined with parole restrictions, were the reason he'd stayed away from Angel all these months. But now, he was on his way to look Angel in the eyes—to try and confirm what he already believed to be the truth.

“So, Angel doesn’t really leave this spot, huh?” Julian said.

"Nah, not really. He'll go to the stash house every now and then, but he pretty much sticks to the store. He deals with the connect. I work the streets and make sure everything's running the way it should. We clean the money through the store, no muss, no fuss, and everybody's happy."

“So, what do you want me for? Sounds like everything is going good.”

“These youngsters, man. They do stupid shit. We need someone we can trust. We’re starting to move more product, and I can’t be everywhere.”

They pulled up to Angel's store before he could respond, so Julian left it alone. Jimmy drove past the store and made a U-turn in the intersection of Throop and Jefferson without slowing for other traffic. The driver of the one car that'd been impeded by Jimmy's driving must have been from the neighborhood because he waited quietly even though he had the right of way.

Jimmy parked the car along the curb a few feet past the store. Julian stepped out of the Chrysler onto the sidewalk and saw Angel standing in front of the store with two of his people.

“*¡Mira aqui!* Motherfucking Julian Serrano in the house!” Angel yelled.

Hearing Angel's voice for the first time in years made Julian chuckle. Angel had always had a soft, velvety tone to his speaking voice, like Bruno Mars or El Debarge. Angel had a pretty good singing voice, which was all but useless in this game, and was close to comedy when he got as loud and boisterous as he was now, like Michael Jackson in the music video for his song “Bad.”

“Get over here, *hermano.*” Angel extended his arms out to his side.

They made their way to each other and hugged briefly. Julian stepped back and inspected Angel. He looked good—slim and healthy, with a full head of high-styled hair and a finely groomed beard. He wore a black Jordan hoodie, designer jeans, and black and red Air Jordan 1 sneakers.

"What's up, Angel? Why are you standing out here? It's cold as fuck," Julian said.

"Just hollering at my boys here and waiting for you. I've been like a bitch on prom night waiting for your ass to show up." He hugged Julian again and stepped back. "Damn, man, you look good. You all swole and shit."

"Doing what I can." Julian looked Angel up and down, making a show of checking him out. "You looking clean as fuck. Those Jordans are dope."

"Well, you know, *what can I say*," Angel said in his best J.J. Evans impression.

Julian chuckled and glanced at the two young men standing by a black Explorer parked by the curb. The big one was block-out-the-sun large and stared down at Julian with an empty expression. The little one tried to hold Julian's eyes with his, a misguided attempt at intimidation. It was a look Julian had seen a thousand times before, both on the street and in prison. It didn't impress him then and was comical coming from this gangster hobbit now.

"Fellas, this is Julian." Angel took a position between Julian and the two young men. "This is Vernon and Little D." Angel seemed to notice Julian's expression when he heard the big one's name. "I know, I know it don't make much sense but just go with it."

"What's up, fam," Little D said.

The one Angel introduced as Vernon gave a slight nod but didn't say anything. Julian figured Vernon had been working hard to move up in Angel's organization, and the sudden reappearance of one of Angel's old partners sent a message. Bringing Julian on let everyone know that Angel had a problem with his people and that Vernon was not the next man up.

"Come on, man. Let's go inside," Angel said. He glanced at Vernon and Little D. "You two, stay out here. We won't be long."

Julian followed Angel and Jimmy inside, and they made their way to the back of the store. He followed them through a door and down a flight of stairs into the store's basement. It was cold, and a moldy smell filled the air.

Shelves stocked with supplies and boxes of store inventory lined the walls. A small wooden desk and matching wooden chair were at the far end of the room. A black plastic chair and an old black leather loveseat were directly in front of the desk.

Angel walked over to the small refrigerator behind the desk and took out three bottles of Heineken. Jimmy stretched out on the loveseat, and Julian sat down on the black plastic chair. Angel opened the three bottles of beer with a bottle opener and handed one each to Jimmy and Julian.

"*¿Entonce, mano?* Tell me what's been going on. How the hell have you been?" Angel sat down behind the desk.

"Ain't much to tell. Just been working, trying to stay clean," Julian said.

"I heard you been cleaning buildings or some shit. That true?"

"Yeah. It is."

"Why the fuck you doing that shit? Why didn't you come see me when you got out? You know I would've put you on."

"I know. And I appreciate that, but I've been trying to toe the line. I'm still on paper for a few more years. I'm trying to be with my kid. You know how it is."

Angel nodded. "How is Tito anyway?"

"He's good, man, getting big. He's smart as fuck, and he's a good ballplayer too."

"Like his pops. Man, I remember when we was hooping every day. We'd go all over the city looking for games. Remember that time at Brower Park?"

"When Ivan and his sister Desi got shot? Hell, yeah, I remember that shit. It was fucked up," Jimmy said.

"Yeah, I remember that. Fucking Ivan used to be cold. He had a crazy handle, and the kid was like five-eight but could reverse dunk and shit," Julian said. He took a sip from his beer bottle. "Fucking Terrence Davis. That kid was a maniac. Blasted Ivan and Desi because Ivan worked him in that half-court game."

"Yeah, I was standing right next to Desi when she got smoked. Game ends, Terrence starts beefing with Ivan, she tries to step in, and boom—it's a wrap," Angel said.

Jimmy breathed out a deep sigh. "Whatever. Fucking Ivan should've known better. Everybody knew Terrence was nutso and was always strapped."

Julian leaned back in his chair till the front legs lifted off the ground. "Maybe. But he didn't have to blast Desi. She was just being loud. Old Desiree was always loud, especially when it came to her brother." Julian shook his head. "Crazy shit."

"Whatever. That motherfucker got his anyway. Heard he got stabbed in the neck up in Attica and bled out in less than a minute," Angel said.

The room grew quiet as they drank from their beer bottles. The conversation had felt forced, and now there was an awkward silence filled with tension and unease.

The strange feelings weren't unexpected. After all, they hadn't seen or spoken to each other in almost nine years. Angel was putting in real work now and couldn't afford a misstep. In this life, old friendships didn't mean shit, and trusting the wrong person could be fatal.

The only thing going for Julian was that he hadn't snitched. He'd stood tall in the interrogation room the night he got arrested. That piece of shit Hawkins had tried to bargain, intimidate, and persuade, but Julian hadn't budged. It'd pissed the cops off bad when he just stared straight ahead and demanded a lawyer. Seeing them get worked up was the last time Julian would smile for a while.

"So, listen. I know you and Jimmy already spoke about all this, but I wanted to see where your head was at. If you really wanted back in," Angel said.

Julian nodded. "Yeah, I think I do. I tried it straight, but it ain't working. I'm not making enough, and I have responsibilities."

Angel smiled. "That's all you got to say, *mano*. We always got you. It sucks that it took this long for you to come back, but you're here now, and there ain't no stopping us." He leaned forward in his chair. "But one thing. You want in, so you're in—no questions asked. I owe you that much. But this ain't the minor leagues anymore. The business has grown, and we're putting in real work now. I know you been away a while, but we're gonna need the old Julian. You think you can get back to that?"

"Angel, man. I'm not asking for a piece of the pie. I just want to be a soldier and make some green. That's it, bro."

Angel studied Julian and didn't speak for a few seconds. "*Bueno*. I'm gonna put you on something easy first. Just a little security work to help you get your sea legs back. Jimmy will get with you in a few days to square everything away."

"That'll work. Thanks, man."

Angel got up from the chair and stepped around the desk. Julian stood up, and they embraced each other in a quick, insincere hug. Angel reached into his pants pocket and pulled out a large billfold. He counted out two thousand dollars and handed it to Julian.

"That's just some walking around money. Call it a welcome-home gift."

Julian took the cash, folded it once, and put it inside the front pocket of his jeans.

"Thanks, Angel."

"If you need anything in the meantime, you call Jimmy. *¿Me entiendes?*"

"*Claro*."

"And say hi to Tito for me, okay. And Nikki, too, with her fine ass. They living out there in Bay Ridge, right? Over there on Ninety-Seventh Street, by Shore Park? They picked a good spot. It's a short walk to Tito's school. That's a nice neighborhood. Good for them, I always knew she'd do good."

They stared at each other. Angel had chosen his words carefully, but the message was clear. Julian's heart began to race, and his knees shook from the adrenaline that flooded his blood. He was angrier than he could ever remember being, and it took everything in him to push it down.

If it wouldn't have ruined his plans, he would have killed Angel right then and there.

CHAPTER ELEVEN

DIANA REGRETTED HER DECISION. SHE HADN'T BEEN IN THE mood to deal with the Thursday morning rush-hour traffic on the Brooklyn Bridge, so she'd decided to take the subway into the city. She planned to conduct a worksite visit on Julian, whom she knew was working overnight cleaning a commercial building on Fulton Street. Diana wanted to avoid coming out in the middle of the night, so she figured if she got there early enough, she could meet with him before his shift ended at eight.

She'd parked her car in front of her office and caught the F Train at the Ninth Street station at 6:30 a.m. Usually, there were only a few people on the train so early in the morning, so Diana thought she'd made the right choice till she'd transferred to the Two train at the Nevins Street station. The Two was packed with morning commuters, and she felt suffocated. Standing in the middle of the train, holding onto the germ-covered metal pole for balance and surrounded by dozens of people in cold weather coats, she remembered why she had avoided the subway the past few years.

Now I know what heifers feel like. Is it heifer or heifa?

Diana got off the train at the Fulton Street station and jogged up the stairs to the street level. It was mid-November cold, and it had rained while she was on the subway. The sun was hidden behind gray-metal-colored clouds, and the air smelled of wet asphalt.

She walked west on Fulton Street to the commercial building where Julian was working, near Nassau Street. It was already almost eight by the time she reached the building. So, she decided to wait in the lobby and catch him as he walked out.

After a few minutes, she spotted Julian stepping off the elevator. He was chatting with an older man. Both wore dark gray coveralls and black tennis shoes, so she assumed they were co-workers.

"Serrano," Diana called out from across the lobby.

He looked in her direction when he heard his name. He seemed alarmed at first but then he smiled, which surprised her. Smiles weren't one of the facial expressions she was used to seeing from the parolees she supervised. She was even more surprised when she needed to suppress her smile.

I'm a professional. This is my job. He's just another ex-con.

Julian made his way to her, with the older guy following behind.

"Ms. Rivera, what are you doing here?" Julian said.

"Worksite visit. I need to make sure the people I supervise are actually working," Diana said.

"You're a little late. I'm done working for the day." He smiled as if they were old friends.

Stop looking at me like that.

"This will work for this part. I can call your boss later for more information."

"Oh, okay. Good." Julian held her eyes briefly but then seemed to remember his co-worker standing beside him. "Man, I'm sorry. This is Eli. We work together here. You probably already figured that out."

"Hello, Eli, nice to meet you." Diana offered her hand for a handshake.

Eli glared at her. "Yeah. How ya doing," he said coldly, keeping his hands at his side.

Diana lowered her hand. She had worked with many people like Eli before and recognized him for what he was. He had the aggressive tone and hostile body language of someone who had spent their entire life committing violent acts and then fighting to survive in the places those violent acts sent them.

She pegged him for fifty to fifty-five years old, and although he was short, he was powerfully built and looked capable of inflicting pain on someone. His deep, raspy voice, a mix of Tone Loc and James Earl Jones, only added to his intimidating presence.

Eli turned his attention to Julian. "*Oye, mano*, I'm gonna take off. Leave you to it."

"Alright, man. I'll see you tonight." They bumped fists, and Eli strolled away without giving Diana another look.

She watched him exit the building and returned her gaze to Julian. "Well, he seems...rough around the edges."

Julian chuckled. "He's a good guy. We're all rough around the edges. He's just a little rougher."

"And his edges are sharper. Yeah, I get it."

"Well, I know you have to go through your questions, but I don't think doing it right here in this lobby would be a good idea. You want to grab some coffee?"

She pondered his question. He was right. It wasn't a good idea to sit in the building's lobby and make the social elite who traversed these halls uncomfortable with their working-class presence. She didn't want to risk costing him his job when the snobs undoubtedly complained.

On the other hand, sitting down over coffee could give off the wrong impression. They'd eaten during meetings previously, but the last few times, the conversations had become more personal and intimate. She didn't believe they had crossed any professional lines and wanted to keep it that way.

But if she were being honest with herself, she liked speaking with him and looked forward to their meetings. Yes, she thought he was handsome, but it went beyond that. She liked how he saw the world and articulated his observations. She thought, if circumstances were different, Julian Serrano was someone she could be friends with.

"Yeah, sure, coffee sounds good. You have a place in mind?"

Julian had suggested a very good but expensive boutique coffee shop about three blocks east of them on Cliff Street. Diana figured he'd thought that was the kind of place she frequented and was trying to impress her. She'd countered with Dunkin Donuts. There was one across the street from where they were that served great coffee and was relatively inexpensive.

They sat at the counter in front of the window and had a clear view of the people and traffic on Fulton Street.

"So, it looks like the job is going well," Diana said.

"For what it is, yeah, sure. It's okay. I mean, *it is* cleaning up after other people. That's not much to be proud of."

"You're staying straight and doing honest work. That's a lot to be proud of."

Julian didn't respond. He took a sip of his coffee and stared out the window. She wondered what he was thinking but didn't ask, deciding to let his silence speak for him.

"Is it, though?" He finally said.

"Is it what?"

"Is staying straight something to be proud of? Is being broke all the time and not being able to take care of your kid something to be proud of?"

"What do you mean?"

"I mean, there isn't anything out here for an ex-con. I made a lot of mistakes, and maybe this is what I deserve, but, damn, it sucks. If this is as good as it gets playing it straight, then maybe playing it straight ain't for me."

She was surprised by his words and the way he spoke. She'd already figured out he was very good at code-switching, using language and mannerisms to navigate between two different worlds effortlessly. But usually, his use of this skill felt contrived—like an actor slipping in and out of character.

But now he seemed dejected, and his guard was down. He was speaking to her as he would someone from the neighborhood. Even though he tried to mask his thoughts as questions, she couldn't help but feel the questions were rhetorical. That he wasn't looking for an answer so much as he wanted to try and unburden his conscience.

"I don't know if I should act like I heard that. You realize you're speaking with your P.O., right?"

"I know who I'm talking to. I'm talking to someone who I trust and whose opinion I value. Besides, it's not like I'm laying out my grand plans to rob a casino in Atlantic City or something." Julian flashed a forced smile.

Diana didn't smile back. This was the first time she regretted the tone of their relationship. She thought she may have misjudged the situation and let her guard down too much.

Goddamn it, I am so fucking stupid. Time to rein this shit back in.

"Let's get a few things clear. First, I'm your parole officer, not your friend. Okay? That's number one. Second, the most important thing for you is to stay out of trouble and stay out of prison. You have a lot going for you and people who are counting on you."

He kept his eyes focused on the view outside the window, seemingly disappointed he wasn't hearing the affirmation he had been expecting.

That was a good speech. I hope he heard me.

After a few seconds, he turned to her. "I didn't mean to overstep, Ms. Rivera. I just meant that there's no one left. Everyone I trusted is gone now or changed to the point that they might as well be gone. Sometimes, you just want to vent, and that's all I was doing. Okay?"

"As long as we're on the same page, venting isn't an issue. Part of my job is to help keep you on the right track. But if it ever sounds like you're about to make a bad choice, you and I will have problems. Fair enough?"

"Fair enough."

"So, how's Tito?"

"Oh, we're back to being friends again?"

"Well, we were never friends, but we can talk. Talking is part of the process." Diana thought she sounded like Dr. Griffin and smiled to herself.

"He's good. We spend time together. We're building something. I don't know where it's going if it can even go anywhere, but I'm going to keep at it."

"That's good to hear."

"What about you?"

Excuse me.

"What about me?"

"Do you have any kids? Are you married?"

This fucking guy.

"What did I just say?" She was incredulous.

He laughed and put his hands up in a surrender pose. "I know, I know, we're not friends. We're more like...colleagues. But colleagues talk, right? They know a little about each other."

"We don't work together so, no, we're not colleagues. This is a professional arrangement, and I'm not answering those questions."

"Okay, here's a professional question—do you like your job?"

She looked into his big, soulful eyes, and for reasons she couldn't explain, she trusted him. Julian had an easy way about him, and she felt comfortable around him. Despite herself, she wanted to speak with him, to confide in him.

"Yeah, I like my job. Actually, I love my job," Diana said.

"Really?"

"Damn, man, don't sound so surprised."

"Nah, I'm not trying to be a jerk or anything. It just seems like it would be difficult supervising a bunch of ex-cons and headcases."

"Don't get me wrong, it can be challenging. But seeing people succeed, whether with a job, beating addiction, or caring for their family. It makes me feel good."

"Are you ever scared?"

She didn't answer immediately. Diana thought about the question and whether she should give an honest answer. "I'm terrified every day."

"Really? You don't act it."

"Thanks, I try." She let out a forced chuckle. "Yeah, I worry about parolees and whether they're staying on the program. I worry about them eating and being able to feed their families. Some of the people I deal with scare me, and I worry they can see my fear. I feel like I've failed a lot in my life, and I'm terrified I might fail at this."

He stared out the window and finished his coffee, silent and ostensibly lost in his own thoughts. Diana stared down at her half-full cup of coffee.

"One day when I was a kid, my uncle Gary brought a garbage bag full of old paperback books to my *abuela's* apartment. Don't ask me where he got them from. He probably stole it from the Bushwick Public Library or some shit," Julian said.

"Damn, your people were burglarizing libraries? With those kinds of role models, it's no wonder you got locked up."

They both chuckled, but he kept his eyes on the view outside the window.

"Most of the books were about old basketball players like Pete Maravich and Magic Johnson, which I ate up. I read every single one. One of the non-basketball books was about Greek and Roman mythology. I read it cover-to-cover when I ran out of books about basketball players. I loved it.

"The stories were...I don't know how to explain it. Anyway, one of the goddesses I read about was Diana. The Greeks called her Artemis, but Greek and Roman mythology got all mixed up when Rome was in charge back then, so they're the same person—or goddess. Anyway, Diana was the goddess of the moon. The book described her as beautiful, brave, independent-minded, and strong."

Where's he going with this?

"They really built her up, didn't they."

"Yeah, they seemed to describe most of their gods and goddesses as brave, strong, and beautiful. But she was also considered the protector of the poor and the lower class. People who were grasping on to the last rung in life turned to her for hope, for salvation. Runaway slaves would even go to her temples for sanctuary."

"That's certainly a lot to live up to."

"You already have—at least from what I've seen you have. You're a lot stronger than you think, and if you're telling the truth about being scared, you do a great job hiding it. Considering what you said about why you love your job, and not to mention how you look, it makes sense that your name is Diana."

Damn.

She wanted to see his face, but his head was turned away from her. She gazed out the window instead. It had started raining again—light at first but then increasing quickly. It poured straight down and heavy, cascading over parked cars. The people caught in the downpour were a blur. The sound of the rain landing on the world outside put her in a slight trance, and she thought about the words he'd spoken.

She'd enjoyed the story and felt a twinge of pride in the origins of her name. Diana figured she had another ten minutes before she had to leave for her next appointment. She held her empty cup close, and she lost track of time as they spoke.

She was an hour late for her next appointment.

CHAPTER TWELVE

Diana hated being late. She had spent her life being compulsively early for almost every appointment, a habit she'd developed during her youth. Rising from bed before everyone else so she could get to school early enough for a free breakfast before class started.

Over time, it got to where she was only relaxed if she was where she needed to be at least an hour in advance. She often found herself sitting in her parked car in the predawn darkness, waiting for doors to be unlocked, smiling and completely at ease.

At this point in her life, being late caused her anxiety and the grating feeling of having forgotten something important. Like she'd left the stove turned on or the door to her apartment unlocked. Now, jogging the block and a half back to her office from the train station, she had that unfinished business feeling.

Diana spotted the man leaning on the big truck from a block away and figured it had to be the person she was meeting. He wore a black overcoat and appeared to be holding a blue "We Are Happy to Serve You" coffee cup. Two visual clichés of the dogged New York City detective. The giant black truck surprised her a bit; it seemed too big and conspicuous for a narcotics detective, but she figured they knew what they were doing. She approached him, but he gave no indication that he was aware of her presence. His attention was on the cell phone that lay on the hood of his truck.

"Sgt. Hawkins?" Diana said.

He turned to face her, and she saw the lit cigarette in his other hand, another cliché confirming her initial instinct. He was average height and middle-aged, with a full head of salt and pepper hair. Diana thought he was plain looking, neither attractive nor unattractive. But there was something unnerving about him. Something behind the icy stare of his blue eyes and his used car salesman smile that made her feel uncomfortable and suspicious.

"Officer Rivera?"

"Yes. Sorry, I'm late."

"No problem at all. I had some emails to catch up on anyway," Sgt. Hawkins said.

"Do you want to go inside?"

He looked past Diana, at the parole office behind her. "Do you mind if we speak out here? I'd rather not be surrounded by a bunch of skells."

Ugh. Here we go. Skells? Alright, Sipowicz.

"Um, okay. So, how can I help you?"

"I had some questions about an ex-con you're supervising, Julian Serrano."

Julian?

"Serrano? What about him? Is he involved in something criminal?" Diana was more concerned than she should have been and hoped it didn't show.

"No, nothing like that. I'm working a case, and his name came up. He doesn't seem to be directly involved, but he's had some past connections to our suspect. We're just doing homework, tracking the perp's movements as far back as possible."

"Has Serrano been in contact with this person? If he has, I need to know. It could put him in violation of his parole," Diana said.

"Like I said, we don't have any information that leads us to believe he's involved in anything...nefarious. I'm just doing some background work."

"Okay. So, what do you want to know?"

“Has Serrano been sticking to the conditions of his parole? Is he working?”

"Yes, he's been working. He's had a job with a cleaning company for a few months now. He works, checks in when he's supposed to, and urine tests are always clean. He's in compliance."

“Do you know if he’s been in contact with anyone engaged in criminal activity?”

What kind of stupid fucking question is that?

“If I knew that, he’d be back in prison. Consorting with known felons or people engaged in criminal activity is a violation of his parole. And like I said before, he’s in compliance.”

The used car salesman's smile faded away as he took a drag off his cigarette. Every instinct Diana had was screaming the guy wasn't telling her the truth. He was a city cop, a narc no less—they were not known for willingly sharing information. But it wasn’t just that. She’d worked with cops before and was familiar with their behaviors and methods.

This was something else. Diana didn't feel this was a professional meeting between two people in a mutual career field. It felt more like he was shaking her down for information, as he would a local store merchant.

“Listen, Officer Rivera—may I call you Diana?”

“Let’s keep this official. I’d prefer Officer Rivera.”

"Fair enough. Officer Rivera, I can imagine being in your line of work—you might grow an attachment to these people.”

What the fuck did you just say?

“How was that?”

The used-car salesman's smile returned to his face. "I'm just saying. You spend all day helping them with their problems, keeping them on the straight and narrow. The lines get blurred, and things can get confusing. Especially when you account for all the estrogen pumping through a woman's body. It makes sense you might be a little protective, not be able to see everything that might be going on."

Estrogen? Between the oversized truck and fake tough-guy act, I’m willing to bet that between the two of us, I have the bigger dick.

"Let's get something straight Sgt. Hawkins. I have a job I take seriously and that I do well. Your bullshit Vic Mackey routine is tired, and to be quite honest, you're not good at it. So, out of professionalism, I'll give you thirty more seconds to finish asking what you need to ask. After that, I'll be walking into my office so I can get back to doing something useful—helping *these people*."

Sgt. Hawkins smiled, took a long pull off his cigarette, and put the rest inside his coffee cup. "Okay, one more question. I saw Serrano did eight years on a twelve-year sentence. Do you know if he made a deal to get out early?"

"I'm not sure I know what you mean."

"Do you know if he agreed to cooperate with law enforcement to secure an early release?"

"Why do you need to know that?"

"Because it would help me with my investigation. If I know Serrano has provided information in the past, it's a fair assumption he'd be willing to do it again. I can approach him for information and not worry about it getting back to my suspect."

Well, that sounds like a bunch of bullshit.

"As far as I know, Serrano worked hard inside, stayed clean, and was approved for parole by a board. If he was working as an informant, I'd know," Diana said.

"How would you know?"

"Because those requests go through me and are approved by the court with jurisdiction. I rarely get requests because they're rejected pretty much every time. And I certainly never received a request about Serrano."

Sgt. Hawkins' lips curled into an obnoxious smirk that made her skin crawl. "Okay, then. That's all I have. I'd appreciate it if you kept this conversation between you and me. Like I said, Serrano isn't suspected of doing anything illegal, but if he is, I don't want him getting hinkey because you asked him questions. That could hamper our investigation. I'll let you know if anything changes, and we think he's involved." He reached into his coat pocket and removed a business card. "Here's my card. It has my personal number on it. You can call it anytime—for any reason." Sgt. Hawkins handed her the card and tried to hold her eyes with his.

She brought the card to her face as if reading it.

What a fucking sleazeball.

He extended his hand, and she hesitated before finally grabbing it and shaking it. His grip was firm, and he held her hand a few seconds too long.

"Thank you for your time, Officer Rivera."

He got into his truck and drove away.

Diana thought about their conversation and his questions about Julian. Despite what Sgt. Hawkins had said she was suspicious and uneasy. She wanted to believe Julian was still on the right track.

But she couldn't ignore the doubts now swimming around in her head. Even though he was a complete asshole, Frank Hawkins was a decorated NYPD cop and a supervisor of one of the Department's high-performing narcotics units. Julian Serrano, she had to remind herself, was an ex-con. A person who had grown up fully immersed in violence and crime.

Whether out of despair, the safe feeling of something familiar, or just plain old not giving a shit, people who had spent their lives doing dirt often returned to their former ways. They relapsed, committed crimes, or just had a beer and a smoke with the wrong person.

Diana was confused, frustrated, and, more than anything, angry. She turned and walked into her office building.

FRANK DROVE through the intersection at Bond Street and First Street two seconds after the light had turned red. Vehicles traveling east on First Street were forced to stop moving to avoid colliding with his truck. A cacophony of curse words and vehicle horns chased him through the intersection, and Frank smiled to himself. He wasn't late for the meeting with his team, but he hated to wait, and he loved driving fast.

He thought about his conversation with Officer Rivera. She'd given him the information he needed about Serrano. But more than that, he couldn't get her out of his head. Despite her best attempts to hide it, he thought she was gorgeous. He thought about the way she spoke, with hot-blooded Latina feistiness, and what she was hiding under all those clothes, and he felt the blood rush to his penis. He fully intended to find a reason to meet with her again.

Frank reached into the center console and grabbed his burner cell phone. He wanted to call Angel Guerra and let him know what he'd learned, get this task off his plate, and move on to the next thing. When Angel had texted him Serrano's name the other day, he hadn't provided any other information.

The name had sounded familiar, and Angel could have made his job a little easier if he had told him who Serrano was; that he was the first chump Angel had served up and Frank had already busted him once. Frank had put Serrano away for twelve years, of which he apparently had only done eight.

But as usual, Frank had only been given a name, so he ran it through the NYPD database. Serrano hadn't been arrested since he got released, and as far as Frank could tell, especially after his conversation with Officer Rivera, Serrano wasn't an informant.

Frank looked up Angel's number on the phone's contact list and pressed dial.

"Yeah," Angel said on the other end of the line.

"It looks like Serrano's clean."

Angel didn't respond for a few seconds, but Frank could hear him chewing something crunchy.

"You sure?"

"Yeah, I ran a check on him. He hasn't been picked up for anything since he got out, so I know he hasn't cut any new deals. And I just got done talking with his P.O. If you want to work someone who's still on paper, you gotta get it cleared through their P.O. and a judge. His P.O. says Serrano isn't working for any law enforcement."

"Alright."

"Not for nothing, but I think you're making a mistake bringing this guy back in."

"It is for nothing `cause I don't care what you think." Angel hung up.

Frank tossed the phone on the passenger seat. He didn't know how much longer he could stomach working with Angel. With his expensive clothes and queer voice, pretending to be better than he was. Now, the little prick was talking to Frank like he was *his* boss—like Frank took orders from him. As far as he was concerned, Angel was a bottom feeder. A catfish pretending to be a Regal Tang.

But Frank couldn't deny how beneficial the relationship had been for him, both professionally and financially. Angel would serve up dealers for Frank's team to take down. Small-timers, far enough down the ladder the losers wouldn't be missed and were easily replaced. Angel would sell them product, then Frank's team would take them down, make a pretty good collar, and pocket whatever cash they found.

In return, he'd left Angel and his crew alone to conduct business. Did his part to keep them off the radar. Hell, since he only needed so much product to make a good case, he would even give Angel back most of the stuff they seized.

And Frank never worried about blowback. His team was rock solid and the dealers they busted kept their mouths shut. And why wouldn't they? Yeah, they lost cash and product. But they were only being charged with a portion of the weight they could have been, so why rock the boat. It worked out well that way—at least in the beginning it had.

But now Angel's ego was out of control, strutting around like he was Stringer Bell or some shit. Not to mention that Frank was in so deep with the sharks, whatever he took off the suckers Angel gave up barely kept his head above water. He was growing tired of the little fuck, and he wasn't making enough money anymore to justify the headache. He knew he would have to make some changes to the arrangement.

Frank parked his truck along the curb on President Street, directly in front of the entrance to Carroll Park. He walked into the park toward the eight-foot-tall bronze and granite monument to soldiers and sailors who'd served in World War One. It was cold outside, but the clear sky and bright sun made it a criminal offense to spend one second indoors. He spotted Tony, Kat, Eddie, and Joe near the benches directly behind the monument.

"What's up, Frank," Tony said, handing Frank a cup of coffee.

Frank shrugged and took a sip of coffee. "Just trying to put something together. What do you guys got for me?"

Although they conducted all their operations as a team, every member of Frank's unit was expected to work up their own cases. That way, they always had irons in the fire. He liked to meet in person, so everyone had a chance to lay out what they each had going. They would prioritize the cases based on which one had the most heat and plan out how they wanted to take down a perp or location.

He nodded at Joe, signaling he wanted him to speak first. Joe was the youngest, and newest, member of Frank's team. He'd joined Narcotics as a detective about a year ago after having spent two years in plainclothes on SNEU—Street Level Narcotics Enforcement Unit. He was a young, fit, hard charger and Frank loved him. He thought of Joe as his protégé.

"I'm working a deal over on Flushing Avenue. It's not ready to go yet, but we may be able to get an undercover in there," Joe said.

"A U.C.? I always like those. Any day I don't have to deal with a bottom-feeding informant is a good day. Keep at it—let me know when it's ready to be served," Frank said.

Joe flashed a thumbs up. "Roger that."

"What else we got?"

"Angel Guerra," Kat said.

"Who?" Frank took a long sip of his coffee, holding the cup close to his face.

"I have a C.I. that put me onto this guy named Angel Guerra. C.I. says Guerra is pushing heavy weight out of this *bodega* on Throop Avenue. I ran his name, but he doesn't have much. Just some petty thefts and assaults when he was a kid," Kat said.

"So, then, why are we talking about him?"

"Eddie and I have been sitting on the store. There's a lot of traffic in and out of the—"

"It's a *bodega*. There's going to be a lot of people in and out of it."

"Yeah, I know that, Frank. But I also know when I'm looking at a bunch of dope boys. There were D-boys in front of that store every day. We followed two of them from the Best Buy on Atlantic back to the store," Kat said.

"So?" Frank said.

"*So*, they waited outside with Guerra until another two showed up and went inside the store with Guerra. The two we followed from Best

Buy stayed outside—probably providing security for the meeting inside," Kat said.

"I'm still not hearing anything interesting. Did you see anything of substance? Did it look like anything was being moved?"

"No. We don't believe it was anything more than a meet and greet. But, Frank, I know what I'm looking at, and my C.I. is solid. This could be a good one—we're just gonna have to put some work into it," Kat said.

Kat wasn't going to let it go easily. She was a firecracker who loved to make cases. If she was pitching a case to him, she was confident in what it could produce. Frank knew he had to handle this delicately. He had to direct her away from Angel without making it obvious what he was doing. Make it appear as if the team was too busy to move on less than solid intel.

"I know you know what you're doing, Kat. That's not what I'm saying. But this just sounds like wannabes hanging out in front of their homeboy's store. We don't have time for fishing trips, not when we have good cases waiting in cue," Frank said.

"Alright, Frank," Kat said.

"Maybe we can look at it again if you get something with meat on it."

She nodded but didn't respond. Frank knew she was pissed at being shut down, but he couldn't worry about that. He could hear Tony going over the details of another investigation, but Frank wasn't paying attention.

His mind was on other things, like who Kat's C.I. was and how they knew about Angel Guerra.

CHAPTER THIRTEEN

The bar was one of three businesses occupying a space in a one-story commercial building. Wedged between a laundromat and a Brazilian restaurant on Nostrand Avenue in Crown Heights, the bar was away from the upscale bars clustered around the now chic area stretching along the East River, from the Brooklyn Navy Yard down to Union Street. It was a comfortable, low-key neighborhood spot filled with the familiar faces of anonymous people.

Diana sat at a table drinking a rum punch. She had been hungry when she'd left work, so she ordered a plate of Asian chili wings from the waitress, an attractive young woman with short black hair that she wore stylishly. The food and drink were a bit expensive, but both tasted great, and the service was good, so Diana didn't mind.

The room was mid-sized, dimly lit, and decorated in a steampunk theme. Tables and booths lined the walls. Several couples occupied tables, along with two separate groups of young adults. Hipster types by the look of their knit caps and multi-colored sweaters. Their discussion, from what she could hear, consisted of a debate of dueling philosophies —Absurdism versus Existentialism, Albert Camus or Soren Kierkegaard. She was tempted to weigh in on the merits of each but thought better of it when she spotted Kat Esposito entering the bar.

Diana waved her arm at Kat to get her attention. After a few seconds, Kat noticed and made her way over to the table. Diana stood up, and they embraced each other in a long hug.

"Hey, girl," Kat said.

"What's up, mama?"

They stepped back, and both grinned. Kat hung her coat on the back of her chair and took a seat at the table.

Kat looked around the bar; she seemed to take in the faces and admire the décor. "I like this spot. A few too many knit caps, but it's away from any precincts, so that means no cops, which is fine with me."

Diana laughed at the irony of Kat not wanting to be around cops when she was a cop herself and had been for over thirteen years. Kat was a narcotics detective in Brooklyn North, assigned to the Eighty-Third precinct, the same as Frank Hawkins.

Kat was also an adjunct professor at the Orange County Police Academy. The two had met when Kat taught Introduction to Policing to Diana's Peace Officer class. She had enjoyed the way Kat had delivered the material. She was direct and honest and didn't indulge in war stories.

They were women, about the same age, and both in a profession dominated by men. Diana had first approached her seeking professional advice. But after years of emotionally charged conversations about professional accomplishments and romantic failures, their relationship evolved into what it was today, a close friendship.

"So, how have you been? It's been a while since we did this," Diana said.

"I know. It's been going well. Busy as heck, but productive. And you? How's life in the parole business?"

"Ah, you know, there are good days and bad. But the good days outweigh the bad, so I still enjoy the work."

"That's good to hear. If you're enjoying what you're doing, then that's all that matters. But you know, if you ever want to change over, we need smart people on the force."

"*Nena,* please, I already tried the city cop thing, and I am way too old to start over. And besides, I like what I'm doing."

The waitress approached their table, and Kat ordered a vodka tonic.

When the waitress left, Kat reached for a wing. "Do you mind? I'm starving."

“Of course not. So, how’s Maya? You two still planning on moving in together?”

“No, we put those plans on hold. We’re on the outs right now. Honestly, I think we’re close to being done.”

“Really? You two were good together. What happened?”

“We *were* good together. I don’t know, things change. She’s different, I’m different.”

“Is there someone else?”

“No. I’m too busy for that crap. That’s one of the problems, time. I don’t have a lot of time to give her.”

“What about her?”

The waitress put Kat's drink on the table. Kat glanced up and thanked her. She and the waitress both smiled and held each other's eyes about five seconds past friendly. Kat took a long sip of her drink as she watched the waitress walk away.

Kat turned her attention back to Diana. “What was the question again?”

“Do you think Maya is seeing someone else?”

“No. Maybe. Who knows? At this point, it doesn’t matter. We had our time together. We had our little love story, and it was a good one. Ours just doesn’t end with the two of us living happily ever after. And you know what? There’s nothing wrong with that.”

“You’re right.” Diana took a sip of her drink.

“And what about you? Any new *papi chulos* you want to brag about?”

“No, nothing regular. I went on a date a few weeks back.”

“Okay, that’s something. Tell me more.”

"Not much to tell. He's a doctor, and he looks like Michael B. Jordan, but only taller."

“Damn. Really?”

"Oh, yeah. His sense of humor was for shit, but he was fairly interesting and very hot, so I slept with him."

Kat leaned back in her chair and flashed a toothy grin. “Oh snap. Details, please.”

Diana smiled and felt her cheeks get warm. “There’s nothing to tell. He was pretty bad in bed.”

"Oh, man. Now see, that's a goddamn shame. What a waste of a perfectly good specimen."

“Tell me about it.”

"Are you going to see him again? I mean, he's a doctor, right? Which means he's probably smart, so he can learn. He's already rich and handsome. You can always teach him how to fuck."

“Yeah, but I’m not interested in projects. Besides, he was unfunny and gave a corny toast. That’s three strikes, *nena*.”

They both laughed and took sips of their drinks.

“So, let me ask you something. You still working out at the Eight-Three?”

“Yeah, for a while now. Why?” Kat said.

“I had a narcotics detective come see me today. Frank Hawkins. Do you know him?” Diana saw the concern on Kat’s face and was surprised by the reaction.

“Frank Hawkins? Yeah, he’s my boss. What did he want?”

Diana leaned back. “What’s with that face?”

“What do you mean?”

“You look like you just found a lump on your tit.”

Kat forced out a phony chuckle. “It’s nothing. I’m just surprised Frank went to see you. So, what did he want?”

“He asked about one of my parolees. He wanted to know if he was an authorized informant.”

“Is that it?”

“Yeah, but it was more than what he said. It was the way he said it. And something in his eyes. I got a bad feeling from him.”

“That’s just Frank. He gives off that sleazy used car salesman vibe. I don’t know if he does it intentionally, but it works for him. So, what’d you tell him about the ex-con?”

“The truth. That he isn’t an informant.”

“Are you sure about that?”

Hold on now.

“Are you pressing me for info now?”

“Hey, relax. I didn’t know anything about this until you told me. Remember?”

"You're right, I'm sorry. I just thought it was weird how this guy Hawkins was acting. Anyway, to answer your question, yes, I'm sure the parolee isn't an informant. Anyone who wanted to work with him would have to go through me. There'd be an official record."

“Not if it was off the books.”

"True. But then, no one would know, including me. They couldn't use the information in an official capacity. Could they?"

“No, not officially. But there’re ways around that.” Kat took another sip of her drink. “So, was that it? With Frank, I mean. Was that the end of the conversation?”

"Yeah, pretty much," Diana said. She studied Kat's face and still felt something was bothering her. "Is there something else I should know about?"

Kat brought her glass up to her lips but didn't drink right away, as if she were taking time to collect her thoughts. "No, it's nothing. Just, fucking Frank is always sneaking around trying to put cases together. I hate that he leaves us out of the loop till the last second."

Sneaking?

“Isn’t that normal for narcotics detectives?”

“Yeah, but not with your own team. It’s just...I’ve been thinking maybe it’s time for me to move on. I’ve done as much as I can in narcotics. If I want a real shot at promoting, I’m going to have to make a move.” Kat smiled awkwardly as she absently thumbed the edge of her menu.

Diana placed her hand on Kat’s hand. “What’s wrong?”

“What do you mean?”

“It just feels really heavy in here suddenly. I know you, and something is wrong. I can tell.”

Kat scanned the room as if she was searching for something. When she finally made her way back around to Diana, her eyes were welled with tears. “It’s nothing. It’s just all the changes. Maya, the job—it can be overwhelming.”

Diana didn’t think Kat was telling her the truth, but she didn’t force the issue. The fact was, Diana was shocked by Kat's reaction. She only wanted to ask about Frank Hawkins and fooled herself into believing the answer would be innocuous. That Kat would tell her Frank was just an old school cop and he was rough around the edges.

But that wasn't what she got from Kat at all. And her feelings weren't based on anything Kat had said but, on her reaction, and the way she'd spoken. It was as if Kat wanted to rationalize her life choices to a priest but was held back by a blood oath of secrecy.

To Diana, Kat sounded ashamed and embarrassed. Diana believed her friend was a good person, and she understood the informal politics and tribal rituals of Kat's profession—like bunting when a pitcher is throwing a no-hitter—the NYPD had more unwritten rules than Major League Baseball.

"No, I understand. I get pretty overwhelmed myself sometimes," Diana said.

Kat laughed and wiped her eyes. "This was supposed to be a good time. Hey, I'm hungry. You want to order some food?"

"Sure." Diana forced a smile.

Kat opened her menu. "What's his name anyway?"

"Who?"

"Your ex-con."

"Serrano. Julian Serrano." Diana searched Kat's face for a reaction at hearing the name.

There wasn't one.

FROM WHERE HE STOOD, Julian felt like he could reach out and touch the Seven train as it passed on its elevated track, curving directly in front of the window. He knew it was an illusion, of course. The train's bright lights filled the apartment, and its speed and mass caused the apartment to shake and its contents to vibrate. The circumstances combined to make the train appear closer than it was.

Julian stood in front of the living room window in an apartment on Roosevelt Avenue in Corona, Queens. The apartment was on the second floor of a two-story walk-up above a pharmacy. The small one-bedroom apartment was dimly lit and smelled like old cooking oil. Jimmy had asked him to go with Vernon and Little D to deliver two keys of stepped-on coke to some up-and-comers in Queens. Jimmy tried to sell it to Julian as the youngsters needing security—and looking after. He figured it was just as much for Jimmy and Angel's peace of mind as for providing security for their product. So, they could see if Julian's head was in the game and if he still had the nerve to be in the life.

When they had arrived at the apartment the up-and-comers were already there. Julian had walked in behind Vernon but ahead of Little D. He'd scanned the room and counted four up-and-comers.

They were all young men, early to mid-20's as far as Julian could tell. Three of the four were average height and slim. The fourth was tall—around six-two—and he looked older than the other three. Julian had spotted the pistol's handle in his jacket pocket and had figured the rest of them were strapped, too.

Vernon and the tall one had greeted each other with smiles and an insincere hug. Vernon had introduced him as Nate. He spoke with a lisp and had a thick Staten Island accent that made taking him seriously very difficult. Nate had introduced the others in his crew, but Julian hadn't paid attention. Nate was the leader and the only real threat.

They'd all taken their positions, and Julian was on full alert.

"So, you guys got it on lock then?" Vernon said.

"You know it. We got a little beef with some Jamaicans out in Queens Village, but they ain't shit," Nate said.

"You might want to be careful with that. Them Jamaicans ain't nothing to fuck with."

"What you mean, son? *We* ain't nothing to fuck with. They gonna see real soon." The voice came from the kitchen and belonged to one of the guys in Nate's crew. He wore a black skull cap with a yellow Nike symbol embroidered on the front.

They should've been gone already. Vernon was talking too much, and this was taking too long. The bravado from Mr. Black Skull Cap had raised Julian's antennae, so he stood silently by the window, scanning the room.

Two anonymous up-and-comers were seated on the couch directly across from Julian. They both wore light-weather black jackets, but one wore a Pittsburgh Penguins baseball cap and the other a Pittsburgh Steelers baseball cap. Penguins Cap had a patchy beard, and his left nostril was pierced with a hoop earring.

Steelers Cap was clean-shaven, but he had a long, vertical scar that started on the outer edge of his left eyebrow and disappeared underneath the brim of his cap. The two passed a blunt back and forth. The one in the kitchen seemed to be texting on his cell phone.

Vernon was seated on one of the two chairs around a small, circular wooden table, and Nate was seated in the other chair. Nate's left hand was on the table, but his right hand hung down by his side, out of sight. Little D was standing against a wall by the kitchen and holding the two kilos of white in a black backpack.

“Alright then, you ready? We got what you asked for. You got the loot?” Vernon said.

“Yeah, we got it,” Nate said.

“Let’s see it.”

Nate's lips curled into a venomous grin, exposing his gold and diamond grill. He reached into his jacket pocket and removed a white letter-sized envelope. The envelope was thick and had the familiar creases of a cash stack.

He placed the envelope on the table but kept his hand on it. "We got a little problem though."

A heavy silence filled the room, and Julian felt the air grow dense and tense. He placed his hand inside his pants pocket and gripped the handle of his .38 snub-nosed revolver.

"And what's that?" Vernon turned in his chair, so he was facing Nate.

“It’s not really a problem. It’s more like a hiccup. I only got thirty,” Nate said.

“That’s more than a hiccup, Nate. You ordered up two keys. That’s only enough for one.”

Nike Skull Cap stood at the kitchen's threshold, about a foot away from Little D. The two seated on the couch had finished smoking and were leaning forward.

This was going downhill fast. Julian felt his heartbeat quicken, and he tightened his grip on his gun.

"I know it. I need you to give me the two for what I got. I'll get you the rest in a few weeks," Nate said.

"What the fuck I look like, a bank or some shit? I don't front shit for nobody, homeboy." Vernon put his finger close to Nate's face. "You either got it or you don't."

"What's up, Vernon? Why you being a bitch? Just hook me up for what I got. I'll get you the rest."

Vernon stood up. "Who the fuck you calling 'bitch,' motherfucker? You trying to play like you, Tony Montana, and your broke ass can't even come up with sixty Gs!" He flexed and pointed dramatically. All eyes were on Vernon, and he seemed to enjoy the attention.

Nate's expression hardened. "Alright, motherfucker, you—"

A loud bang filled the room, and the back of Nate's head exploded in a cloud of blood and flesh as the bullet penetrated his eye. Julian quickly pivoted to his right and shot the two on the couch once in both heads. Nike Skull Cap must not have had a gun because he tried to run out the front door.

Little D grabbed him by his coat collar and threw him on the floor. He landed on his back and was looking up when Julian stepped over him and shot him in the forehead.

"Yo, what the fuck!" Vernon yelled.

"Grab the envelope. Let's go," Julian said.

"Why did you fucking kill them? I had it handled."

Julian stepped over to the table and grabbed the envelope. He was moving quickly but not rushing. People in these neighborhoods seldom called the cops, and when they did, the response was slow at best.

"You didn't have shit handled, you stupid motherfucker." Julian pushed the table aside and pointed at the gun in Nate's hand. "You talk too much. That motherfucker was gonna smoke your stupid ass. Now, let's go."

Julian pushed past Little D and out the front door. Vernon and Little D followed behind, exiting the building together. It was after two in the morning, and the streets were empty.

They walked four blocks south on 104th Street. Julian had insisted they leave the Ford Explorer somewhere away from the deal, so they parked it curbside in front of a church on Forty-Second Avenue.

They entered the Explorer, and as they drove away, all Julian could think about was how nothing good ever came out of leaving Brooklyn.

CHAPTER FOURTEEN

"We got a problem," Frank said.

"Yeah? And what exactly is *our* problem?" Angel said.

They'd met on the second level of a three-level parking garage underneath a twenty-five-story apartment building on Worth Street in Manhattan. It was early afternoon on a Friday, and the garage was mostly empty. They were far from his precinct, so Frank wasn't too concerned about running into a familiar face.

He'd insisted they meet in person. He didn't want to leave a paper trail by communicating through text message. And he didn't trust that Angel would be the only one listening during a phone conversation.

"Your name came up," Frank said.

"What do you mean by that?" Angel took a drink from a small glass bottle of apple juice.

"One of my people pitched you as a potential case. Says one of their informants threw out your name."

"So, what does your guy have?"

"*She* doesn't have anything so far. They sat on your spot for a few days and followed two of your guys around, but they didn't see anything I couldn't dismiss."

"Then what's the problem?"

"The '*problem*' is you got a rat in your crew. How else would your name come up?"

"Who the fuck knows? I'm not Keyser Soze. I'm not an urban myth. People know me. It can be anyone. There's always some little piece of shit basehead selling names for ten dollars a pop. As for my people—do you know if any of them got picked up?"

"No. Not from what I can tell. But that doesn't mean somebody isn't being worked off the books," Frank said.

Angel rolled his eyes and checked his watch. "Anything else?"

"Are you hearing me? You're on the radar now, so you gotta be careful. This is a problem that can affect me, and I won't allow that. You gotta lay low for a while."

Angel scoffed. "That's not gonna happen. I got too many things happening, and I'm too far down the road to stop now. Do your part, keep your people in line, and run interference on everyone else. That's not too hard, is it?"

"Listen to me, you little spic motherfucker. You don't run shit around here. Do you understand me? We have an arrangement where I get something, and you get something—that's it, and that's that. And remember one thing, I have the full weight of the NYPD at my disposal. If I wanted to, I could end you—just like that." Frank snapped his fingers.

Angel smirked. "You keep telling yourself that, Frank, and maybe you'll even start believing it. In the meantime, I'll keep getting rich, and you'll keep licking my balls for the chump change I lose between my couch cushions."

Frank lit a Marlboro Red and didn't respond. He thought about the Faustian deal he'd made with Angel Guerra eight years ago and how it wasn't paying off like it used to.

He had been on the job for over fifteen years when he met Angel. Frank had done good work in those fifteen years, put a lot of shitbags in prison, and he'd done what he needed to do to keep his side hustles a secret. But now it seemed his error in deciding to work with Angel would wreck what was left of his world.

Frank's team had been working with the feds on a mean son of a bitch out of Yonkers named Isaac Jimenez. He was a distributor hooked up with a cartel out of Honduras. Isaac had been bringing in fifty kilograms a month of uncut cocaine and supplying dealers in all five boroughs.

Frank and Tony had been conducting surveillance when they picked up Angel coming out of one of Isaac's stash houses in Greenpoint. They'd conducted a stop and frisk on Angel and found a pound of Honduran snowflake in the front pocket of his New York Giants hoodie. After a lengthy question-and-answer session in the backseat of Frank's Dodge Magnum, they'd made a deal.

Isaac was going down. There'd been no doubt in Frank's mind about that. But he'd figured he could insulate Angel from the investigation. He'd ensure Angel wasn't part of the indictment and help him get his own thing going. Keep the whole thing at a level where everyone made money, but the feds didn't pick up the scent.

It'd been going good at first, too. Angel had given up the deal at the tire shop to show he was all in. He told Frank that he and his boys had ordered two kilos from Isaac. But they weren't going to pay for it and had planned to rob Isaac's guy.

It couldn't have worked out better. Frank's team had hit the spot, and Angel had disappeared with the coke in the confusion. Frank pocketed the cash and arrested everyone else on the weapons charges.

He hadn't been worried about the optics of not finding any drugs in a narcotics raid. It wasn't the first time a narcotics unit had hit a spot and come up with a dry hole. But he'd had the weapons charges, so the bosses had been happy.

When they'd first started up, it'd worked out just like Frank wanted. Isaac and his crew were indicted on a RICO beef a few weeks later and were out of the picture. Angel had taken the two kilos and started his little empire, even managing to connect with the Hondurans along the way. Frank's team made good collars with the information Angel fed them, and Frank made some extra cash from time to time.

Why not, after all? Didn't he deserve it? All those years being first through the door on different dope houses all over Brooklyn, one heartbeat from being shot to death. All for what? For a pension so shitty, he would have to get a full-time job as a security guard just to survive. Screw that. That wasn't going to be the last chapter of his story.

But just when Frank was getting close to riding off into the sunset and retiring, he went on a losing streak and got in deep with the sharks. Now, he couldn't afford to retire, and as much as he hated to admit it, he needed Angel's chump change. At least for now—till he could get square and get gone.

"What about Serrano?" Frank said.

"What about him?"

"You sure you can trust him? It seems to me these problems started popping up when he entered the picture."

"First of all, you cleared him, so there's that. But to answer your question, no, I don't trust him. But that don't mean nothing. I don't trust anybody."

"So, what do you want to do?"

Angel stepped away from Frank and didn't speak for several minutes. Frank figured he was running things through in his head, trying to find a way to shake loose of these new problems.

"I got a deal coming up with the Polish. Piotr Grabowski been talking about stepping up his game for a while now. I guess he finally saved up enough because he ordered up ten keys."

"Ten? That ain't much, but alright," Frank said.

Angel rolled his eyes as he finished his last sip of apple juice.

"Ten keys at thirty a key? That shit is definitely alright. But you're missing the big picture."

"Enlighten me."

"You're gonna take that shit down."

"Really? Are you sure you wanna turn off that faucet? Seems to me like the Polish are just getting started. They're going to be ordering more down the line."

"I ain't worried about customers. I'm the only one in the city bringing in shit this pure. Motherfuckers can step on my shit four times and still have the best product on their block. The Polish are ruthless. It's only a matter of time before they try to push me out the way and take over the distro. Nah, I gotta nip that shit in the bud now. You see where I'm going with this?"

Frank took a long drag off his cigarette. "Yeah, I think so. You're gonna send Serrano with the product. As soon as all the kids are in the sandbox, my team takes everyone down, and they all get tucked away upstate for the next twenty-five years."

"Close. Julian needs to go to sleep. For good."

"I don't think that's the right way to go. It would be easier and cleaner to just bust him and charge him with delivery. With his priors and being on parole, he probably won't ever get out of prison."

"Nah. He'll figure he got fucked, so he'll be looking for payback. Besides, he's got a kid. He ain't gonna want to go back inside. He'll snitch. He'll go straight to the feds and start cooperating. Nah, locked up won't work. He's gotta go away."

“What about the rest of your boys? I’m assuming Serrano won’t be going alone.”

"No, he won't, but it ain't no loss. As long as I can keep Jimmy away, I don’t give a fuck about the rest of them.”

“You sure?”

“Those kids are like pipes under a house—they have value when they work, but they end up full of shit and need to be replaced at some point.”

"That's pretty cold, but okay."

“It is what it is.”

"Alright, but you know this is a serious ask, so it'll cost extra."

"Just bring me my shit back and seventy grand for the two keys you'll need to make the delivery charges stick. You keep the rest of the cash."

“Seventy? I thought it was thirty a key?”

"Taxes." Angel pulled out his cell phone and walked away without saying anything else.

Frank smoked his cigarette and watched Angel take the elevator back to street level. He thought about Angel's plan and smiled because it wasn't half bad. He'd probably have to make some changes, but it was a solid idea. Angel would get rid of two problems and even make himself ten grand.

Frank did the math in his head and chuckled. After holding back sixty grand to make the delivery charges stick and giving Angel his ten, he stood to clear two hundred and thirty large. Even after the split with his team, he would have more than enough to clear his debts and start fresh.

Frank climbed into his truck and sped out of the garage, grinning widely as he thought about the horses running in the first at Aqueduct.

WHEN ANGEL first got in the Toyota Camry, the Uber driver tried to engage him in conversation. She was an older, MILF type with nice tits, but Angel wasn't feeling any conversation. When he didn't respond to her remarks about how nice Brooklyn had become, she got the message and stopped talking.

The driver turned up the volume on the radio, which was set to a classic rock station. Pretty soon, Stevie Nicks' soothing voice filled the silence. Angel leaned back on the headrest and thought about his conversation with Hawkins.

He hated Hawkins from the moment they'd first met. With his beady little eyes, Angel thought he looked like one of those lizards on the nature channel. The ones that seemed all dangerous and predatory when the camera was tight on their faces.

But then the camera would zoom out, and the whole lizard would be revealed for what it was—a tiny little thing that ate bugs, hid from its enemies in trees, and ran away whenever it felt threatened. Eight years into this bullshit arrangement, and he still had this dirty lizard cop breathing down his neck.

There was a time when the arrangement had worked for him. A time when knowing he had cover from the cops and a way to get rid of some competition made it easier for him to make some bold moves. But that time was done, and Hawkins was confused about the situation. The dirty little cop puffed out his chest and spoke like he was running shit, and Angel wasn't having it. He knew it was a situation he would have to deal with soon.

But he couldn't be completely mad at Hawkins for throwing out the idea that Julian was a snitch. The fact was, Angel had been suspicious when Jimmy had first mentioned bringing Julian into their operation. Angel and

Julian had been tight since junior high school, but he'd been back on the street for five months and hadn't so much as spit in Angel's direction. Suddenly, he wanted back in, and Angel felt something wasn't right.

Yeah, Julian was on parole, but so what? Guys hit the street every day on parole and go right back to putting in work. The truth was, Julian was way too smart to not suspect some foul shit went down the night he got busted.

Angel had given him up. He'd given them all up, actually, but he'd done his best to make sure his boys didn't do too much time. He'd taken the coke and made sure Hawkins took the money. That way, all they'd get was weapon charges. Jimmy didn't have any prior violent felonies, so he'd only done three years on the gun charge. Julian did twelve because of his priors, but it was all for the greater good.

While they were locked up, Angel had built the business up and created something for them to come home to. Except Julian had got out and didn't want any part of it. At least at first, he hadn't.

But then they'd spoken, and Julian had said his piece. Angel only believed half of what he'd said—the part about needing money. But Jimmy loved Julian, and Angel felt like he owed him something. So, Angel gave Julian a shot, albeit with a clear warning.

He had to be honest with himself. What had happened the previous night had Angel questioning his instincts. Julian had gone into Queens and held it down. He showed the young ones how a real G handled business. Angel was proud that his boy hadn't lost a step and was still cold as steel, but it made the whole situation even more confusing. No one snitching to the cops would be murdering people.

But Hawkins suggestion that Julian is the snitch made sense. Before Julian showed up, Angel's name didn't come up in shit. No, he wasn't going to risk it—he was too close. He had built something out of nothing and wasn't going to let it slip away.

With his hookup in Honduras and the network he was creating, Angel was on his way to the top, and nothing was going to stand in his way.

CHAPTER FIFTEEN

HIS BACK FILLED UP THE ENTIRE TELEVISION SCREEN. THE room's occupants tried to play it cool, but curious eyes undermined their attempts. Kat had already reviewed the video footage that'd been recorded on her button camera. So, she knew the screen would clear up, and they'd all have a clear view of what they came to see.

After a minute or two, the considerably large Tony Bruno moved out of view of the camera. The video footage showed a small open floor safe containing several stacks of U.S. currency. Kat used a remote control to pause the video.

"That turned out to be eighty grand, Eddie and I counted it. But it was never vouchered into evidence. We also located four kilos of coke and a Glock handgun inside the residence. The coke and pistol were turned in," Kat said.

She looked around at the three other people seated at the large, oval-shaped oak table, but no one said anything. Kat sat in one of the oversized black leather chairs near the foot of the table, right in front of the wall-mounted fifty-inch high-definition television. Captain David Harris, the NYPD Internal Affairs Bureau commander, sat to her left. Enriqué Doñes, the Assistant Agent in Charge of the FBI's New York

Office, sat at the head of the table. One of his special agents, Giselle Alaniz, sat on the other side of the table, directly across from Kat.

They were in the third-floor conference room of a thirteen-story commercial building on Wilkinson Avenue in the East Bronx. With Friday's rush hour traffic, it took Kat almost two hours to get to the meet location. But it was far removed from where she lived and worked, so she felt it was well worth the drive. If for nothing else, Kat had peace of mind there was little chance she would run into any familiar faces.

"Tell them what happened to the money," Captain Harris said.

He had a hard time masking the contempt he undoubtedly felt, if he was trying to hide it at all. Captain Harris was the only person on the job who knew she was ratting on Frank Hawkins and his team. She'd been under Captain Harris' thumb for over a year—ever since the feds got her on tape blabbing like Chelsea Handler on Ritalin.

A year ago, she had lunch with her cousin Paul "Paulie" Colella in Palladino's on Hester Street to discuss money laundering. Paulie was a Columbia University-educated commodities broker for a small brokerage firm on Wall Street. He also happened to be a low-level associate of the Genovese Crime Family whose only value to them was his ability to clean dirty money.

She had a lot of cash to clean from her work with Frank, so she'd met with him to discuss it. Paulie had gone into precise detail about putting her money in mobile commodities like gems and gold so it could be moved around more easily. They'd also spoken about investing in real estate through shell companies and how easy it was to open fake accounts through online banking institutions. He'd explained how they could use Bitcoin to make it harder for anyone to detect the money transfers.

They'd spoken about a lot, and Kat had thought she'd been smart by not talking over the phone or communicating through text message. She hadn't considered that Paulie, forever the wannabe gangster, would arrange for their lunch to take place in a restaurant owned by a made guy the F.B.I. was surveilling. The restaurant was wired for sound, and the feds recorded the whole conversation. It turned out they hadn't even known who Paulie was and getting the conversation on tape had been a happy accident.

ASAC Doñes and Captain Harris were old friends from way back when, so they'd kept the recording between them. Captain Harris had cornered Kat while walking out of her apartment building. Escorted her to the office they were in now and had a little show and tell of the audio recording. After some back and forth, he'd convinced Kat it was in her best interest to cooperate with a joint Justice Department and I.A.B. investigation of Detective Sergeant Frank Hawkins and his band of merry men.

"We did what we always do—we split it up. Tony gave me my cut a few days later. He handed me an envelope with twenty grand. He even told me I did a good job," Kat said.

"What's the significance of that?" ASAC Doñes said.

She glanced nervously at ASAC Doñes. He had medium brown skin and a neatly trimmed mustache, and his curly hair was more salt than pepper. His face was emotionless as usual, and he didn't seem to blink. Kat thought he must be a great poker player.

"I've been on the team for almost nine years now. Tony has never complimented me or told me I've done a good job."

"Any idea why that is?" ASAC Doñes said.

"Tough love? I don't know. He doesn't really speak all that much, so I never took the lack of compliments personally. He's not really the mentor type, but we all love him anyway."

"Well shit, it's good to know you all love each other so much," Alaniz scoffed.

Kat glared at Alaniz. She was average height, but four years of division two wrestling at Colorado Mesa University, followed by three years chasing her dream of fighting professionally as a mixed martial artist, had left Alaniz with a powerful build and cauliflower ears. She was also fighter pilot cocky and rude as hell.

"What about the coke? How's the split go on that?" Alaniz continued.

"There is no split. We make cases. That's why the bosses leave us alone."

Alaniz rolled her eyes. "Yeah, why mess with something that helps feed the stat monster."

"So, you're turning in all the narcotics you seize?" ASAC Doñes said, interrupting the standoff.

"I didn't say that. Since I've been on the team, we've vouchered in the dope on *most* of our cases. We turned in enough to make solid cases on the few that we held back product."

"So, what happens to the rest of the dope in those situations?" Alaniz said.

"I can't say for sure. I don't think Frank sells it because I've never received cash from any sale, and we split everything. But I have a theory."

"Please share," ASAC Doñes said.

Kat's right leg shook rapidly under the table. "Every time we've made a case through one of Frank's informants, we've held back on the dope we vouchered. All except this last one. This one came from one of Frank's snitches, but this time, we turned in all the dope."

"Why?" Alaniz said.

"It was almost two days from when we started working the case to when we hit the residence. And when we got inside, there was baby laxative everywhere. It was obvious Lugo had already stepped all over the coke, so it wasn't as pure as when he first got it," Kat said.

"So, what's your theory?" As usual, Alaniz took over the meeting.

"Frank's C.I. is a dealer, and Frank is helping him stay in business. I believe Frank is helping his C.I. rid himself of competition. I think the C.I. is selling his product to dealers and then telling Frank when and where to hit. We hit the spot—Frank makes some money and returns the product to his C.I. if it hasn't been stepped on."

Alaniz and ASAC Doñes glanced at each other.

"Sounds thin," Alaniz said.

"Well, if you think that's thin, you're going to think this one is Karen Carpenter. I'm pretty sure I know who Frank's C.I. is," Kat said.

"Well, don't stop now, Esposito, you're on a roll." Skepticism dripped off every word Alaniz muttered.

Kat stared at Alaniz's smirking face and had to take a few breaths to control her anger. Captain Harris and ASAC Doñes sat stone-faced, waiting for her to continue.

"I'm pretty sure his C.I. is a guy named Angel Guerra."

"And what makes you believe that?" ASAC Doñes said.

"One of my snitches called me last week and gave me Guerra's name and where he's moving product out of. Guerra owns a building and *bodega* out in Bed-Stuy. So, Eddie and I sat on it for a few days, and everything seems to fit."

"Did you see anything substantive? Any transactions?" ASAC Doñes said.

Kat chuckled.

"Did I say something funny, Detective?"

"No, sir. It's just that Frank asked me the same exact questions."

ASAC Doñes didn't seem amused by the irony and pressed on. "And what was your response?"

"No. But, like I said, everything fits. The way Guerra held court outside the *bodega* and the way his little minions provided security. I'm from Bed-Stuy, okay. I can recognize corner boys when I see them. And I've been on the job for a long time. I know what I'm looking at."

"Oh yeah, you're a regular old Jenny from the block. So, what happened next?" Alaniz said.

"Frank shut it down. I gave him what we had, and he completely dismissed it. He said we needed to work on other cases."

"Maybe Hawkins is right." ASAC Doñes leaned back in his chair. "Look, Detective Esposito, you're doing good work, but I have to be honest, I don't care about Sgt. Hawkins' informants. What I do care about, however, is collecting the evidence we need to arrest him and his co-conspirators. Do you have anything beyond conjecture or supposition?"

She thought about Diana and her visit from Frank. "There's something else."

"What's that?" Alaniz said.

"Frank's been looking into an ex-con named Julian Serrano."

Alaniz shrugged. "So? Looking into criminals is part of the job, correct?"

"I'm pretty sure Serrano and Guerra are partners," Kat said.

"Please expand, Detective Esposito." ASAC Doñes said.

After Diana mentioned Serrano's name at dinner, Kat thought she had done a good job of masking her recognition of the name. Her recollection hadn't been immediate initially, but there had been enough familiarity in the name, combined with Frank asking Diana about him, for Kat to become curious enough to do some homework. She had gone back to the station, looked up Serrano, and it had all come back to her.

Kat remembered the night they'd arrested Julian Serrano.

"We put Serrano in prison for twelve years," Kat said.

"Again, so what? What's so weird about Hawkins looking up people he locked up already? We all know most of them go back to doing dirt as soon as they get out," Alaniz said.

"Exactly my point. Serrano just got out, so he's trying to get back in the game. My guess is Frank was vetting Serrano for Guerra." Kat looked around the table. "The night we busted Serrano was all bullshit. Frank sold it as a tip from a C.I. about a big dope deal. So, we sat on a tire shop out in Brooklyn. I remember thinking it was strange that we didn't have every possible route away from the garage covered. How unorganized that seemed for someone who made as many cases as Frank. But I was new to his team, so I kept my mouth shut. Three perps eventually showed up and entered the shop, but I didn't get a good look at any of their faces. Frank had information that there were at least two people already inside.

"After a while, Frank gets a text message and calls the entry. We hit the spot, but all we found were some yahoos with guns—at least, that was what I was told. I was new so I was assigned to prisoner control. I wasn't part of the search.

"According to Frank, no drugs or money were located. He said one got away and put the dry hole on that person. Frank's story was that more than likely, the runner took the dope and money with them when they escaped. The bosses bought it and chalked up the dry hole to being part of the game. They were content with the weapons charges and happy the operation wasn't a total waste of resources," Kat said.

Alaniz's face softened, and she seemed intrigued. "So, Serrano is one of the unlucky ones that got arrested. What about the one that got away? Do you know who he was?"

"I don't have any proof, but I'm convinced it was Guerra. He and Serrano are known associates in the system. Those two have been joined at the hip for a long time. If it was Guerra who escaped, then it makes sense he's Frank's snitch. Frank was getting texts from someone inside the tire shop that night. And now he's dismissing Guerra as a good target—and vetting Serrano. You know as well as I do that there are no coincidences in our line of work."

"Okay. So, Guerra gives up the tire shop deal to Frank. Frank lets Guerra walk away with the dope and the money. And the two have spent the last eight years in a quid pro quo relationship? Am I tracking you right?" Alaniz said.

"Close. Guerra took the dope, but Frank kept the money."

"But if Frank kept the money, you would know more, wouldn't you? Didn't you get your cut?" Alaniz said.

"Not at that point. The team still didn't trust me. I didn't get my first taste for a while—almost six months after I joined the unit."

Alaniz sat back in her chair and nodded. "Well, it's nice to know they have standards."

Kat ignored the remark. "I think, more than anything, it was like a test. That deal established the ground rules for Frank and Guerra's relationship."

They were all quiet for a few seconds.

"Interesting story, Detective Esposito. Nevertheless, I'm more interested in information, or evidence, that either proves or disproves there are other law enforcement officials involved in Sgt. Hawkins' illegal dealings," ASAC Doñes said.

She looked at ASAC Doñes, and while she disliked him and found almost everything he said patronizing, she couldn't disagree with his point. She had been video-recording their operations for the past six months. The feds and Captain Harris had more than enough to move on Frank, Tony, Eddie, and Joe. The only reason they hadn't was because she'd convinced them Frank's schemes might involve other people in law enforcement, including some on the federal level.

Kat had no evidence of this and had never seen anything to support it, but she was trying to delay the inevitable for as long as possible. She knew when there was no more juice to squeeze, her life as she knew it would be over. She wouldn't be a cop anymore.

Indictments would be handed down, and people would go to prison. Kat didn't want to deal with the reality that soon, her friends would know she betrayed them, and they may come looking for payback.

"No, sir, nothing solid yet. But there must be other people involved. There's no way he does this for as long as he has without help from above."

"Alright, let's do this—we'll continue investigating Hawkins and the rest of his team. There's no harm in waiting a little longer. Esposito will brief Special Agent Alaniz on everything she has so far, and we can go from there. Let's see where it takes us." Captain Harris looked at Kat and Alaniz. "Will you two excuse us, please? We have some boss-type business to discuss."

Kat and Alaniz stood up, exited the room, and made their way to the elevator shoulder-to-shoulder.

"So, that went well," Kat said.

"If you say so."

Kat stopped walking. "What's your problem, Alaniz?"

Alaniz turned and faced her. "You're my problem. You and Hawkins and every dirty cop that makes the rest of us look like shit."

"Listen, I know I fucked up, but I'm trying to get square."

"Who are you kidding? You're trying to save your ass, so save me the born-again bullshit. The only reason you're here is that you got caught. Not from some deep-rooted feelings of guilt for betraying the badge. I'd respect you more if you just owned your shit."

Kat was quiet for a few seconds. "I am aware of who I am and what I've done. Regardless of how I got here, I'm here, so let's make the best of it. We don't have to like each other, but we're stuck together, so let's try to get through this without killing each other."

"Fair enough." Alaniz turned, and the two started toward the elevators again. "So, this Guerra angle is actually kind of intriguing. You said a C.I. put you on him?"

"Yeah, I signed him up a few weeks back. A uniform pushed him my way. This guy is a trip. I'll tell you what."

"How so?"

"Well, he's short—about my height, which is short for a guy. But he's massive, with a big chest, thighs and arms, a round face, and a soft belly. He's really intense, and he looks mean as fuck. Picture Danny DeVito after twenty-five years in Attica."

They both chuckled.

"Wow, that is certainly an interesting image. Anything else I should know about Mr. DeVito?"

"He has this deep, sandpaper voice."

"Really?"

"Yeah, he sounds like Harvey Fierstein if he gargled glass."

"Harvey Fierstein sounds like he *did* gargle glass."

"Fair point." Kat chuckled.

"So, you have a Danny DeVito, Harvey Fierstein gangster Frankenstein working for you as a snitch. That is pretty freaking awesome."

"I don't know how awesome it is. He's—um, well, let's just say he's a very interesting person to meet in person."

"Well, if you want some company next time you debrief him, I can make myself available."

"Nah, he looks the part, but I'm pretty sure I can handle old Eli."

CHAPTER SIXTEEN

JOSH HAD SENT JULIAN'S TEAM BACK TO THE TWENTY-STORY commercial building on Fulton Street. Usually, the cleaning crews rotated locations weekly, so working in the same building two weeks in a row was a rare occurrence. Julian was vacuuming an area rug in one of the executive offices on the eighteenth floor when he got the call from Ms. Rivera. She'd told him she was on her way to see him and would text him when she arrived so he could meet her in the lobby.

He got back to vacuuming. It was a little after eleven-thirty, and he wondered why Ms. Rivera would come out to visit him at work so late on a Friday night. It couldn't be on account of what went down in Queens yesterday. Some shit that bloody, if the cops knew it was him, they'd send a tactical team to pick him up. Kick in his door while he slept—try to catch him with his guard down.

Nah, her visiting him had to be about something else. Maybe he pissed dirty. He hadn't smoked since he'd got out, but he'd been around Jimmy a lot, and that fool got blazed damn near every day. If that was the case, he figured he could explain the situation. Ms. Rivera was good people. She wouldn't violate him just for being around the shit.

At least, he hoped she wouldn't. He could tell she liked him, and he liked her too, maybe too much. She showed compassion and legitimate interest in whether he made it. He didn't want to disappoint her and felt bad knowing he would.

Julian was staring at the rug trancelike, lost in his thoughts when he heard the text message alert from his cell phone. He pulled his cell phone out of his pants pocket and read the message from Ms. Rivera, letting him know she was downstairs.

THIS TIME, Diana decided to drive into the city. It was close to midnight on a Friday night, so she had assumed correctly that traffic on the Brooklyn Bridge would be light. It was a clear, beautiful night, and the moon's reflection danced on the moving waters of the East River.

She had called Julian before she'd left her office to let him know she was on her way. She listened to Julian's voice on the call for any sign of concern. It was well into the evening, and they had never met after business hours. As usual, his voice was even and calm, and he'd given no indication that her visit surprised him.

Diana could have met him earlier. She could have called him during the day to arrange a meeting or just showed up at his apartment for a site visit and asked her questions there. But she'd spent the day going over her meeting with Hawkins, her dinner with Kat, and following up on information. The meeting with Hawkins had made her uneasy, but her conversation with Kat had made her suspicious.

The funny thing was that when Kat taught Diana's class, she always said there were no such things as coincidences in police work. She told the class they should look deeper if they were ever faced with a confluence of seemingly unrelated occurrences. Now, here Diana was amid some strange coincidences and doing exactly as she had been taught.

She had spent the day researching Julian's case. As a parole officer, she only had immediate access to information directly pertaining to Julian. Police reports were not part of Julian's case file, so she made some calls and got what she needed to dig into what exactly had happened the night Julian had been arrested and who else had been involved.

Four people were inside the garage but only three had been arrested and charged—Julian, James O'Donnell, and Benjamin Sheffield. The fourth, someone named Hector Franco, didn't have any weapons on him, so he wasn't charged. He was listed as the victim in the reports but hadn't provided any statements and had refused to cooperate with the prosecution. According to the court records, since they didn't have prior felony convictions, James O'Donnell and Benjamin Sheffield had both received three-year sentences on weapons charges.

Diana's blood boiled when she discovered that two of the detectives listed in the case file were Frank Hawkins and Katalina Esposito. It had been almost nine years and Kat had been on hundreds of operations since then. Diana wanted to believe her friend hadn't remembered Julian's name when she'd mentioned it at dinner. But she couldn't get there. Not when she considered her meeting with Hawkins.

Hawkins asking her about Julian as if he didn't know him was another red flag. The man was a seasoned detective. Even if he didn't remember Julian when he first learned of him, Hawkins would have undoubtedly run Julian's name and figured out he'd already had dealings with him.

Diana knew she was missing something and hoped Julian could fill in the blanks. She had texted him to let him know she was outside his building. She waited outside, watching for him through the glass front door. After a few minutes, Julian emerged from the elevator.

He spotted her and started toward her with a smile on his face.

When he stepped off the elevator, Julian scanned the room and outside the giant glass windows surrounding the entire first floor. He was relieved to see Ms. Rivera was the only person waiting for him and genuinely happy to see her, so he smiled. She didn't return the smile, and he was embarrassed.

He made his way to the front door, cutting between the leather couch and seats arranged conversation-style in the middle of the lobby. He unlocked the front door and stepped aside so she could escape the cold.

"Hi, Ms. Rivera."

"Hello, Julian." Ms. Rivera walked inside and stopped a few feet away from him.

He locked the door and turned to face her. Ms. Rivera wore a dark blue three-quarter-length navy wool coat buttoned up over light blue jeans and tan Timberland boots. A dark blue wool ski cap was pulled over her head, covering her forehead just above her eyebrows. Her eyes were watery, and her nose was red from the cold.

"Why are you out here so late? Is something wrong?" Julian said.

"I wanted to ask you about something," Diana said.

"And it isn't something you could have asked me on the phone?"

"No. I like to see who I'm speaking with."

"Okay."

"Can we sit?"

"Sure." Julian stepped past Ms. Rivera and led her to the leather couch and seats in the middle of the lobby. She sat in one of the leather seats, so he lowered himself into the other. "What's going on?"

"Frank Hawkins came to see me."

DIANA SEARCHED Julian's face for a reaction, but there wasn't one, at least not one she noticed.

"Do you know who that is?"

Please, don't lie to me.

"Yeah, of course I do. What did he want?" Julian said.

"He wanted to know about you."

"What about me?"

Diana waited to answer. As much as she liked Julian, he was still an ex-con, and as much as she disliked Hawkins, he was still a cop. Something was going on, and people were lying—that much she was sure about. She knew she had to tread lightly until she was sure who was doing what.

"Let me ask you something first. How do you know Frank Hawkins?"

"He put me in prison. But you already know that. Right?"

She ignored his question. “What were you doing there that night? At the tire shop.”

"Like I'm sure you've already read, we went to rob it. We didn't find anything, so we tried to leave, but the cops got us before we could get out."

He was being evasive, and it was pissing her off. As much as she tried not to, she had stopped seeing him as a parolee and was as comfortable around him as any of her friends.

“That’s what the official record says, but I want you to tell me what you were really doing there that night.”

Julian remained silent for several seconds and stared at her like he was studying her. He leaned back in his seat and placed his hands on his stomach, fingers interlocked as if he were watching television in his apartment.

“Why are you here, Ms. Rivera?”

“What do you mean? You’re under my supervision. I can meet with you wherever and whenever I want.”

"No, I get that. But why the urgency? You could have called me to your office or visited during the day like you've done a dozen times before. Why are you out here now, asking questions like you're Veronica Mars?"

Veronica Mars? I prefer Clarice Starling, thank you very much.

She removed her cap and surveyed the room. It was beautifully decorated but cold and impersonal. The floor was made entirely of dark gray ceramic tiles—large square tiles that, depending on the observer's point of view, connected to create strange geometric shapes.

The area where they were sitting had been arranged in the middle of the room, and long hallways led to offices on either side of them. Large stone sculptures were placed along the walls in front of each hallway, like sentinels standing watch over the building's occupants.

She stared at Julian, thought about his question, and decided it was time for a real conversation.

Time to ante up.

“I don’t believe you were in that garage just to commit a robbery. Which, to tell you the truth, doesn’t really matter. You got caught and did your time. But Frank Hawkins is a narcotics cop. He was then and he is now. He came to me and said your name came up in an investigation. So, I'm asking you straight up, are you involved in something illegal?"

"No."

Liar.

He'd hesitated when he'd answered. It had been barely perceptible, and Diana almost hadn't picked it up, but it had happened—she was sure of it. She didn't say anything immediately, choosing to sit silently and study his face.

"I guess I have to take you at your word."

He looked out the window contemplatively and then down at his hands. "Have you ever been sad, Ms. Rivera?"

She was caught off guard by the seeming randomness of the question. "Of course, I have. Everyone has been sad at some point or another."

"I don't mean a 'my dog just died' kind of sad. I'm talking about an unbearable sadness. The kind that gnaws at your soul and makes your heart cry."

Diana heard his voice crack when he spoke the words, and she thought about her own heartache—she thought about Isabel. The logical part of her brain was telling her to end the conversation—to not engage anymore and just leave. But the other part, the emotional part, was pushing her in the opposite direction, and she wanted to respond to his question. She wanted to vent to someone she wasn't paying by the hour, and she wanted someone to share an emotional experience with.

"Yes," Diana whispered her answer like she was speaking to herself more than him.

He brought his head up and met her eyes with his. "Me too. Only, I feel that way every day. Right here, right now, sitting in this chair, I'm holding back tears. You asked about the night in the garage. Well, that night, I lost everything."

"Julian, I—"

"Don't get me wrong, I put myself in that situation and own it. Every fucked-up thing I ever did or was ever into was all of my own choosing. But things happened that night and I went away for a long time. And because of that, I lost the love of my life."

"What do you mean?"

"Laila, my wife. Her sister hates me. She says it's my fault Laila died. And you know what? She's right."

"Didn't she die from cancer? You can't blame yourself for that—people die from cancer every day."

"And people beat it every day, too. Maybe she beats it if I'm not locked up when she gets sick. Without me, she couldn't afford the best doctors. If I didn't go to prison, I could have paid for better medical care, and she would have gotten better treatment.

"At the very least, I would have been by her side when she got the bad news. Maybe she would have been stronger because she wouldn't have been stressed out worrying about me. Maybe she wouldn't have given up."

"Is that what you think? That she gave up?" Diana said.

"I don't know, maybe. All I know is Laila's not here and I wasn't with her when she left this world. I didn't get to hold her hand or kiss her goodbye."

I KNOW THE PAIN! I FEEL IT EVERY DAY TOO! And as much as I want to, I will not—I cannot share that experience with you.

"Julian, I've never experienced the kind of loss you're talking about, but I have felt the overwhelming sadness you described."

"If you had the chance to do something about it, would you?"

"What do you mean? The only thing you can do is let time pass and not drive yourself crazy waiting for the wounds to heal."

"Did that work for you?"

"I'm still waiting."

They both breathed out tension-releasing chuckles.

"That's what I'm talking about, Ms. Rivera. That kind of hurt doesn't ever go away. But what if you could do something to at least make the score zero-zero again—get back to even?"

The tone of his voice had changed, and she had an uneasy feeling. It was as if his worst enemies had just entered the room and sat on his lap.

"Julian, I'm not really understanding what you're hinting at, but it doesn't sound good."

He stood up and looked down at her. "It's nothing, Ms. Rivera. I'm just venting a little. I have to get back upstairs. Eli is probably pissed that I left him alone cleaning the bathrooms."

"Alright, Julian, I'll let you get back to it." She stood up and he escorted her back to the front door. He unlocked the door, and she stepped out into the cold night. She turned and gazed into his eyes. "Remember one thing, Julian. Life is about choices. The choices you've made led you here, for better or worse. You may not like the options, but you always have a choice. Think about your son and choose wisely."

"Good night, Ms. Rivera." Julian smiled and locked the door.

Diana watched him walk back to the elevators and wondered if anyone ever got back to even with their demons.

CHAPTER SEVENTEEN

Angel had told everyone to meet at his store at three in the afternoon. Jimmy offered a ride, but Julian declined. He told Jimmy he had errands to run and would meet him there. He didn't have any errands, but he didn't like rolling with Jimmy. It wasn't like it used to be between the two of them.

Too many years had passed, and the old feelings had changed. The conversation and good times that used to come easy were now awkward and forced. He could blame it on the time away. But if he was being honest, even though he loved Jimmy, he just didn't trust him anymore. Julian had plans for Angel. And if nothing else, Jimmy was loyal. But his loyalties were with Angel now.

It was cold outside, but it was only a few blocks from his apartment on Dekalb Avenue to Angel's place, so Julian decided to walk. He thought about his conversation with Ms. Rivera and how it could impact his plan. Hawkins asking his parole officer about him all but confirmed his suspicions that Angel was working with Hawkins and always had been. But now Ms. Rivera was suspicious and poking around, and that wasn't something Julian had planned for.

He was still a block away from Angel's *bodega*, but he could already hear hip-hop music booming from the car radio inside Little D's Ford

Explorer. When he got close Julian spotted Little D, Vernon, and two other people he hadn't met before standing on the sidewalk beside the Explorer.

Little D met him on the sidewalk. "Yo, what up, Julian?" They pounded fists and Little D turned toward Vernon and the other two men. "That's Flaco and Dennis. Fellas, this is Julian."

"What's up fellas," Julian said.

Flaco and Dennis nodded at him but didn't say anything. They looked to be in their early twenties. Both men had that aura of violence Julian was so familiar with from growing up in these streets and his time in prison.

Flaco was tall and thin, and he wore thick, black-framed eyeglasses. Dennis was about Julian's height and had an elaborate black-and-gray tattoo that took up the entire left side of his neck. Julian could make out a crown, but the rest was indecipherable from where he stood. Dennis held a lit blunt and was drinking from a forty-ounce Old English beer. An expensive-looking gold grill was revealed when he pulled the bottle away from his face.

"Julian, Vern—you two come inside."

Julian turned when he heard Jimmy's voice. He was standing in front of the *bodega*'s front door. Julian and Vernon entered the *bodega* and followed Jimmy down to the basement.

Angel was already seated behind his desk. Julian and Vernon sat down on the old couch, and Jimmy took a seat in the plastic chair next to Angel's desk.

"We got some business coming up on Tuesday," Angel said.

"It's about time." Vernon leaned forward in his seat. "Who with?"

"Grabowski," Angel said.

Vernon looked confused. "The Polish? Since when we fuck with them?"

"Since now. They ordered up ten keys."

"Ten? Really? That's a lot, especially after they cut it. I wonder what they got going." Vernon was working hard at the smart soldier bit.

"Who cares. As long as we're the plug, it don't matter what they do with it."

"Facts," Vernon said.

“So, what’s the plan?” Julian said.

“You and Vern gonna make the delivery. I’m not sure where yet, but it’ll be one of their places,” Angel said.

“Just us? What about security?” Julian said.

“You’ll take Little D, Dennis, and Flaco with you to watch your back. But, Vern, you make sure you the only one handling the product or the money. You understand?”

“A hundred percent. I got you. Don’t worry about nothing.” Vernon glanced at Julian and smirked.

"Cool. Jimmy will get with you before the meet on Tuesday to pass off the product." Angel locked eyes with Julian for a few seconds and then turned to Vernon. "Vern, go ahead and step out for a second. I want to holla at Julian real quick.”

Vernon hesitated. He glared at Julian with envy and anger as he got up and left.

Angel waited till Vernon was gone before he spoke again. "So, what you think?"

Julian shrugged. “It sounds alright. Just some security work, no big deal.”

"It's a little more than that. I told Vern I want him to handle everything, but that don't mean anything. I gotta make sure wild ones like Vern stay loyal. He might go off the reservation if he thinks I'm pushing him aside for you. And then I gotta put him down and I'm not ready to do that yet."

“Angel, man, you ain’t gotta explain anything to me. This is your shit. I don’t want anything more than what you’re giving me now.”

“Nah, Julian, you don’t get it, man. You’re my brother. You and Jimmy both. I love you motherfuckers. We in this shit together. We're close to what we started, man. This deal is just a taste of what's coming for the three of us." Angel rose from his chair, removed three bottles of beer from his refrigerator, and used a bottle opener to remove the caps.

Angel walked around his desk and handed Jimmy and Julian beers. "This is to us, *hermanos*.” He held out his bottle to toast their success. “We made it.”

Julian stood up. He looked at Angel and although he was filled with hate, he smiled and jutted his bottle toward Angel. In front of him, speaking of loyalty and love, was the man who betrayed him and destroyed his life.

Julian's hand shook with rage as he drank from the bottle.

THEY'D both lied to her. She was sure of it. Diana was about twenty minutes into her two-hour drive upstate to visit her sister Rosa in New Windsor. She'd spent every minute thinking about her conversations with Julian and Kat and was upset.

She'd half expected it from Julian. He was an ex-con after all, and she was always prepared for one of her parolees not to make it. As hard as most of them tried not to, they failed. Things got difficult, so they relied on old instincts and made bad decisions. Diana knew all this. She dealt with it every day. She was still disappointed.

It's a tired trope used in bad movies to say she thought Julian was different. That he was a flawed person seeking redemption. If she was being honest with herself, she'd seen it in his eyes the last time they'd spoken.

At first glance, Julian appeared to be shrouded in an overwhelming sadness that made her want to reach out to him. But when she looked deeper, she saw it—a furious anger that filled her with dread. Although charismatic and kind, Julian had an aura of violence about him, like a beautiful jungle cat searching for prey.

As for Kat, she knew they weren't as close as they once had been. An expected byproduct of too many hours spent at work trying to avoid the realities of her own reality. But they were still friends. Diana had seen the despair on Kat's face and heard the pain in her voice. Frank Hawkins was a wrong cop; Diana was sure of it, and now she believed someone she loved was mixed up with him.

It was after five in the evening, and dusk was already setting in the city. It was Saturday evening, so the traffic was light. The Bluetooth speaker in her car connected to her cell phone, so she listened to her favorite songs on shuffle mode. She was lost in her thoughts and made it over the George Washington Bridge right as "Nothing Even Matters" by Lauryn Hill ended.

Diana had a lot of paperwork to catch up on but felt isolated and alone. She hadn't seen her sister in a few months, but it was more than that. After everything that had happened, she wanted to be around people she loved and who she knew loved her unconditionally.

When Diana arrived at her sister's home, Rosa met her outside, and they hugged. Diana held on to her sister a few seconds longer than usual, enjoying the safe feeling of her embrace. Diana stepped back, looked at her sister, and smiled. For her, seeing Rosa was like seeing their mother. Her dark, silky, thick hair and hazel-brown eyes made Rosa the spitting image of their mother.

You look so beautiful.

They went inside the house, where wonderful smells flooded Diana's senses and filled her with nostalgia. When she had called Rosa earlier in the day and asked if she could come by, her sister told her it would be more than fine and promised a home-cooked meal. Diana stood in the middle of her sister's kitchen, and the smell of *pernil y arroz con gandules* made her happy and hungry.

"It smells so good in here," Diana said.

"Uh-huh. I don't know why you always ask me to make that. All you do is pick out the *gandules*," Rosa said.

"Because I like the way they make the rice taste, but I hate the texture of the peas."

Her brother-in-law Junior joined them for dinner, and afterward, he fixed them drinks before he went to bed. Diana and Rosa sat in the living room, kept warm by the heat from the fireplace and the sips of rum they drank from their glasses.

"Remember when we used to live on Willoughby?" Rosa said.

Hell, yes, I do. Met some of the finest papis out there on Willoughby Avenue.

"Yeah." Diana smiled widely. "Those were good times."

"Yeah, but they were hard, too," Rosa said.

That's not how I remember it.

"For *Mami* maybe, but not for you and me. We were young and having fun."

"But now we know how hard it was for her. Doesn't that change how you remember everything? Or at least how you feel about our experiences?"

"No, not at all. I mean, I was always aware that *Mami* was raising us alone and that she had to work two jobs for minimum wage to take care of us. But she didn't talk about it, so I don't remember considering it a big deal. My memories of back then are good ones. I love that I have them."

"I see it differently. I understand what you're saying about *Mami* not discussing the hard stuff when we were kids and how that impacts your feelings about our childhood. But knowing now how much she was struggling. It changes it for me. I don't remember it as fondly anymore."

"You should. *Mami* worked hard but didn't complain. She created an environment where we were only aware of the difficulties much later. *Mami* kept us out of the hard stuff. It was an act of love."

"But don't you think it was all a lie?"

"Sometimes you have to lie to protect the ones you love."

"Maybe." Rosa sipped her drink and was quiet for a few seconds. "So, what's going on with you?"

"Oh, nothing really. Just work stuff."

"Bullshit. You didn't sound too good on the phone, and you wouldn't make the drive up here just because things at work weren't going well."

I can't say too much, sis.

"I just wanted to see you guys. Be around you, Junior, and the kids for a little bit. Is there anything wrong with wanting to be around my family?"

"No, not at all and you're more than welcome any time. But I know you, and I know it's more than that. So, what's up?"

Diana took a drink and waited a few seconds before answering. "I'm just exhausted. I'm tired of being disappointed by people."

"In your line of work, I would think you would be used to that by now," Rosa said.

That is definitely a fair assumption.

"You would think so. No, it's more than that. I'm just tired of misjudging people. It's got to the point where I'm questioning every one of my instincts."

"You shouldn't. You've always been good at getting a feel for people.

"Maybe, but lately, people I've put faith in are turning out to be liars. And I don't know if I'm angry that they're lying or that I was stupid enough to believe them."

"I don't think you should be angry at all. People are going to be who they are. It's not really anything we can control. You just need to continue doing what you do the best way you know how. Unfortunately, that may lead to disappointment sometimes."

When did you get so smart?

"Maybe you're right."

"Are you still seeing the shrink?"

You stupid bitch!

"*¡Ay Rosa, que mucho tu jodes!*" Diana felt bad for raising her voice, but she was angry. They'd had this discussion before, and Rosa knew how Diana felt about sharing that part of her life.

"Calm down, I was just asking."

"Listen to me. I love you, and I know you're only asking out of concern for my well-being, but it's been nearly four years. Yes, I miss Isabel every day, and it can be difficult sometimes, but I'm getting better."

Diana looked at her sister and for the first time, she was beginning to believe her own words. She thought she'd presented herself well over the past few years. Whenever she was around people who knew her story, Diana would put on her best face and say what she thought she needed to say to appear as anything other than what she believed she was—broken.

The truth was, for the longest time, she had been holding on by the thinnest of threads. When her daughter died, and Derek left her, having said the things he'd said, she felt defeated and insignificant. But that was before she realized how strong she truly was and found value in herself and what she did. Diana found that she was capable of so much more than she'd ever thought.

She'd met new people and became the pillar they leaned on for support. She was having new experiences, not aware that she was getting better and that she was healing. Now that she thought about it, she figured no one is aware they're getting better till the day the bandage comes off, and they see their wounds have healed.

“I’m sorry. I love you, and I worry about you sometimes,” Rosa said.

"Well, don't. I'm a Rivera, and we *are* Puerto Rican after all—loud, stubborn, and proud till the day we say goodbye to this world." Diana smiled. "Come on say it with me."

“I’m not saying that. It’s corny and it’s too late to be yelling.”

“It is not corny. It’s our battle cry and you know you want to say it.” She raised her glass to toast. “Come on, say it with me.”

Rosa smiled and raised her glass.

“*¡Yo soy Boriqua, pa'que tú lo sepas*!” they yelled in perfect unison.

They laughed and spent the rest of the night talking about Isabel, their mother, and the good times on Willoughby Avenue.

CHAPTER EIGHTEEN

A TINY CRYSTALLINE SNOWFLAKE LANDED ON THE chessboard, distracting him momentarily. Frank raised his head up and toward the gray sky. The powdery white snowflakes floated down slowly and featherlike as if being shaken loose from a pillow.

Frank loved being outdoors, especially in the cool weather that was the norm this time of year. The surprising appearance of snow made it even more pleasant for him. Being cooped up in the office, especially on a Monday, surrounded by old-timers scared to leave because they were close to collecting their pension, was unbearable to him. Like a junkie needing their fix, he needed the sounds of the street.

Tony sat across from him, chewing on his bottom lip. He studied the board and contemplated his next move, oblivious to the falling snow. They were seated at one of the game tables at McNair Park on Washington Avenue, near the Botanical Gardens.

Frank scanned the area for onlookers and busybodies, but there were none to be found. He had directed Eddie, Joe, and Kat to rendezvous with him and Tony in the park but set the meeting for a time that gave the two old friends space for a quiet game. Their shared affection for chess was one of the things that had helped them connect when they were first partnered up as uniforms in Coney Island. They'd played a lot in the beginning before life told them there were other things they should be doing. Now, they played when they had time, stolen moments that were hard to come by but easy to lose.

"How are the girls?"

"They're good. They start winter break in a couple of weeks. It's going to be good having them home," Tony said.

"I still can't believe they're both at Penn State. I remember when they were still running around playing Hide and Go Seek. Time really does fly, brother."

"Yes, it does. And it's expensive, too."

They were well into their third game. Frank moved his knight to the C6 square and captured Tony's bishop.

"Check."

After Tony moved his king out of harm's way, Frank shifted one of his pawns to the D4 square. Tony captured Frank's D4 pawn when he moved his pawn to the D3 square.

"Nice move." Frank glanced at Tony. "What's expensive?"

Tony kept his gaze on the board. "Time, my brother—time costs a lot. Every year, it becomes more expensive. First, it's braces, then sweet sixteen parties, high school graduation gifts, and college tuition. It won't be long before I'm footing the bill for a couple of weddings."

They each made several moves. When it was Tony's turn, he moved one of his pawns to the C1 square on the board, capturing Frank's Bishop and promoting one of his pawns to queen. Frank moved his rook to C1, capturing Tony's newly appointed queen. Tony moved one of his pawns to the D4 square.

"Checkmate," Tony said.

"Fuck," Frank whispered. He analyzed the board and went over his mistakes.

"You see it?"

"Yeah, I see it. Man, I'm rusty."

"We both are. This game is a perishable skill, brother, like shooting a gun. Got to keep at it to be any good." Tony took a sip from his cup of coffee. "So, have you heard from Gloria or the girls?"

"No." Frank thought about his wife, who'd left him, and his daughters, who wouldn't speak to him, and wanted to change the subject.

“That’s an expensive habit you got, Frank. Look what it’s costing you.”

"Yeah, I know," Frank said. He drank from his cup of coffee and stared at Tony. "So, speaking of expensive. I have something coming up that will set us all up for a good while if we handle it right. Help you out with that list you just went through."

"Not the smoothest of segues, but I guess it'll have to do. When?"

“Tomorrow.”

“Tomorrow? Frank, if it’s as big as you’re hinting at, that’s cutting it close. Why the rush?”

"I just got this from Guerra yesterday. I'm still not clear on where or when. I just know the delivery's supposed to go down tomorrow."

“Who’re we looking at?”

“Small crew out of Bed-Stuy. They’re going to be delivering ten keys of white to Piotr Grabowski.”

“Grabowski? Frank, that’s a serious crew, and this other group is probably a bunch of wild-ass gangbangers. There’s going to be a lot of guns out there. Are we using ESU?”

“No, just us.”

“Are you serious?” Tony didn’t bother to mask his surprise that Frank didn’t plan to include the Emergency Service Unit. Grabowski’s crew was dangerous, so it made sense to use tactical teams. But that would mean a lot of people, and for what Frank had planned, the fewer eyes, the better.

“That’s how it has to be. One of the delivery guys can’t leave breathing.”

“So, Guerra wants one of his own people whacked. Why?”

“He didn’t say, and I didn’t ask. Look, it doesn’t matter why. Guerra wants us to take care of it, so that’s what we need to do.”

Tony looked away from Frank. When he turned his head back, anger covered his face. “First, I don’t work for Guerra, so fuck him. And second, what the fuck is going on, Frank? Are we fucking assassins now?”

“We’ve done it before.”

Frank didn’t feel bad about reminding Tony of their past. Nine years ago, they pulled the card on Agon Dervishi. He was a low-level dealer connected to the Albanian Boys out in Pelham Parkway up in the Bronx.

Agon had used a cell phone to record Frank squeezing him for ten grand. He'd tried to hold it over Frank's head in exchange for protection, so Frank and Tony made the problem go away.

Dervishi took two rounds in the chest from Frank's service pistol when they served a search warrant at Dervishi's apartment in Gravesend.

"Yeah, but that was different," Tony said.

"How so?"

"First, Dervishi was a murdering psychopath. Second, and most importantly, it was about survival. Dervishi had you on tape. We couldn't risk that shit getting out. What you're talking about here is... it's fucking murder for hire."

"It's just some little piece of shit that's probably killed more people than you and I could count. Tony, this is gonna pay out huge. I'm talking two-hundred-and-thirty grand huge. And more where that came from down the line. Guerra's been a honey pot for us going on almost nine years now, and he's only getting bigger. We need to do this. We need to keep Guerra on the hook till he ain't no use to us anymore."

"And when will that be?"

"I don't know, but I know it ain't now." Frank tried to read Tony's face for an emotion other than disgust. "What do ya say?"

Before Tony could answer, Frank spotted Eddie and Kat walking toward their table. He shook his head at their matching dark blue jeans and black leather jackets and thought they might as well be in uniform.

"What's up, fellas?" Eddie said. He remained standing and nodded at the chess board. "Who won?"

"Can't you tell?" Frank said.

"Not at all. That game is like trying to read hieroglyphics to me."

Frank sneered at the comment. He had heard that analogy before and thought it was a weak statement for weak minds.

"Big man won." Frank pointed at Tony.

"Cool." Eddie's dismissive tone raised Frank's temperature a few degrees. "So, what's up, Frank? What'd you want to talk about?"

"Where's Joe?" Frank said.

"Some child support thing came up. He had to go meet with his attorney. What's up?" Eddie repeated.

"We got something coming up?"

"When?" Eddie said.

"Tomorrow."

Kat's eyebrows arched. "Tomorrow? Damn, Frank, that's quick. So, who are we going after?"

Frank decided to tell them everything he'd just told Tony. Everything except the button job on Julian Serrano. He wanted to keep that between him and Tony. Like all officer-involved shootings, this one would be investigated. He figured it'd be easier for Eddie and Kat to lie if they didn't know they were lying.

"The Pollocks, huh? Are we using ESU?" Eddie said.

"Nah. It's better if we keep the eyes on this to just us," Frank said.

Kat and Eddie exchange confused glances. They had worked with ESU plenty of times and had always been able to get what they wanted. The tactical team would hit the location, secure everything, and clear the scene. Leaving Frank's team alone in their investigation.

Frank figured the change in how they did things would make them curious and maybe even cause them concern. But he believed the fewer details Eddie and Kat had, the better. Besides, he was guessing he didn't have to be specific. They were smart people and good cops. They'd probably figure out why he wanted to keep the number of cops involved limited to their team.

"Fuck, Frank, that's a serious ask. Where is this happening? What time?" Kat said.

"Late afternoon, early evening—somewhere around there. My CI will have the where and the when to me before the end of business today."

They were all quiet for several minutes. Each stared off in a different direction and seemed to think about the possible outcomes.

"Screw it." Tony went from face to face, putting eyes on everyone. "We've taken down big numbers before. It's what we do."

Kat and Eddie nodded in agreement.

"So, I'm clear on the Pols. Do we know anyone from the other group?" Eddie said.

Frank glanced up at Eddie. "One of them we do. At least, Tony, Kat, and I do. You weren't with us the first time we dealt with this joker. Turns out we took him down eight years ago on some weapons charges. Man, we were really scraping the bottom of the barrel back then. Some hump named Serrano."

KAT SAT in the front passenger seat of a department-issued 2016 Chevy Impala. She chewed on the knuckle of her right index finger and stared absently at the passing snow-covered streets outside her window.

"Kat?"

She turned and looked at Eddie when she heard him say her name. "Yeah?"

"Did you hear me? I asked you what you thought about Frank's deal."

She'd been lost in her thoughts and hadn't heard him speaking. "Honestly? I think it's fucked. We're moving too fast. Especially when you consider that it involves the crazy-ass Pols and some knuckleheads from a crew we don't know anything about. *And* he doesn't want to use ESU."

"We've gone without help plenty of times before."

She didn't answer and returned to the view outside her window. The snow was falling heavier now, covering the black and gray concrete and asphalt streets in a white blanket. The people outside wore heavy winter clothing. Dark and anonymous, Kat thought they looked like silhouettes on the other side of a giant white screen.

She went over the meeting with Frank in her head and was worried. She was confident she knew why Frank didn't want to use ESU. First, he'd lied to them about Guerra. And now, based on what she knew about his meeting with Diana, he wasn't telling them everything about Serrano.

It'd been almost a week since he'd gone to see Diana about Serrano, so Frank didn't just get Serrano's name yesterday. Only one thing made sense. He was going to whack this Serrano guy, and he couldn't risk having outsiders around.

She caught her reflection in the window, and another dark thought entered her mind. What if Frank knew she was ratting? What if this was all a play to clean house? It'd be easy for him to arrange for her to be gunned down during the deal. Make it look like Serrano was the shooter, and they took him out in the exchange. Frank would be rid of all his headaches—maybe even get a medal out of it.

Kat pondered her situation and weighed her options. The way she figured it, she could do only one thing.

She studied the table and worked the angles in her head but couldn't figure out any other way to play the shot.

CHAPTER NINETEEN

There were two minutes and twenty-three seconds left in regulation when Kawhi Leonard hit a three-point shot to give the Toronto Raptors a two-point lead over the Brooklyn Nets, ninety-six to ninety-four. After a timeout, Spencer Dinwiddie made a hook shot over Toronto's Fred VanVleet, tying the game at ninety-six.

Julian rose from his seat to cheer the made shot and glanced down when he felt Tito grab his arm.

"Did you see that?" Tito yelled excitedly.

Julian turned his attention back to the game and watched the players run up and down the court. He realized that even though he adored basketball and spent his entire life playing and watching games on television, he'd never appreciated how truly amazing the game was until seeing professionals play live. He and Tito were seated in the fifth row of section nine at the Barclays Center and had a great view of the court and players.

With one minute and nine seconds left in the game and Brooklyn leading by two points, Pascal Siakam tied the game with a three-foot shot in the lane. After a couple of attempts to score by each team in the last minute of the game, Leonard blocked Dinwiddie's shot at the end of regulation to send the game into overtime. Tito sank back in his seat dejectedly.

Julian sat down and leaned in close to Tito. "What's the matter?"

"They had the win, and they blew it. Now they're going to lose."

"What do you mean? It's not over. We're going into overtime."

"It's the Nets. They'll lose."

"Have faith." Julian smiled and pulled the front of Tito's Nets ski cap down over his eyes.

Although Julian tried to project confidence, he thought Tito might be right. The Nets hadn't won more than thirty games in any of the past three seasons and, despite their current four-game winning streak, had lost eighteen of their first thirty games this season.

Regardless of the game's outcome, Julian was the happiest he'd been since he'd gotten out of prison. Jimmy handed him three Gs after that thing out in Queens, so he'd decided to take his son to a basketball game. He took some of the money and bought two tickets for the best seats he could afford and spent a little more on Nets gear for him and Tito.

It was the first time for either of them at a live NBA game. When Julian was a kid, Brooklyn didn't have a team, and going to Madison Square Garden to see the Knicks was too expensive. By the time he could afford his own ticket, going to the Garden wasn't a priority.

He scanned the arena, taking in the spectacle of it all. The shiny brown parquet court with the black-and-white Brooklyn Nets emblem at center court was glorious. Biggie's "Juicy" blasted from the arena speakers, creating a feeling of electricity. The good energy and positive feelings in the crowd were palpable.

Toronto led Brooklyn by one point with one minute and forty-five seconds left in overtime. Julian watched the two teams exchange fouls and missed shots for the next few seconds. He glanced down at Tito. He was on the edge of his seat, a look of concern on his face.

Jarrett Allen made a layup with one minute and four seconds left, giving the Nets a one-point lead. For the next sixty-four seconds, the Nets played lock-down defense and still had the lead with one second remaining in the game. After a timeout, VanVleet took and missed a three-point shot at the buzzer, giving the Nets a one-point win, 105-

106. Julian and Tito rose to their feet and joined the roaring crowd in cheering for their team.

"They did it!" Tito yelled.

They hugged, and Julian pulled Tito close, burying his nose in his son's right shoulder. He pulled back enough to look Tito directly in the eyes. "Sometimes a little faith goes a long way."

THE LATE AFTERNOON start time for the game meant it ended a little before seven, and they were both hungry. The snow had stopped, so Julian recommended they walk the few blocks to Junior's Restaurant and Bakery. Tito spoke about the game the entire stroll.

He bent Julian's ear about different plays each team ran throughout the game, and Julian was surprised at his son's recall of small details. He knew Tito liked to play basketball and truly appreciated the game and its history. But the things he said affirmed how much of a hoops fanatic Tito was, and that they had one more thing in common.

After a thirty-minute wait for a table, the hostess seated them at a booth by a large window. Julian hadn't been to Junior's since before he'd gone to prison, and he was eager to taste their food again. The restaurant was a Brooklyn landmark renowned for its cheesecake, so Julian had anticipated they would have to wait for a table.

From where they sat, they had a view of the heavy pedestrian and vehicle traffic on Flatbush Avenue. Waves of people, walking fast and with purpose, passed by. The area was already a tourist attraction for out-of-town visitors, but the post-game crowd added a considerable amount to the congestion.

The restaurant was busy and filled with diners. But their waiter, a friendly middle-aged man who introduced himself as Phillip, quickly made it to their table and asked them for their drink orders. Tito requested apple juice, and Julian settled on an egg cream and a glass of water.

After Phillip left to get the drinks, Julian and Tito sat in silence across from each other, looking over the menu. The restaurant was famous for its cheesecake, but it also offered a variety of breakfast, lunch, and dinner options. Julian loved their pastrami sandwich and knew that's what he wanted.

When Phillip returned with their drinks, Julian ordered the pastrami with American cheese on an onion roll with a side of onion rings. Tito ordered a grilled cheese sandwich with French fries on the side. After Phillip departed, they both sipped their drinks.

Tito eyed the egg cream curiously. “What’s that?”

“This? This is an egg cream. You’ve never had one of these?”

“No. What’s in it?”

"Milk, chocolate syrup, and soda water. It sounds simple, but it's one of the best things I've ever tasted. Supposedly, it was invented in Brooklyn in the late 1800s, but we could only get it in certain places when I was a kid."

"So, no eggs or cream? What does it taste like?"

Julian studied the drink and thought about the question. “It tastes like...memories. You want a sip?”

“Sure.”

Julian lifted the tall, cool glass of egg cream slightly off the table and placed it in front of his son. Tito picked it up and took a sip through a straw. After he was done, he licked his upper lip and smiled broadly.

"Did you like it?" Julian said.

“Yeah, that’s really good.”

“Want one?”

“Maybe. Let me finish my grilled cheese first.”

Tito placed the glass cup on the table and nudged it toward Julian. They were both quiet for a few seconds, but there was no awkwardness in the silence.

“So, how was school today?”

“It was alright. We’re doing a lot of reviewing. My teachers want to get us ready for our last tests before winter break,” Tito said.

“Will Alex picking you up early today screw you up?”

“Nah, we covered most of the material before lunch.”

“That’s good.”

He thought about the steps he had to take to spend time with his son. Nikki still wouldn't let Tito and Julian spend time together, so Alex was playing the middleman—picking up and dropping off Tito as often as possible.

The arrangement made sense at first. He was fresh out of prison and pretty much a stranger to Tito. But over the past few months, they had gotten to know each other better, so his attachment to Tito had grown. Stolen moments weren't enough anymore, and he wanted to be with his son all the time.

"Can I ask you a question?"

“Yes—I mean, no. I don’t mind if you ask a question,” Tito said.

“Would you ever want to come live with me?”

Tito didn't answer for a few seconds and seemed to struggle with the question. Julian had just asked his young son a very tough question, and it may have been unfair of him to do so, but he couldn't help himself. Julian was curious and wanted to know how Tito felt. He had some things planned over the next day or two, and knowing if his son even wanted to be with him would impact the choices he made.

“Yeah. Maybe. I don’t know. Titi Nikki and Alex have been good to me. I wouldn’t want to hurt their feelings. I—”

“You know what? You don’t have to answer that right now. We have plenty of time for that down the road. Let’s enjoy our time. So, anything else interesting going on at school?”

“We’ve been doing this exercise in my history class. I know my teacher, Mr. Holmes, only does it to run out the clock at the end of the day, but I think it’s interesting. Want to try it?”

“Sure.”

Tito sat up straighter, and his eyes grew wide with excitement. Julian knew he had a curious mind. Tito was always asking questions and getting excited when he learned something new. Julian was proud that his son was smarter than him.

"So, Mr. Holmes asked two questions. We all took turns telling the class our answers to each question and why we answered the way we did."

“Okay, I’m pretty sure I understand. So, what are the questions?”

Julian glanced up when Phillip arrived with their food. He placed their food on the table and walked away. They both took bites out of their sandwiches.

“Man, that is so good.” Julian closed his eyes and savored it. The taste of the smoke, black pepper, and coriander from the pastrami and melted cheese flooded him with memories. Julian couldn’t tell what was more delicious, the sandwich or the feeling of nostalgia. “How’s your grilled cheese?”

“It’s good.”

“Okay. So, you had some questions you were going to ask.”

"Yeah. First, if you could be any fictional character, who would it be and why?"

“Wow, that’s a tough one. ‘If I could be any fictional character, who would it be?’ I guess I would be Edmond Dantès from *The Count of Monte Cristo*.”

“Okay, why?”

“Have you read it?”

“No.”

"Give it a shot when you can. It's a great book. It's basically about this guy who goes to prison for something he didn't do. While he's in prison, he improves himself through education and eventually escapes. Edmond makes his way to the island of Monte Cristo, where he finds a treasure that makes him rich. After a few years, he returns home and gets even with the men who set him up to go to prison."

“Is that what happened to you? Someone lied on you. Got you sent to jail?”

Julian realized he and Tito had not spoken about his going to prison. Tito had been six when Julian got locked up, old enough to know he had a father and to ask questions when Julian wasn't around anymore. Laila, always his ride-or-die, told Tito he had been away on business making money. She told him Julian would come home after he'd made enough money, and they'd live in a big house together.

Laila would tell that tale for the next year and a half till the cancer stole her voice. He'd figured Nikki had told Tito the truth about him. It was a suspicion Alex had confirmed during one of their pickup basketball games.

He'd known this conversation was coming and thought he was ready for it. But sitting there looking into his son's inquisitive eyes, Julian had no idea how to respond.

"So, we haven't really talked about this, have we?" Julian said. Tito shook his head subtly. Julian nodded and continued, "No, no one lied on me. I deserved to go to prison."

"Really?"

"Yeah. I did a lot of bad things growing up. I could sit here and try and give you a dumb reason why, but I'd be lying, and I don't want to lie to you. I made a stupid decision and went to prison for it."

Tito kept his eyes focused on Julian as if he was trying to read his thoughts. "I understand."

It got heavy at the table, so Julian decided to redirect the conversation back to the good place they were at five minutes earlier. "So, what's the second question?"

"Okay. If you could have dinner with any person, dead or alive, who would it be?"

Julian thought about the question and immediately wanted to say Laila. It was the truth, after all. He would give almost anything to spend one more minute with his wife again. But he thought their conversation had gotten too serious, so he didn't want to pile on an extra dose of melancholy by speaking about her.

"Probably Prince. He's my favorite musician, and I never saw him play in person while he was alive. It'd be mad cool to go to Paisley Park for a private concert and then share a meal with him."

"I thought you were going to say, Mom."

Julian stayed silent for a few seconds, trying to decide whether to tell Tito the truth. "To be honest, I was, but I didn't want to upset you."

"You wouldn't have upset me. My answer to that question is Mom. I would love to spend time with her again."

Julian felt the sadness swell up inside him. He had a knot in his throat, and he could feel the corner of his mouth twitching with emotion. He didn't respond for a few seconds, trying to compose himself before he spoke. "Yeah, me too. I would give almost anything for that."

"*Almost*?"

"Well, yeah. I mean, I wouldn't give you up for that chance. She wouldn't want me to. Shit, she'd kill me if I even thought about it."

They both laughed.

"She was pretty tough, huh?"

"Toughest person I've ever known. The smartest, too. That's where you get it from."

"I'm scared I'll forget her." Tito's eyes welled up with tears, and he looked down at his food.

"Hey, look at me," Julian said. Tito raised his head. "That'll never happen. You're too much like her for you, or anyone else, to forget her. You look like her, you're smart like her, and you fill the room with happiness and good energy like she did. Shit, man, you even tug on your ear lobe when you're thinking about stuff like she did. She's with you every day—in your heart. Every time your heart beats, you feel her love."

They finished their meals silently, content to let the words they'd shared about Laila be the music that played as they finished their dinner.

CHAPTER TWENTY

ANGEL STARED AT THE WALLS INSIDE HIS STORE, TRYING TO visualize what a different color might look like. The walls had been the same dark shade of orange since he bought the place three years back. He didn't like the color back then and had always intended to have the walls painted, but time and laziness got the better of him.

Now he stood, holding his usual morning cup of *café con leche* in one hand and his e-cigarette in the other, surveying the landscape of his little kingdom. He smiled because the planned changes encompassed more than just his store.

He took a long drag off his e-cigarette and thought about everything he had going down later today. He went over the details in his head and was confident he had everything set up how it needed to be. Grabowski's man called him last night and told him the meet location would be at a construction site out in Ridgewood, which he'd figured it might be. The Pols had a lot of territory in that part of Brooklyn, so it made sense they'd want to deal where they felt secure.

It made no difference to him where the deal went down; he wouldn't be there. And if that piece of shit Hawkins handled his business, he was going to get most of his product back anyway. He would even rid himself of some headaches in the process.

Angel thought about Julian and felt a twinge of remorse for what he had in motion. They had, after all, been lifelong friends and had a lot of history. Julian, Jimmy, and he had put in a lot of work together while growing up. And there'd been plenty of good times, too.

But Julian never saw the big picture, and that's why he had to go away eight years ago. Because as smart as Julian used to be, he'd never had the balls to make the hard choice. And that's why Angel believed he should have always been running things. He knew making hard choices and being comfortable with the consequences of those choices was where he thrived.

He was good at reading his opponents. He'd anticipated their moves and did whatever was necessary to counteract those moves. If that meant sacrificing a few people along the way, so be it. Angel made peace with the fact that there wasn't room for compassion in this game long ago.

He heard a ping sound in the front pocket of his green NY Jets hoodie, alerting him he'd received a text message on his cell phone. He put his coffee on a shelf and grabbed the phone. Jimmy had sent a message telling him he was waiting outside the store. Angel grabbed his coffee off the shelf and walked toward the store's front door.

"Bino, I'm going to be busy for a little bit. *¿Estás bien aquí verdad?*"

"*Claro,*" Bino said.

Balbino "Bino" Dominguez was sixty-seven years old and worked harder than anyone Angel ever knew. He had given Bino a job because he needed someone dependable to work the counter. Bino had moved to the States from his hometown of Ponce, Puerto Rico, fifty years ago and had been working hard ever since.

Bino was a tough old man who reminded Angel of his pops. They both did whatever honest work they could find to take care of their families. Angel admired their work ethic, but that's where his admiration ended. He thought people like Bino, and his father were fools. They spent their lives doing back-breaking work for pennies before dying alone and anonymously.

Angel stepped outside into the frigid morning. The sky was filled with dark gray clouds, and it was evident the sun would not be making an appearance today. Jimmy stood by his Chrysler 300. He wore a light gray North Face jacket, dark blue jeans, and black boots. His long, salt and pepper hair blew wildly in the strong wind as if made of metal and being pulled away from his head by a magnet.

“It’s cold as fuck out here. Let’s go inside,” Angel said.

They entered the building through the main entrance for residents and climbed one flight of stairs to Angel's apartment on the second floor. They entered the apartment and Angel slipped into the small kitchen as Jimmy headed for the living room.

“Want some coffee?” Angel said.

“Sure.”

“Did you get the stuff?”

“Yeah. I picked it up early this morning.”

“Good. You got a spot set up with Vern to pass it off?”

“Yeah. We’re gonna meet in Scarangella Park later.” Jimmy sounded distracted and there was a heaviness in his voice. “So, I’ve been thinking about how you want to do this, and I don’t think it’s a good idea. I think I should go too. Julian is a G, no doubt. But the Polish ain’t nothing to fuck with. We can’t just send him out there with Vern and the three other youngsters.”

Angel put two cups in the tabletop microwave and turned it on. He looked up at the ceiling and took a long, silent breath. He knew how Jimmy felt about Julian. At one point, the two had been closer than brothers. Although time and distance had altered the relationship, Jimmy still loved Julian.

"Nah, that can't happen," Angel said.

“Why not?”

Angel walked into the living room and sat on the recliner. “Because they’re not going to make it out of this one.”

“What the fuck are you talking about?”

Angel had been thinking about what he would say to Jimmy. He loved and trusted Jimmy, and he wanted to keep him close. But there was no way Julian, and the fellas could go down today without giving Jimmy some sort of explanation. Angel knew he had to tell Jimmy something about what he had planned.

"The thing in Queens. I got word the cops are getting close on that one," Angel said.

“What? Where the fuck are you getting this from?”

"Hawkins hit me up the other day. He told me the Homicide Squad out in Queens had a line on who did the murders."

"And you believe him?"

"Why wouldn't I? He doesn't have anything to gain by lying. The bottom line is the cops are getting close to putting those bodies on Julian, and when they do, who's to say he won't start informing? We can't risk that he won't snitch to make it easier on himself."

Jimmy rubbed his large hand along the side of his heavily stubbled cheek. Angel could see the wheels turning in his head. Jimmy was trying to make sense of what he'd heard and probably trying to work out a different way through the mess.

"Julian would never snitch. No fucking way. He's always stood tall."

"What if he does? Do you really want to risk what we got going? He just got out. You know there's no way he wants to go back." Jimmy looked down at the floor. Angel imagined his head was spinning with what he'd just heard. "We gotta clean house, Jimmy. It's the only way we'll be sure."

Jimmy lifted his head and stared at Angel. "So, what happens now?"

"Hawkins is going to do what Hawkins does. He's going to take down the whole thing and return our product. Everybody goes away for a long time, including the Polish who were becoming a problem anyway. And as for Julian—well, Julian is done."

"Man, this is so fucked up. Julian is our brother, Angel. How can we do this to him?" Jimmy's voice was hoarse, and he sounded like he was begging for his own life.

"Because this isn't yesterday, Jimmy, and shit has changed. We gotta look out for our own shit. Like it or not, Julian is on the outside looking in."

Jimmy stared into the distance and didn't say anything. Angel searched his face for a hint of what he was thinking, but there wasn't one. He'd lied about the cops having a line on who committed the murders in Queens, but he hoped the story would help Jimmy make peace with betraying their friend again.

Because as much as he loved Jimmy, Angel had come too far and wouldn't let anything stop him. If Jimmy couldn't let go of Julian, Angel would put him in the ground, too.

DIANA MADE sure to leave Rosa's house early. She'd stayed a day longer than she'd planned and wanted to make it into Brooklyn before the inevitable traffic jams occurred. The previous day's snow and overnight rain had left the roads an icy mess that was sure to have a detrimental effect on the morning rush-hour commute.

Traffic was light all the way down New Jersey and through the Holland Tunnel into Manhattan, but it backed up a little when she reached the Battery Tunnel. Despite the slowdown through the Battery, traffic was still much better than it would be in an hour, and she made it back to her Brooklyn office before anyone else had turned on the lights.

She sat at her desk and thought about the last few days. The time with her sister had helped put some things in perspective. However, she had other things in her personal and professional life that needed attention. She decided the issues with Julian and Kat would have to wait for now.

She reviewed the organizer on her phone and saw she had some time after lunch. Even though it had only been a week since she'd last seen him, Diana decided she'd make a job site visit on Jan Zajac. Zajac hadn't committed any overt violations when she had last seen him, and his boss had given her a glowing report. But there weren't any rules as to how often she could, or should, check on parolees. And besides, he still hadn't come by the office to give a urine sample.

But the truth was, she didn't like the way he'd made her feel the last time they'd spoken. Zajac had tried to intimidate her, and he'd succeeded. After their meeting, she was ashamed that she'd allowed someone to make her feel weak and inconsequential. She wanted to look him in the eyes again, but it wasn't enough to just face him.

If that was all she needed, she could just call him and have him come to the office, threaten him with violating his parole if he didn't. No, she wanted to go at him where he felt safe. So, he would know she wasn't one to be intimidated.

Diana wanted Zajac to know that if he made a wrong choice, he'd have to deal with her, and there was nowhere he could go that she wouldn't follow.

CHAPTER TWENTY-ONE

Frank told the team to meet him at his house on East Twenty-Seventh Street in Sheepshead Bay. They usually used a conference room on the second floor of the Eighty-Third Precinct for their mission briefings, but he didn't want to risk anyone outside the team listening in.

Angel had sent him the address a few hours earlier, so Frank knew the deal was going down at a construction site in Ridgewood sometime this afternoon. In preparation, he had his team carry out their responsibilities the same way they would before any operation.

Tony was pulling the criminal histories on Grabowski and the sacrificial lambs Angel was sending, as well as collecting all available data on the location of the hit. He'd sent Eddie and Kat to conduct reconnaissance on the construction site to try and determine all possible exit points and identify any structures on the premises. Joe was double-checking all the equipment, ensuring the team had everything needed for this sort of hit.

Frank pulled a fresh Marlboro Red cigarette from its pack. He placed it between his lips and used the cherry of the almost-finished cigarette he held in his other hand to light it. He paced the first floor of his two-story single-family home as he waited for his team members to arrive.

He was more excited than nervous or scared. His adrenaline was pumping, so sitting on the couch wasn't an option. This opportunity couldn't have come at a better time, and he was eager to get his hands on the cash. Frank had spent the last few months suffocating in debt, and this money would provide the oxygen he needed to breathe easily again.

He crossed in front of the fireplace in the living room and stared at the pictures on the mantle. Six photos of varying sizes in frames of different colors and styles—each frame as much a time capsule as the picture it held. Photos of his three daughters, Annie, Tina, and Yvette. All grown and living their own lives, unable or, he thought more likely, unwilling to make time for him. Memories of the happier times, the in-between times when his job and his vices didn't make their lives miserable.

He took a long drag off his cigarette. Deep down, he knew the smiling faces in the pictures weren't an honest representation of the life he'd made for his family. He figured no one ever took photos of the hard times. Frank doubted he would ever go into someone's home and see proudly displayed pictures of their wife leaving with her bags packed. Or of their kids mugging for the camera as they say "fuck you" to their father one last time.

The doorbell rang once, followed by the familiar six-knock rendition of "Shave and a Haircut." He walked to the door and looked through the peephole. Tony and Joe stood on the other side. Frank pulled the front door open, gave them both a hard look, and stepped back so they could enter the house.

He glared at them as they walked past him into the living room. "It's about time. Where have you guys been?" He slammed the door shut.

Tony turned to face him. "What are you talking about, Frank? It's only been a few hours since you called me. That's pretty good time if you ask me. And we've been standing out there for five minutes. What took you so long to open the door?"

"I was taking a shit." Frank stomped by them. "Where's Eddie and Kat?"

“Don’t know, we haven’t heard from them,” Joe said.

“Will you call them or text them, Joe? See what’s taking them so long,” Frank said.

“On it.”

Joe took his cell phone out of his jacket pocket and started typing a message when the doorbell rang. Tony pulled the door open without checking who was on the other side first, which pissed Frank off even more.

Eddie strutted in. “What’s the motherfucking dee-lee-o.”

Kat followed behind him.

“You’re late,” Frank said.

“I didn’t know we set a time but, okay, if you say so, Frank,” Eddie said.

Frank glared at Eddie. After he rid himself of Angel, he would send Eddie packing. Everything wouldn't be perfect, but at least he'd remove two checks from his life's shit column. "Everyone, have a seat so we can discuss what we got going."

The living room furniture was arranged to encourage conversation, with the couch at the center, flanked by a love seat on one side and an oversized chair on the other. A heavy oak coffee table took up space in the middle, and there was no television anywhere to be found.

The setup was something Frank’s ex-wife Gloria read about in a magazine and decided to try in their home. He thought it was dumb at first. What American family didn't have a big-screen television in their living room? But after a while, Frank grew to like how everything was configured and left it as it was—even after Gloria had up and left him.

“Alright, so what do we have so far?” Frank remained standing and lit his fourth consecutive cigarette.

"Nothing on Grabowski we don't already know, and there's no intel on how many people he's going to have out there or who those people are," Tony said. He was seated on the oversized chair, holding a manila folder in his giant hand. "As for the other crew, we got them identified as Dennis Roberts, Javier "Flaco" Flores, and Julian Serrano."

Frank knew Tony wouldn't reveal anything that would give too much away, but he was still relieved when Tony didn't mention Vernon

Miller and Damon "Little D" Horowitz. Kat and Eddie had already connected the two to Angel Guerra, so hearing those names now would only evoke questions Frank didn't feel like answering.

"Any evidence they're anything more than just some street-level gangsters?" Eddie said.

Tony pulled photos from the folder and dropped them on the coffee table. He spread the photos neatly on the table. "Like Frank mentioned at the park, me, him, and Kat put this Serrano guy away eight years ago. We were working a spot based on a tip from one of Frank's snitches, but there wasn't any dope when we hit it. We got three, including Serrano, on weapons charges."

He slid the picture of Serrano out of the way and pointed at the other photos. "Now, these two could possibly be a problem—Dennis Roberts and Flaco Flores."

"*Flaco Flores*, give me a fucking break. Where do they come up with these names?" Eddie sneered.

"Yeah, well, don't laugh too hard. Anyone willing to stand by a nickname that stupid has to be taken seriously," Joe said.

"You're not too far off on that guess. I ran all the names through Anti-Crime and the Gang Squad, but those two were the only ones that rang any bells. They're both affiliated with the Crown Heights Hitters and are suspects in multiple armed robberies and aggravated assaults. Al Velasquez in Anti-Crime told me the Homicide Squad is looking at this Flores guy for at least three murders," Tony said.

"Nice," Eddie scoffed.

"Alright. What about the location itself?" Frank said.

"Not much. It's on Linden Street, just west of Fairview Avenue. The property is owned by some company out of Ohio." Tony flipped to a new page in his notepad. "Dusza Construction Company. The owner is listed as Magdalena Grabowski. Grabowski's seventy-year-old mother," Tony said.

"That figures. Alright, what else? Eddie, Kat, what do you two have for us?"

Eddie glanced at Kat, but she didn't seem like she was in a speaking mood. "It looks like they're putting up a commercial building. The place is surrounded by a chain-link fence with only one entrance on Linden. It looks like they keep the entrance gate wide open during business hours. They're still working on the foundation, so the only structures on site are an office trailer and a port-a-potty. It's a safe bet they'll be meeting inside the trailer."

Eddie pulled out his cell phone and tapped on its screen. "I just sent everyone some pictures we took of the site. It looks like we can set up on Linden and Fairview. It'll take us five seconds to drive from the entrance on Linden to the trailer."

Frank studied the photos on his cell phone for several seconds. He looked up and noticed Kat sitting quietly on the loveseat. She was staring blankly at the coffee table and didn't seem to be paying attention. "Kat, you've been quiet. Is there anything you want to add?"

She looked at Frank as if it was her first time seeing him. "Nah, Eddie covered everything. It looks like a pretty simple hit, actually. Mind if I use your bathroom?"

"Of course not. Go ahead." Frank watched her disappear down the hallway and then turned his attention back to the meeting. "Joe, have you got everything set on your end?"

"Yup. Everything we'll need is clean, operational, and in the van."

"Alright, good. Okay, here's the plan—I'll set up on Linden just west of the main entrance. Eddie and Kat will be on Fairview, a little south of the location. Tony and Joe, you guys will be on Linden east of Fairview. Since you're in the soccer-mom minivan, you can sit in front of that *bodega* without attracting too much attention. Any questions?" Frank gave them a few seconds to chime in, but no one spoke. "Alright. Let's get one final equipment check and get to the spot. The deal isn't supposed to happen till this afternoon, but I want to have eyes on the location within the hour."

KAT BENT over the sink and splashed cold water on her face. The frigid temperatures that had enveloped the city over the past few days made the faucet water much colder than usual, and it felt like needles on her skin. It shocked her awake, so she welcomed the discomfort.

She stared at her reflection in the mirror. Deep, dark purple-blue circles filled the space beneath her eyes. Her cheeks were sunken and drawn, and her hair was disheveled. She thought she looked like one of the junkies she leaned on for information.

Kat glanced down at her cell phone, which lay on the edge of the sink. She had already sent a text message to Alaniz letting her know about what Frank had planned. Alaniz made it clear the feds weren't interested in the dope deal, and with her credibility about to go up in smoke like a Cheech and Chong movie, Kat didn't want to pass the intel on to another group. She figured she was out of options as far as the deal at the construction site went.

Kat didn't care much about the dope anyway. A few dirtbags moving some weight was the least of her problems. Anyway, she had other things on her mind. Despite everything that was going on, she was thinking about Diana and the ex-con Serrano.

So, another drug deal goes down uninterrupted, what else was new. But this Serrano guy was putting in work and making her friend out to be an asshole. The least Kat could do after lying to Diana's face was give her a heads-up about Serrano. Diana would have what she needed to violate his ass back upstate somewhere.

At least one of those assholes would put on some bracelets. Kat knew she couldn't risk any information getting out too early, so she used her cell phone to type Diana an email and scheduled it to be delivered later in the day. After finishing the email, Kat took one last look at herself in the mirror and exited the bathroom. She entered the living room and saw everyone gathering their belongings and preparing to leave.

"Feeling better?" Joe said.

"What do you mean?"

"You didn't look too good earlier. Actually, you still don't."

"Thanks a lot, Joe. That's just what a single woman over thirty-five wants to hear."

"No, I was just saying you look like you might have the flu or something. You know what, forget I said anything. You're gorgeous."

They both smiled, and Joe headed for the front door. She walked to the loveseat, grabbed her jacket, and took her time putting it back on.

All the guys walked out the front door except Frank, who held the door open as he glared at her.

"Are you coming?" Frank said.

"Yeah."

She walked past Frank, out the front door, and toward the stairs leading to the street. Tony, Eddie, and Joe had already made it to the sidewalk when Kat spotted the black SUV turn onto East Twenty-Seventh Street from Avenue W. She turned in the other direction and saw two more black SUVs turning onto East Twenty-Seventh from Avenue X. There were no sirens, but the vehicles' windshields were lit up with red and blue lights.

The SUVs reached the front of Frank's house almost simultaneously, and multiple FBI agents quickly exited the three vehicles holding AR-15 rifles and wearing body armor. The letters F-B-I were bright yellow and clearly visible on the front and back of their body armor.

The FBI agents took cover behind their SUVs and pointed their rifles at her teammates. Her guys raised their arms to show they weren't holding any weapons.

Kat turned her head back toward the house. Frank was standing by the open front door. He looked at her, his facial expressions running a gamut of emotions: confusion, hate, disappointment, and finally, acceptance.

Frank grabbed the doorknob and pulled the door shut. He turned back to the feds and reached for the gun in his hip holster.

Everything felt as if it was happening in slow motion.

"Frank, don't—" Kat yelled.

She looked back at the FBI agents. Several of them pointed their rifles at Frank. Kat dropped to her knees, covered her head, and glanced back at Frank. He raised his 9mm Glock service pistol and pointed it in the direction of the agents.

Kat jumped at the sound of the rounds being fired from the FBI agents' rifles.

Three different shots spaced less than half a second apart. Two of the bullets hit Frank in the chest, and the third entered through his forehead. A mixture of flesh, skull fragments, and brain matter burst out the back of his head as the bullet exited in a red fog. Frank's lifeless body fell to the floor. His hand still held the gun in a tight shooter's grip.

His index finger was off the trigger and outside the trigger guard—not ready to shoot.

CHAPTER TWENTY-TWO

Vernon had picked Julian up in his Ford Explorer, and they'd headed out to Scarangella Park to get the product from Jimmy. The meeting with Jimmy had gone quickly, and they hadn't even left their cars. Jimmy had already been waiting when they'd arrived at the park. He had been in his Chrysler 300, parked along the curb on West Thirteenth Street, next to the basketball court.

Julian had been sitting in the front passenger seat. When they pulled the Explorer up beside his car, Jimmy passed the duffel bag full of coke to him. Jimmy held on to his side of the bag for half a second longer than he needed to, and there was sadness in his eyes.

"You good?" Julian said.

Jimmy hesitated. "Yeah." They stared at each other for a few heartbeats. "Be careful out there, alright. Them Pols are dangerous."

"Yeah, of course." Julian glanced at Vernon, and they drove away. He thought about the exchange with Jimmy and wondered if he was warning him about something other than the Pols.

They were twenty minutes into their drive from the park to Little D's apartment on Wilson Avenue, and Vernon still hadn't shut up. It was all trash—random, trivial topics, none of which Julian had more than a one-word response. Not that the lack of interest on Julian's part dissuaded Vernon from running his mouth.

They pulled up in front of Little D's apartment and double-parked next to a red Hyundai Elantra. Vernon used his cell phone to send Little D a message, and after a few minutes, Little D, Flaco, and Dennis emerged from the building. All three got into the backseat of the Explorer. Julian glanced over his shoulder and noticed they had blank expressions on their faces and smelled of burned marijuana.

Vernon pulled the Explorer onto the road and headed for the construction site in Ridgewood. It was a little after four in the afternoon, but the light of day was already fading. The familiar sound of metal slides being pulled back and bullets loading into the chambers of semi-automatic handguns emitted from the backseat. Julian used the inside of his elbow to feel for the .38 snub-nosed revolver he'd put in his jacket pocket before he left his apartment.

"How do you think this is going to go, Julian?" Little D said.

"It shouldn't be a problem," Julian said. He kept his eyes on the view outside his window.

"Damn right, it won't be a problem. Those motherfuckers don't want no smoke," Vernon said.

Julian rolled his eyes. "The Polish are businesspeople, and they're trying to get into the dope game. They're not going to fuck around and risk losing the connect."

"Yeah, that makes sense," Little D said.

Julian didn't have to look at Little D to know he was afraid. For as big as he was, Little D was still a kid in this game. He and Vernon ran around playing gangster without any real idea of what it took to get ahead in this life. Julian wasn't worried about them at all.

Dennis and Flaco, on the other hand, were going to be problems. He'd known it the moment he'd laid eyes on them. Violence pulsated off them like heat from a radiator. Those two were remorseless killers. Julian knew it and figured he had about an hour to decide how to handle them.

Diana had left her office much later than she'd intended and was now caught in afternoon traffic on Fulton Street. Mr. Bad Toast himself, Carter, the doctor, had sent her a text message earlier inviting her to a New York Islanders game later tonight. She didn't like ice hockey much, but he was friendly and attractive, so she accepted the invitation.

With her new plans in mind, she'd adjusted her schedule so her site visit on Zajac out in Ridgewood would be her last appointment of the day. Diana had figured she'd handle her business with Zajac and then take Myrtle Avenue to the Jackie Robinson Parkway, straight out to the Nassau Coliseum in Uniondale.

But she'd decided to check her emails before leaving her office and was delayed when she opened Kat's email. The email was short and vague, but it still caused Diana concern. She couldn't remember ever receiving an email from Kat before. But for some reason, Kat had decided to send her a one-paragraph email in which she apologized for a reason not made clear. While at the same time informing her that Julian Serrano was involved in illegal narcotics trafficking.

She read the email twice and then spent twenty minutes trying to contact Kat. Her phone kept going straight to voicemail, and the watch commander at Kat's precinct couldn't provide any information about her location. Diana had figured Kat was in the middle of an operation and decided to try her again when she was on her way to the game.

Now, she was sitting in traffic thinking about the email and what Kat had written about Julian. Diana had suspected he'd lied to her the last time they'd spoken, but she didn't think he would be selling drugs. The last time they'd spoken, Julian looked and sounded like a person staring into the abyss.

He seemed obsessed with righting a perceived wrong, so much so that he was willing to sacrifice who he was to do it. Diana didn't know what to believe and knew it was an issue she would have to handle sooner rather than later. Julian would have to face the consequences if he was involved in something illegal

Diana also questioned Kat's motivation for providing information about Julian. Diana ran the possible reasons in her head. Reason one: Julian's name had come up in one of Kat's investigations, and she'd decided to give Diana a heads-up. Reason two: an informant mentioned Julian to Kat, who remembered his name from when she and Diana had dinner the other night. Reason three: Kat's conscience finally got the best of her, and she was coming clean about the dirty shit she was into with Frank Hawkins?

As Diana turned onto Linden Street, she hoped the truth was reason one but feared it was reason three.

CHAPTER TWENTY-THREE

VERNON DROVE THE EXPLORER THROUGH THE FRONT GATES of the construction site around a quarter to five in the afternoon. Julian surveyed the area. The site took up about a quarter of a block and was on the corner of Linden Street and Fairview Avenue, and there weren't any workers around.

Vernon steered the Explorer toward a single-wide office trailer at the back of the lot. The trailer was about forty feet by ten feet and too big for a site this size. The outside had light-gray aluminum siding and two entrance doors. The entrance doors were about two feet off the ground, so there was a four-step steel stair system, complete with handrails, in front of each door.

Vernon parked the Explorer in front of the trailer. Two men stood in front of the trailer's doors. They looked like bouncers at a bar. One of them wasn't much taller than Julian, maybe a little over six feet. But he was heavy. Julian guessed he weighed at least 250, and he looked even heavier with the cold-weather gear he was wearing.

The other one, however, was a monster. He looked well over six feet five inches and like he'd left 250 behind a long time ago. They both wore sunglasses and dark ski hats pulled low over their foreheads. He couldn't tell from where he was sitting, but Julian figured it was a safe assumption they were both carrying handguns.

"Damn, that motherfucker is bigger than you, D," Vernon said.

Little D leaned forward and peered through the windshield. "Maybe so. Why the fuck are they wearing sunglasses? The sky is grayer than rotten meat."

"Maybe they're in the music business. I'm thinking a hip-hop-and-speed-metal fusion act. Insane Clown Posse meets Lamb of God or some shit like that," Vernon said.

"It's a show. They're trying to show us they hard. Trying to scare a motherfucker." Dennis said.

"Exactly." Julian angled his body so Vernon and the three seated in the back could see his face. "Remember, this shit is all a show. They just want to do business and get us out of here as quickly as possible, the same as us. Keep your mouths shut and watch each other's backs, alright?"

No one answered, but Little D nodded nervously.

"Let's go." Julian grabbed the duffel bag off the floorboard between his feet and exited the vehicle. The others got out behind him, and Julian approached the bouncers. "What's up, fellas?"

"Only one of you goes inside," the monster said. He had a thick Brooklyn accent that surprised Julian. He'd half expected the large man to have an Eastern European accent, like Ivan Drago in *Rocky Four*.

"Alright." Julian turned and looked at the guys standing behind him. He spotted a figure standing by the front gate entrance and hesitated for a second. "Vern, I got this. You guys chill out here."

Before Vernon could object, Julian walked up the steps and entered the trailer.

THE CONSTRUCTION SITE'S front gate was still open, but Diana didn't see any workers. She was frustrated and quickly headed toward being angry. When she'd started her day, Diana had been determined to have a face-to-face conversation with Zajac and let him know what's what. But lousy traffic and the nebulous email from Kat had thrown her off schedule.

It wasn't precisely five o'clock yet, and she could see people walking around the yard. Diana decided to wait a while longer and watch for Zajac. There was only one way off the site, so he would have to go this way.

You're not getting away that easy, fuckhead.

Diana found a parking spot on Linden Street. From where she sat, she could see straight to the foreman's trailer at the back of the site. A Ford Explorer was parked in front of the trailer, so she assumed the foreman was still there.

She spotted a huge person standing in front of the trailer and was confident it was Zajac. He appeared to be wearing a hat and sunglasses, so she couldn't make out his face. But outside of being at a pro football game, Diana thought it unlikely she would find more than one person that size in the same place.

Come on, Zajac, sunglasses? Really?

Diana decided she liked her chances the large person was Zajac and exited her vehicle. She'd crossed the street and reached the front gate when she saw five people get out of the Ford Explorer. Her instincts and training told her something wasn't right with this picture, so she decided to stay by the fence and watch. The person who'd been sitting in the front passenger seat walked over to Zajac.

The person was carrying a duffel bag, and there was something familiar in their gait. The person spoke briefly with Zajac before turning and saying something to the four people behind him.

She felt lightheaded when she thought she'd recognized the person's face.

Julian?

ANGEL WAS STANDING outside the store taking a break when he heard "Vivir Mi Vida" by Marc Anthony start playing over the speakers. Bino was busy with a customer, so Angel ran behind the store's counter to turn up the volume. The song had been out for over five years, but he still loved it. With its pulsating, infective beats and lyrics about seizing opportunities and living life to the fullest without regrets, he couldn't think of a better song to use as a personal anthem.

Angel stepped out from behind the counter and danced a little. He was happy and felt invigorated. Business was good and only getting better. And he was about to rid himself of some current, and possibly future headaches.

He decided he would head into Manhattan and hit up a club tonight. He could convince Jimmy to put on his best clothes and come with him. He needed to do something to get Jimmy out of his funk. He was still a little emotional about Julian, but Angel knew Jimmy would get past it at some point. He was confident Jimmy would eventually see the big picture, especially after their pockets got fatter.

Angel checked his cellphone and saw it was five o'clock on the dot. He figured it would be going down anytime now, so he decided to head upstairs to his apartment and wait for Hawkins's call. Afterward, he figured he would take a nap. He wanted to make sure he had plenty of energy for the celebration he had planned.

"*Bino, voy arriba. ¿Estás bien aquí verdad*?"

"*Claro*," Bino said.

Angel smiled as he exited the store. That's all Bino ever said, "*claro.*" The old man was just happy to be employed, so he did and said whatever he needed to make sure he stayed that way. Angel wished everyone who worked for him had that same attitude and work ethic.

It was funny. The honest people, the ones who kept their heads down and played everything straight, always attracted the least attention. And that seemed to be exactly how they wanted it.

But the people who colored outside the lines, the outlaws and criminals who would be better served by keeping their heads down, were loud and flashy. They acted entitled and were quick to challenge authority. It was a sad truth that led to the fall of a lot of cats in this game.

Angel looked up at the dark gray sky and took one last pull from his e-cigarette. He put it in the front pocket of his jacket as he made his way to the front door of the building entrance leading up to the apartments. He used his key to unlock the door and stepped inside.

He heard car doors open behind him and turned to see where the sound came from. Two men, both dressed in dark clothing and carrying shotguns, ran toward him.

He tried to push the door closed, but it was too late. The two men used their momentum and weight to push the door open, and Angel fell to the ground, hitting his upper back on the bottom step. He reached behind his back for the Ruger 9mm handgun he had in the waist of his pants.

"*Mira pendejo*, whatever you got back there ain't gonna help you," one of the men said.

Angel left the gun where it was and slowly brought his empty hand where it could be seen. He glared at the two figures. They were covered from head to toe in dark, cold-weather clothing and wore ski masks. The one who spoke's voice was slightly muffled by the ski mask, but it was deep and gravelly. He was shorter and rounder than the other one.

For some reason, Angel thought about Devon and what his girl Karen had told Jimmy about the shooters. He stared at the ski masks and shotguns and figured these guys were the two that'd smoked Devon.

"I don't keep anything here, so you're wasting your time," Angel said.

"I don't think we are," the deep-voiced guy said.

He crouched down so Angel could see his eyes. They were a deep, dark brown, almost black, and the skin at the edges was light brown and lined with wrinkles.

"What do you want?"

The deep voice guy used his glove-covered right index finger to poke Angel in the forehead. He applied enough pressure to force Angel's head to snap back slightly.

"Take a guess."

Angel stared into the man's absent and cold eyes, and for the first time, he was scared. He imagined it was what divers saw when they swam with sharks.

He tried to collect himself and appear as if he wasn't worried, but he felt the tremble in his knees. Angel took a deep, silent breath to try and steady himself. He wanted to say something, but he didn't want his voice to reveal the fear he was feeling.

"You're fucking up. You know that, right?" Angel gave deep voice guy his hardest stare. "There ain't shit for you here, and my boys will be back soon. I ain't seen you so I don't know who you are. If you leave now, there won't be no smoke."

The deep voice guy chuckled as he stood up. He turned his shotgun to where the butt was facing Angel. "*Mira, pendejo,* you keep practicing, eh. One day, you might get the tough guy act down."

Angel watched him pull back and swing the shotgun forward with speed and bad intentions.

He heard the man laugh as everything went black.

CHAPTER TWENTY-FOUR

JULIAN SCANNED THE INTERIOR AS HE STEPPED INTO THE trailer. Doors were to the left and right of where he stood. Another door was attached to a small L-shaped wall directly in front of him, which he assumed was the bathroom. Three small vials sat on a small table beside the bathroom door. The paneled walls were white, and the vinyl floors were the same gray as the exterior.

Julian heard the door to his right opening, so he turned toward it. A man stepped through the open doorway. He was a little shorter than Julian and had a thin build. His hair was slicked back and shiny from whatever hair product he used. His sneakers were white and out-of-the-box clean and seemed even brighter when set against the black tracksuit he was wearing.

They exchanged nods, and the guy glanced down at the bag. When his eyes returned to Julian, he was wearing a wide grin.

"How's it going, man? I'm Bogdan."

"Julian."

"Is that the stuff?"

"Yeah."

"Show me."

Julian unzipped the duffel bag and tilted it so Bogdan could see the packages inside. “Where’s Grabowski?”

Bogdan ignored the question and extended his hand. “Give me one of the packages.”

Julian reached into the bag and handed him one of the kilos. Bogdan grabbed it and walked over to the small table by the bathroom.

“Where’s Grabowski?” Julian repeated.

“Why would you think he would be here?”

“Because we’re doing business.”

Bogdan used a small knife to puncture a hole in the top of the package and scoop out a piece of the tightly packed cocaine. He picked up one of the vials that was on the table and put the cocaine inside it. Bogdan put the knife down, placed a cap on the vile, shook it, and waited for the results.

“My uncle does a lot of business. Why would you think he’d have time for something this small?”

“I didn’t realize this was that small of a deal.”

"Well, it is." Bogdan eyed the vile and seemed satisfied with the results. "It looks good. If we continue working together, you guys will be dealing with me."

“'*If* we continue working together?'"

“Yeah, well—I’m not big on commitments. One deal at a time, alright?”

“Works for me.”

Bogdan stepped back into the room he had left earlier and returned with a dark blue backpack. He walked over to Julian and handed him the backpack.

“Check it.”

Julian unzipped the backpack, looked inside, and saw multiple stacks of cash, each held together by rubber bands. He placed the bag on the floor and crouched down beside it. He took a few stacks and ran his finger through each one, verifying every bill was U.S. currency. Every note was a one-hundred-dollar bill, and each stack represented $10,000. Julian reached inside and counted thirty stacks. Satisfied there was $300,000 inside the bag, he zipped it shut and stood up.

“I guess we’re done here.”

Bogdan nodded and smiled. "Yeah. For now."

Julian turned, opened the door, and stepped outside without looking back.

DIANA WAS ALMOST certain the guy with the bag was Julian, and she was sure the giant he was talking to was Zajac. She hurried back across the street and got into her car. Her head was spinning, and she was angry.

These assholes think they can play me.

Diana thought about calling the NYPD, but, at this point, she didn't have an actual crime to report, and she knew they wouldn't come out. She removed the Glock 9mm from her side holster and press-checked it, ensuring a round was in the chamber. She placed it back in its holster, turned her car on, and pulled away from the curb.

Linden Street was too small to turn around, so she made a U-turn in the middle of the intersection at Fairview Avenue. She drove back down Linden Street and pulled into the main entrance of the construction site. One guy was standing by the gate. He motioned for her to stop and approached her vehicle's front driver's side window.

She lowered the window.

"This is a closed site, lady," the man said.

"I'm here to see Jan Zajac. I'm his parole officer."

He glanced over his shoulder at Zajac and then back at her. He appeared unsure about what to do next.

"That's him over there by the trailer. This is an official visit, so I need to see him."

He stood straight up, pulled a cell phone from his pocket, touched the phone's screen a few times, and started speaking. Diana peered at Zajac, who was also talking on his cell phone. After a few seconds, Zajac started her way.

"Park over there. He'll come to you." The man motioned to a spot a few feet inside the fence.

Diana parked and exited her car. She only made it a few feet before Zajac reached her.

"What are you doing here?" Zajac said angrily.

"I'm conducting a site visit."

"You just did one."

"Yeah, but it's been a week, and you still haven't come by to give a sample. I was wondering if there was a problem."

"The only problem is you being here. I already told you once not to come here."

Keep it up, dipshit. You're not going to win this one.

"Yeah, well, I'm not the best listener. At least that's what my boss keeps telling me."

Zajac stepped closer, invading her space. He was trying to use his size to intimidate her. Diana's pulse quickened, and her hands shook, but she held her ground. She didn't want him to see her fear, and she had to resist the urge to put her hands inside her coat pockets. If this went south, the last place she needed her hands was in her pockets.

She stepped to her left and made a show of looking at the people standing by the trailer. "What's going on over there?"

Zajac kept his gaze fixed on her. "Nothing. Just some workers waiting to get paid."

"Really? They're not dressed like construction workers. Now, Mr. Zajac, you wouldn't be consorting with felons now, would you?"

He leaned over slightly; his warm, foul breath blanketed her forehead.

"Lady, play time's over. Get in your car and get the fuck out of here!" Zajac yelled.

Uh oh.

His outburst surprised her. Diana stepped back to create distance. She looked at the group behind Zajac and saw them staring back. Julian emerged from the crowd and approached her, with the group close behind.

So, this will either be passably good for me or unfathomably bad.

WHEN HE EXITED THE TRAILER, Julian saw the monster standing a few feet away with his back to them. It looked like he was talking to someone, but the guy was so big Julian couldn't see who he was speaking with. He cleared the stairs in two steps and headed back to the fellas standing by the Explorer.

"How'd it go?" Little D still sounded nervous.

Vernon nodded at Julian. "We good?"

"Yeah, we're good."

"Well, let's see that shit." Flaco reached for the bag.

Julian pulled the bag back. "Nah, you can look at it when we get back to Angel's. Let's just get—"

He peered in the monster's direction when he heard him yell. It looked like a woman was standing in front of him. Julian stepped a little closer to get a better view. The woman stepped back, and he saw it was Ms. Rivera. He was confused and shocked.

He thought about their last conversation and worried Ms. Rivera was following him. That her concern for him might have put her in a dangerous situation. There was something else, though. Julian felt protective toward her and was pissed off the monster was yelling at her.

"Fuck," Julian whispered. He put the backpack over both shoulders as if heading to school and approached her.

"Julian, man, what's up?" Little D said.

He ignored the question and sped up his pace. The group fell in behind him. They followed closely, murmuring in curious anticipation.

When he reached them, the monster turned and faced Julian, staring down at him menacingly. "Can I help you with something?"

Julian locked eyes with Ms. Rivera. "You okay?"

"Yes, Julian, I'm fine. What are you doing here?"

Julian heard Dennis' voice from behind. "Yo, Julian, you know this bitch?"

He glanced over his shoulder, careful to keep an eye on the monster. Everyone, including the big guy's partner, was standing behind him.

He turned back to Ms. Rivera. "We're looking for jobs. What are you doing here?"

She gave him a look like she knew he was full of shit but didn't have a chance to answer.

"That little motherfucker asked a good question. How do you know this fucking cop?" The monster's voice was thick with suspicion and anger. His eyes darted back and forth between Ms. Rivera and Julian.

Dennis stepped away from the others. "Who you calling motherfucker, motherfucker?"

The situation was escalating quickly, and Julian was flustered. This was not how this was supposed to go. He planned to make the deal and get far away from this site before dealing with Vernon and the other clowns.

He'd have time to get the money somewhere safe before settling things with Angel and Jimmy. Then he could pick up Tito and get the hell out of Dodge. Ms. Rivera showing up like this threw everything into flux, and he knew he had to figure a way out of this quick.

"She's my P.O., but it looks like she came here to see you," Julian said.

The monster shook his head. "Nah, something ain't right. I just saw this bitch a few days ago. There ain't no reason for her to be here today."

Ms. Rivera's eyes narrowed, and Julian could see the wheels turning in her head. The guy that'd been standing by the fence had moved and was now behind her.

"Look, everybody, calm down," Ms. Rivera said. She noticed the guy standing behind her, so she stepped to her right and pivoted so she could face everyone. "I'm not a cop. I'm a parole officer. I was just conducting a job site visit on Mr. Zajac here. Everybody can go to their neutral corners and take a break."

"Nah, fuck that. Something ain't right, and nobody's leaving till we get some answers." Zajac motioned at the guy he'd been standing with earlier. "Mike, take these little motherfuckers over by the car, make sure they don't go nowhere." He turned back to the guy standing by Ms. Rivera. "Pete, take that bitch inside the trailer."

There was a loud bang, and the left lens of Zajac's sunglasses exploded in a haze of plastic and blood. Julian was standing so close to Zajac when the gun was fired, he felt warm droplets land on his face and head. The giant man fell to the ground as if he had been dropped off the roof of a ten-story building.

"I said don't call me 'motherfucker!'" Dennis yelled.

Four more gunshots rang out. Julian crouched down and pulled the

.38 from his jacket pocket. He turned to Ms. Rivera. She was crouched and holding a gun in a shooter's grip. The guy Zajac called Pete was lying on the ground next to Ms. Rivera. He was motionless, and there was a gun in his hand.

Julian turned around and noticed Little D and Vernon were racing back to the Explorer. Dennis stood over Mike's lifeless body, and Flaco ran into the trailer. Two more gunshots went off inside the trailer, and Julian figured either Brogdon or Flaco was dead. Flaco walked back outside a few seconds later, and the question was answered.

He sprinted over to Ms. Rivera. "You okay?"

"Julian, what the fuck is going on?"

Before he could answer, Julian caught movement in his peripheral vision and looked to his left. Dennis was walking quickly toward them.

Julian dropped his hand and tucked his .38 behind his leg.

"We have to get you out of here," Julian whispered.

Dennis pointed at Ms. Rivera. "Yo, Julian, put that bitch to sleep so we can get outta here."

"Nah, leave her alone. Let's just bounce before the cops get here."

"What is you crazy? We ain't leaving no motherfucking witnesses. Dead that bitch right now."

Before Julian could say or do anything, Ms. Rivera lifted her gun and pointed it at Dennis. "No one is doing shit. We're all going to just wait here till the cops arrive."

Her voice was intense but also calm and steady. He looked past Dennis and noticed Flaco looking in their direction.

"Bitch, I'm gonna take that gun and shove it in your pus—"

Julian shot Dennis in the jaw, just under his ear. The side of his face exploded, and the sound of the blast echoed in the yard as Dennis's body fell to the ground.

Flaco and Vernon hurried toward them.

"Get in the car," Julian said, motioning at Diana's car.

Ms. Rivera was staring at Dennis's body and didn't move.

"Get in the fucking car!" Julian yelled.

She got into the passenger seat. Julian jumped into the driver's seat and tossed the backpack in the backseat. He turned the ignition and stepped on the gas, pulling the steering wheel hard to the left. The car skidded in a half-circle till it was facing the entrance gate.

Julian drove the car through the gate and made a left onto Linden Street. They were half a block away when Julian checked the rearview mirror. The Explorer had exited the construction site at a high rate of speed.

By the time Julian made the left on Forest Avenue, the Explorer was so close that its headlights filled the mirror.

CHAPTER TWENTY-FIVE

Angel was disoriented, and everything was completely black. But the pain shooting through his head let him know he was awake. In a panic, he blinked his eyelids furiously. He felt the fabric tight against his eyes and forehead.

The freezing cold wind blew sharply into his face, and he could smell the ocean. The unmistakable blend of seaweed, brine, and sea life filled his nostrils. He was lying on his side, and his hands were behind him and tied together at the wrist. He could feel the wet sand and grass on his fingers. They'd brought him to the beach.

Although it was quiet, he knew he wasn't alone. He felt their presence in the darkness—close by, watching him.

"Hello?" Angel said.

A mocking laugh interrupted the silence. "How you doing there, An-Gel?" The voice was deep and rough like sandpaper, so he knew it was coming from the fat one who'd knocked him unconscious.

Angel moved his head from side to side. "Yo, what the fuck is you doing, motherfucker? If you want something, cut the shit already and say it."

He was scared but also angry and tired of the games. He figured if they were going to kill him, they would have done it already. And since he wasn't dead, maybe he could negotiate his way out of this.

"I don't want anything, *mano*. I'm doing this shit for fun. But my boy Benny here—he definitely wants something. Ain't that right, Benny."

Angel heard footsteps landing heavy and fast on the sand. Then, someone stood over him. A hand was on his face, pulling away the blindfold. At first, the image in front of him was blurry and filled with tiny white dots.

He blinked his eyes rapidly, trying to clear out the messiness in his brain. Slowly, the image became focused, and he saw a man's face. He drew back a little to get a better view, but Angel didn't immediately recognize the person in front of him.

"Who the fuck are you?"

"Think on it a minute. It'll come back to you," the blurry face said.

Angel stared at the man's face, searching his memories for a reminder of who this person was. The man looked familiar, but Angel couldn't pinpoint how he knew him or from where or when. The man had short blond hair and a scar on his forehead.

Then he remembered and could put the man's face to a place and time.

The tire shop—eight years ago.

Angel knew there wouldn't be any negotiating.

DIANA GRIPPED the door handle as the Sonata sped north on Forrest Avenue toward Metropolitan Avenue. Traffic was stopped for a red light at the intersection. Diana didn't feel the car slowing, so she glanced at Julian. His attention seemed divided between the reflection in the rearview mirror and the traffic ahead.

"The light's red." Diana heard the panic in her voice.

"I see it."

They closed in on the car that was stopped in front of them. She pushed back into her seat, bracing for impact.

Julian pulled the steering wheel slightly to the left at the last second, maneuvering her car into the southbound traffic lane. They barely avoided a head-on collision when the driver of a red minivan yanked the steering wheel to the right.

They were in the intersection within three seconds, turning left onto Metropolitan Avenue. Diana looked in her rearview mirror and saw the Explorer skid onto the road behind them.

She remembered her cell phone in her coat pocket and took it out.

"What are you doing?"

What do you think I'm doing?

"I'm calling the cops."

Julian snatched the phone out of her hands. "No cops."

"What the fuck are you doing? What is going on, Julian?"

"What were you doing back there?" Julian said, ignoring her questions.

"I was doing my job. I was checking on Zajac. That's where he works."

Traffic was stopped for a red light at the intersection of Flushing Avenue, and they were coming up on it fast. She braced herself for another harsh maneuver.

He turned the steering wheel abruptly to the left, and they drove across traffic into the parking lot of a Carvel Ice Cream. He drove around the backside of the business and exited onto Troutman Street.

"You fucked everything up. You're not supposed to be here," Julian said.

I fucked everything up? That's not how I remember it going down.

"What are you talking about?"

"I was just going to get the money, get my son, and get out of here."

It seemed like he was reciting an inner monologue rather than speaking to her directly. Diana glanced at the backpack lying on the backseat and guessed the money was there.

She checked the rearview mirror and saw a set of fast-approaching headlights. The lights moved left to right and back again as if they were trying to move around or next to them. Troutman was a one-way street. Vehicles were parked parallel along the curb on both sides of the road, so there was no way for the Explorer to pass their car.

They sped toward an apartment building at the end of a T-intersection. Julian made a wide right turn at Evergreen Avenue, looping far left into the bike lane. He slowed the vehicle slightly and made a left turn back onto where Troutman Street reconnected.

They drove south one block, and he made a hard left turn onto Bushwick Avenue. It was a wide, two-lane street, and traffic was light.

He stepped on the gas.

"Julian, you need to stop the car. What you're doing is crazy. You killed that guy back there."

"He was going to kill you. They probably would have killed me, too."

"Okay then. Let's go to the police. Right now. We can explain this. I was there. I saw everything."

"Ms. Rivera—Diana, listen to me. This won't stop if I don't finish it tonight. Give me a few hours to sort everything out."

Julian turned onto Gates Avenue, drove a block, and then turned the car onto Broadway. Diana was staring at the elevated train tracks when he stopped the car in front of a Walgreens.

"The train station is right there. Wait in the Walgreens till they pass, then take the train and go home."

He handed the cell phone back to her.

"Julian—"

"I'll call you in a few hours, I promise. Now get out."

Diana exited the vehicle and ran into the Walgreens.

She heard the car's engine as Julian drove away and turned around in time to see the Explorer speed by after him.

CHAPTER TWENTY-SIX

JULIAN CHECKED THE REARVIEW MIRROR AND SPOTTED A SET of headlights coming up fast from behind. They were still on him and closing fast. He heard the J train passing on the train tracks above him.

It was a clear, cold night. The snow and ice that had blanketed the city the past few days had melted away, so the roads were dry. Despite being early in the evening, vehicle traffic was light, and there weren't many people on the streets.

Julian wasn't used to being the rabbit, and he was pissed. He kept the car above seventy miles per hour and tried to formulate a plan on how to end this chase. He sped up to create some distance, but not enough that they would lose sight of him. He turned the car onto Conway Street, drove through the intersection at Bushwick Avenue without slowing, and into Evergreens Cemetery.

The road inclined slightly and curbed to the right. Large stone memorials, statues, and tombstones were on both sides of the road.

Bright headlights reflected in his rearview mirror.

Julian followed the road for about half a mile and stopped the car by a large stone mausoleum.

He turned off the engine, exited the vehicle, and sprinted to the back of the large, walk-in-style mausoleum.

It was dark out, and the only light source came from above, provided by a full moon that looked big and powerful in the clear sky.

The Explorer's engine grew louder as it approached, and its headlights turned off as it was still rolling. The vehicle was moving slowly, so he waited until it passed by before he moved to the other side of the mausoleum. He heard the vehicle stop but didn't hear its doors open.

Julian positioned his body so he could see the Explorer. It was stopped on the road, directly behind Diana's car. There were three silhouettes inside the vehicle. The person in the driver's seat moved their hands animatedly as if they were giving directions. The guy was tall and slim, so Julian guessed it was Flaco.

He figured they were putting together their version of a search plan and thought they'd get out of the SUV any second. Julian removed the .38 from his pocket and held it firmly as he jogged toward the front driver's side window.

When he reached the SUV, the left side of Flaco's face was fully exposed. Julian extended his arm and squeezed the trigger. The glass shattered, and Flaco's head jerked violently to the right. Vernon, in the front passenger seat and covered in blood and flesh, watched in shock as Flaco's lifeless body slumped over the center console.

Julian stepped around the front of the SUV, keeping his gun pointed at Vernon and Little D, seated in the back.

"Get out of the car," Julian said.

Vernon raised his hands, showing Julian he was unarmed. "Julian, man, we didn't—"

"Out," Julian repeated.

Vernon and Little D exited the SUV. Julian patted each of them, first Vernon and then Little D, on the outside of their clothing, feeling for weapons. They both had a handgun in the front right pocket of their coats. Julian removed their guns and threw them in the back of the Explorer.

Julian took a few steps back. "Alright. Today is moving on up day for you two. You're the bosses now. It's all yours."

"What is you talking about? Where's Angel?" Vernon said.

"Don't worry about Angel. He's in the history books. Vern, you know where the stash house is, right?"

Vernon nodded.

"Alright, then, forget about everything that happened today. Go home, take a shower, and smoke a blunt. Tomorrow, you go take everything out of the stash house, move it to a new spot, and start your own shit. You wanted to be bosses? Here's your chance," Julian said.

Julian examined both of their faces. He couldn't recall them ever looking more like children than they did right now—scared little children.

"What about you?" Little D said.

"Don't worry about me. You have about five minutes before Five-O is all over this place. Dump that motherfucker in the tree line somewhere and get the fuck out of here."

Julian got into Diana's car and drove away.

He pulled out his cell phone and typed a message to Eli, letting him know he was on his way.

AFTER SHE LOST sight of the Explorer, Diana walked quickly to the Gate Avenue Station entrance on Quincy Street. She climbed the stairs, two at a time, and used her Metro card to gain entry at the turnstile. She raced up another flight of stairs to the train station platform and sat on a wooden bench. She pulled out her cell phone and stared at it, trying to decide if she should call the police.

What the fuck are you waiting for? Make the call you idiot.

She ran through the chain of events in her mind and was dizzy. It was like trying to remember a dream. Everything felt surreal like she'd spent the last few hours staring at a Salvador Dali painting.

Diana knew she needed to call the police.

Put aside the fact that she had just witnessed a massacre. Julian was being chased by maniacs and could be in danger. But he'd saved her life; all he'd asked for was time. Didn't she owe him that much?

She called Julian's phone, but it went straight to voicemail.

Goddammit, answer the phone, you dick.

Diana thought about the reasons Julian was out there in the first place. On its face, it was exactly what it looked like—he'd been out doing dirt, and shit had gone haywire. But her gut was telling her it wasn't that simple.

Everything that had happened somehow tied into what he'd been hinting at the other night. When he'd talked about making the score "zero-zero again" and about "getting back to even." The look in Julian's eyes when he'd said the words had given her pause that night, and now she was convinced this wouldn't end well unless she did something.

She knew if she called the police, Julian wouldn't make it out of this alive. If the police had him cornered, Julian would force a confrontation, and they'd have to react.

Diana believed she could save him. Julian was going back to prison —there was no doubt about that. But Diana thought she could bring him in alive if she could find him. New York was a big city, and she didn't think Julian was going to reach out to her and offer to meet her at the top of the Empire State Building or some crap like that.

She searched her memory, trying to remember anything that would give her a clue where to start.

Diana heard her cell phone ring, and she looked at it hurriedly, hoping it was Julian calling her back. The caller identification read "Unknown Number," which caused her to hesitate for a split second before answering.

“Hello?”

There was a silent pause, and she could hear someone breathing on the other end of the line. She held her breath, hoping to hear Julian's voice.

“Diana.”

“Kat? Where are you? What’s going on?”

“I’m home. They just released me.”

“What do you mean ‘they just released you?’ Kat, what the fuck is going on?”

"The Feds. I fucked up. I've been fucking up for a few years now, and the bill finally came due. F.B.I. took down my whole team today. Frank Hawkins is dead."

Diana was shocked at what she was hearing. She heard Kat's words, but nothing made sense. It sounded like one of her best friends, one of the people she trusted most in the world, was a liar and a wrong cop.

“Kat, I still don’t understand. What’s going to happen to you?”

"I cut a deal. That's the only reason I'm out now. The rest of my guys are probably fucked. They might've had a shot at a deal if Frank was alive. He was the one the feds really wanted. But with him dead—who knows? Look, I’m exhausted. I can’t worry about that right now. I called to check on you. Did you get my message about Serrano?”

With everything she'd just heard, Diana wasn't about to say anything about what had happened tonight to Kat.

"Yes." Diana didn't have the energy or desire to speak anymore.

"I understand. Listen..." The line went silent for a few seconds, and when Kat came back on, her voice was heavy with tears. "I'm sorry for everything. I truly am. I love you."

The call disconnected, and Diana dropped her hand heavily onto her lap. Her head spun, so she took a few deep breaths—trying to collect herself. It was almost too much to process, and she laughed out loud to keep from crying.

She leaned back against the wall behind her and felt the sting of cold metal on her head. She turned around. The source of the sting was the edge of a metal frame that enclosed a stained-glass mural. Diana was surprised she hadn't noticed it when she'd first sat down.

She was too close to make out what was depicted in the artwork. So, Diana stood up, took a few steps back, and saw six murals. The artwork was beautiful—rich, vibrant colors on top of black backgrounds. The images of people walking with their children using the transit system exploded off the glass.

I think I know where to find Julian.

CHAPTER TWENTY-SEVEN

It took Julian fifteen minutes to drive to Shirley Chisolm Park in East New York. He took Pennsylvania Avenue over the Belt Parkway and through the park's main entrance. He steered the vehicle onto Red Tall Trail and followed the road down to the beach.

The road was unpaved and consisted of gravel, sand, clay, and silt. It was configured in a snake-like pattern and sloped downwards. Overgrown grass and tall weeds filled the fields on both sides of the road.

He parked the car along the edge of the grass and walked into the field.

The air was filled with waves breaking on the shore and wind blowing through the tall grass. He heard Eli's deep voice in the distance and headed toward the sound. The grass reached just above his waist, and he could feel the sand and dirt beneath his feet with every step he took.

Julian reached the edge of the field, which opened to a small sand-filled area. Just ahead of him, Ben and Eli were standing over Angel.

Julian walked over and glared at the man he used to call his friend. Angel was lying on his side with his hands tied behind his back. The side of his face was covered with dried blood.

"We been doing a little stroll down memory lane," Eli said. Julian kept his gaze fixed on Angel. “He tried to play dumb at first, but it all came back to him.”

"Oh yeah?" Julian said. He glanced at Ben and then back down at Angel. "Is that right, Angel? My man Ben been catching you up?"

Ben had been in the tire shop the night Julian went to prison. An unwilling pawn in Angel’s fucked up game. He’d gone there thinking he was making a simple delivery and ended up doing three years. One of which was spent at Eastern Correctional with Julian.

About a year into his bit, Julian spotted Ben in the prison yard and recognized him immediately. Ben had been holding up a fence, minding his business, so Julian stepped to him. Pretty soon, they were hanging out every day, going over the events of that night and sharing information about the case they'd each received from their lawyers.

At first, all Julian had was what his gut told him—that someone in that garage had snitched them all out. Only two people got away that night, Angel and Hector. And Hector, fortuitously for Angel, ended up dead. Unable to bear witness.

But all that was just circumstantial at best. At least until they'd started watching the operation. Keeping tabs on Angel and Hawkins and all their little flunkies.

It hadn’t been hard to pick up the pattern, especially after Angel’s man Devon delivered to that kid Lugo. Hawkins and his people kicking in Lugo’s door right after he re-ups with Angel probably would have been enough for Julian. But then he’d had Eli make a call to one of Hawkins’ people and get himself signed up as a snitch.

Eli gave the lady detective Angel's name, and just like Julian had hoped, it had got back to Hawkins. Made him nervous enough to slip up. Then Eli followed Hawkins and saw him meeting with Angel in that garage across from the Brooklyn Bridge. For Julian, that was it, the proverbial nail in the coffin.

“Yo, Julian, man, what the fuck are you doing? What is this shit, bro?” Angel said.

"It's the end." Julian glared at Angel and saw the look of despair on his face.

“What? You going to kill me, motherfucker? For what? Cause I did what you couldn't? You a weak-ass motherfucker, Julian. You always was. That's why your ass had to go."

"I have one question for you. If you tell me the truth, I promise I won't kill you." Julian crouched and was face to face with Angel. "Did Jimmy know?"

"Did Jimmy know what?" Angel said.

Julian didn't repeat or expand on the question. He just held Angel's gaze and let his eyes explain.

Angel sat up and spit sand out of his mouth. "Yeah, of course, he knew. He wasn't supposed to get locked up with you that night. He was just too slow." He pursed his mouth in a mocking smirk.

Julian turned his head up and looked toward the sky. He took a deep breath. He wasn't really surprised to learn that Jimmy knew, but he was sad. With the truth about Jimmy out, he knew that was it—there was no one left.

The last living good memory of his youth was gone.

He looked down at Angel. He was covered in blood, dirt, and fear, and Julian didn't feel anything for this person he'd once loved like a brother. He didn't feel anger or hate, compassion, or remorse. All he wanted was for this to be over.

Julian turned to Ben. "Do your thing, bro. When you're done, meet me at my car. I have your money."

Julian walked into the field and back toward his car.

Even though he was waiting for it, Julian still flinched when he heard the gunshot.

JULIAN CHECKED HIS CELL PHONE. Three missed phone calls, and five text messages were waiting. They were all from Jimmy asking where he was and what was going on. Angel had confirmed what Julian had already suspected. Now, he had to decide how he wanted to finish this.

Julian had settled up with Ben and Eli, giving each fifty thousand dollars. Between that and the sixty grand they'd taken off Devon the night Ben had smoked him, Julian was confident he was square with them.

For the first time in a while, Julian felt like he was ahead. He had a bag of money and a head start on whatever was coming. He could forget about Jimmy and everything that'd happened. Cut his losses and leave right now—not look back.

He found Jimmy's phone number on his cellphone and pressed send. Jimmy answered on the second ring.

"Yo, what the fuck is going on?" Jimmy yelled from the other end of the call.

"Can't talk on the phone. Meet me on the roof in twenty minutes," Julian said. He ended the call and tossed his cell phone on the passenger seat.

He knew Jimmy would know he meant the roof of his grandmother's old building. When he was a kid, Julian's grandmother lived on the sixth floor of a thirteen-story building in the Bushwick Housing Projects, city-built affordable housing for low-income families. Housing developments like this could be found in every borough.

A collection of mini-cities where giant skyscrapers encompass communities of parks and pedestrian-only roads, all built with the intent to transform a city of tenements into a modern metropolis. Unfortunately, the wind-up was better than the follow-through. Years of rampant crime, crippling recessions, and overall neglect and indifference from city leaders resulted in impoverished and oppressed communities.

The three of them had grown up in these communities where poverty and violence were the norm.

As children, they'd play Tag in the building, using the stairwell to run from floor to floor. Sidestepping used hypodermic needles and homeless people as they tried to avoid getting tagged by whoever was "it."

When tired, they'd go to the roof, soak up the sun, and enjoy the breeze. They'd talk about girls and drink stolen beer. As they got older, trips to the roof became less and less frequent until they stopped altogether. The three of them moved on to adulthood and put away childish things.

Julian parked the car on Humboldt Street and entered the building through the back entrance. He took the elevator up to the thirteenth floor and used the stairwell to walk the flight of stairs leading to the roof.

He half expected to run into one of the many homeless who used these stairwells to sleep and defecate, but there was no one around.

The stairwell was filled with the overwhelming smells of human waste. He hurried to the door to the roof, pushed it open, and walked out into the cold, fresh air.

He ambled to the roof's edge and pressed his lower body against the three-foot metal fence surrounding the roof's perimeter. He placed his hands in his jacket pockets in a futile effort to stay warm and looked out over the edge, taking everything in.

The night sky was so clear he felt he could count every star. Everything below was small and indistinguishable. And although the city sounds reached his ears, they were unintelligible and meaningless. He figured when you're this high up, everything below is inconsequential.

He thought about Ms. Rivera—Diana—and was hopeful she'd give him the time he asked for before she made any calls. He was tempted to call her to make sure she was okay, but then he pictured the strong, confident woman he had just seen and decided against it.

He was gone after tonight. With any luck, he would become just another person from the block who may or may not have existed. A vague "do you remember that guy, from that place" kind of memory.

He turned around when he heard the roof door swing open. Jimmy walked quickly toward him, anger and confusion in every step. Julian gripped the .38 in his pocket and took a few steps toward Jimmy. Instinctively, he scanned Jimmy's hands and saw he wasn't holding anything.

"What the fuck is going on? Where is everybody? Where's Angel?"

"Angel's gone. It's over," Julian said.

"What the fuck are you talking about? What's over?"

Always the fighter, Jimmy's hands were balled into fists, and veins bulged in his neck and face.

"I know, Jimmy. I know what you did."

Jimmy's look of anger dissolved into shame, and he uncurled his fingers. He walked past Julian and looked out over the edge.

"We tried to work it out another way, but that fuck Hawkins wouldn't deal unless Angel gave up some people. We figured you'd do two or three years. And with the protection we were working with, we'd build our shit up. Give you something good to come home to," Jimmy said.

"But that's not how it worked out, is it?"

Jimmy turned and faced him. "Yo, I did three years off that shit too."

"Fuck the years. I lost Laila and my son. For what? Cause you motherfuckers didn't think we were moving fast enough?"

"I'm sorry, Julian. On my mom's grave, I'm sorrier for this than anything in my whole life."

"I thought we were brothers. But it's not like this was an accident or something. You two sat down and discussed this shit. Said my name out loud when you were planning it. You didn't think twice about who would get hurt. You stole my life, Jimmy. You took everything I loved—that I still love, and you shit all over it."

Jimmy lowered his head for a few seconds, and tears were in his eyes when he raised it back up. He looked remorseful, but his shoulders weren't hunched like a man begging for food. Jimmy stood with his chin up and his back straight as a steel pole.

"I don't know what else to say," Jimmy said.

"There's nothing else to say," Julian said.

He pulled the .38 out of his pocket, pressed it against Jimmy's forehead, and squeezed the trigger. He felt the warm blood spray on his hand and watched Jimmy fall backward onto the cold rooftop.

Julian stared at his friend's lifeless body, and he cried.

He turned and walked to the roof door. He wiped the tears from his face with his forearm and wondered if everything that happened this high up meant anything to the people below.

CHAPTER TWENTY-EIGHT

It was close to eleven at night, and all the lights inside their home were turned off. Julian stood outside Nikki and Alex's Bay Ridge home, full of envy and sadness. It was a lifetime ago, but this was what he had planned for his growing family: a modest but beautiful single-family home out on the farthest edge of Brooklyn. Far away from the madness of where they grew up, but close enough that they wouldn't forget where they came from.

The house didn't look that big outside, maybe fifteen hundred square feet. It wasn't a mansion, but it was perfect for them. It was a two-story home with a red brick exterior and a long driveway that led to a detached garage for their minivan. It was a dream—not his anymore, but it was definitely someone else's dream.

He texted Tito to ask him to come to the back door when he arrived. Several minutes passed without a response, so he texted him again. After a few seconds, a light came on in one of the windows on the side of the house overlooking the driveway.

Julian reached into the car, grabbed the backpack, and walked underneath the window. He sent Tito another text message, and after a few seconds, his son's face appeared in the window. Tito looked down, and Julian signaled for him to go to the back door. Julian walked to the back door and waited. After a few minutes, the door opened, and Tito walked out.

"What are you doing here? Is everything okay?" Tito said.

"Yeah, everything is fine. I just wanted to see you. How are you? Is everything good with you?" Julian was nervous and rubbed his hands together to keep warm.

Tito looked confused. His hair was messy, and sleep was in his eyes. He shut the door behind him and sat on the step beneath it. "This is kind of weird. Are you sure you're okay?"

He'd had it all planned out. After getting the money he needed and dealing with Angel and Jimmy, Julian would pick up his son and they would leave together. Go somewhere they could live like a family. A place where he could get back some of the time he'd lost.

But he looked at his fourteen-year-old son, a young man on his way to adulthood, and realized that wouldn't happen. No matter how much money he had, what Julian needed most was time.

He needed back the time he'd lost with his wife and son.

It was the price Julian had paid for the life he'd led and the decisions he'd made. He realized that no matter what role anyone played in the things that happened in his life, he was the star of that movie. It was all him.

"Yeah, I'm good. So, listen. I won't be around for a while," Julian said. He handed the backpack to Tito. "Give that to your uncle. He'll know what to do. But don't let your titi see, okay?"

"What's going on? Where are you going?"

"I just have to...I have obligations I need to take care of, and I have to leave to do it."

"Will I ever see you again?"

"Probably not."

"Why not?"

Tito said, his voice cracking.

Julian didn't speak for several seconds, trying to hold back his tears. "Someone once told me life is about choices, and for better or worse, we have to live with our choices. Well, I've made a lot of bad choices in my life, so now I have to deal with the consequences."

Tito was quiet for a few seconds and seemed to be processing Julian's words. "I think I get it, but it still sucks."

"Yeah, it does. But please remember one thing, I love you. I love you more than you could ever imagine."

"I love you too, Dad."

When he heard the word, Julian realized it was the first time Tito had called him Dad, and he cried. He knew a part of it was sadness and despair over the chance that he probably would never see his son again, but Julian realized a lot of what he was feeling was happiness and peace.

He was happy that he'd gotten to know his son and was able to communicate his love for him. And he finally felt at peace with the ghosts of his past.

DIANA WATCHED him park her car on Ninety-Seventh Street. She'd braved the frigid night air waiting for him to show, almost bowing out once or twice because it was so cold. Diana was proud that she had found Julian unassisted and was glad she stayed.

After spending some time on everything that had happened, she'd figured Julian would visit his son at some point. For what reason exactly, she wasn't sure. But Diana figured he would, and she had guessed correctly.

She'd thought hard, trying to recall everything she knew about Julian, and remembered his son was living with the aunt in Bay Ridge. She'd even remembered on what street.

From the end of the block, Diana watched Julian get out of the car and stand on the street in front of the house where his son slept. She considered approaching him with her gun drawn and taking him into custody—end this whole thing right now. But then she thought about what she would do if she were him and decided to give him some time.

What are you doing over there, Julian?

After a few minutes, he took the backpack out of her car, walked toward the house, and she lost sight of him. The time passed slowly as Diana waited and watched. Unsure of what he was doing and second-guessing her decision not to immediately arrest him, she walked to her car. When Diana reached the car, she pulled on the driver's door handle. While she was happy to get out of the cold, she was a bit dismayed to find the door unlocked.

Damn, Julian, it's not that good of a neighborhood.

Diana scanned the car's interior for contraband. Satisfied there wasn't any, she got into the driver's seat. Peering down the long driveway, she didn't see anyone, so she leaned back and waited.

After ten minutes, Julian strolled into the light without the backpack. He appeared to be typing on his cell phone as he walked down the driveway toward her car.

Julian looked up from his cell phone, and their eyes met. He stopped and scanned his surroundings. After a few seconds, he continued toward the car. He walked around to the front passenger door and got in the car.

"How long have you been here?"

"Long enough. Where's the backpack?" Diana said.

"I left it with my son. What's inside was always supposed to be his anyway."

"He's a kid, Julian. He won't know what to do."

"I just sent his uncle a message. Alex is smart. He'll handle everything."

Julian shifted in his seat, and she turned to face him when she felt his eyes on her.

"Thanks for giving me the time," Julian said.

"Did you do what you needed to?"

"I had a chance to say goodbye to my son. That was what was most important to me. You gave me the opportunity to do that, so thank you."

They were silent for a few seconds.

"I lied to you," Diana said.

"What do you mean?"

"When I told you I'd never experienced the loss you talked about." Julian didn't say anything, and Diana started to doubt herself for saying what she'd said. But looking into his sad eyes and knowing exactly how he felt, she felt compelled to share her story. "I had a daughter...Isabel."

"Had?"

"She died. Almost four years ago."

"I'm sorry to hear that. How did she die?"

"She was born with a congenital heart defect. She fought for as long as she could but died when she was three." Diana wiped the tears from her eyes. "I don't know why I'm telling you this now. I should be dragging your ass to the nearest precinct." She let out a small, awkward laugh. "I...I don't know. I've bottled everything up for so long. It just got old, you know? People patting me on my back and telling me they understood what I was going through. I know they meant well, but I didn't believe them and resented them for saying it. I mean, how could they really know what I felt?

"But I want you to know I truly understand what you've been going through. The overwhelming sadness—it's like this monster tearing at your insides, and it doesn't go away. But what I've come to realize is that I'm not alone. It's okay to say I'm not okay and to ask for help."

He didn't respond, but the silence didn't feel uncomfortable. She felt relieved somehow and a strange sort of joy.

"So, what happens now?" Julian said.

"Well, you violated more than half of the rules in that handbook I gave you when we first met. So, you'll be going back inside. For how long exactly will be up to a judge," Diana said.

"So, you're taking me in on a parole violation? What about everything else?"

"That's up to the police to figure out. But I'm not real clear on everything that happened tonight or who was involved." She looked at him and noticed the dirt and dried blood that dotted his clothes and hands. "Right now, I'm hungry. There's a cool little all-night diner in Brooklyn Bridge Park that sits right on the East River and serves great pancakes. I figured you might want some time alone, you know, to throw something in the river and make a wish."

Julian turned his eyes to the front of the car and smiled as he handed her the keys. She turned the car on and drove into the waiting night, guided by the light from the moon.

ABOUT THE AUTHOR

J.J. Hernandez was born in Brooklyn, New York and raised in Brooklyn and Miami, Florida. He is a graduate of Sam Houston State University and has been a law enforcement officer in Central Texas for twenty years. He lives in Austin, Texas with his wife and two daughters. This is his first novel. Visit him online at www.authorjjhernandez.com.

www.ingramcontent.com/pod-product-compliance
Lightning Source LLC
Chambersburg PA
CBHW020501310726
48979CB00016B/2754/J
* 9 7 8 1 7 3 7 1 0 1 3 2 1 *